FINDING JOY

LAURIE WOODWARD

ONE

JOY

I was seventeen when the bong years came to a close. When the pipe's gurgling water morphed from concentric circles on a pond, to a drowning undertow. Jolted from a Kodachrome dream of psychedelic turquoise, I struggled to the surface, back toward the beautiful light.

Why should you give a shit about another stoner kid inhaling her last? You'd probably think she was just another fuck-up doing something stupid. And you'd be right. I'd done a friggin' factory of idiotic things during the bong years. From taking downers before chugging Coors, to sneaking the car out while my parents played golf, I'd churned out more stupid widgets than'd fill a Pakistani sweatshop.

But you know, every stunt made perfect sense in my daydreaming head. I'd work out the details on how bitchin it'd be when *everyone* saw me cruising through the park, tunes cranked, flicking Marlboro ashes out the window. Of course, I didn't count on my uncle being there with his kids, or running out of gas two blocks from home.

Shit.

When I was seventeen, the sweet ambrosia of Hawaiian,

Thai Stick and Columbian Red turned to bitter resin. The chamber's glowing bowl flared and spat embers while I fought to stoke that dying flame. I searched both purse and pockets, but all of my matches had burned, leaving the rolling smoke withering to ash on my tongue.

That year, you could have changed my name to Naïve. Or Dreamer and Head-in-the-clouds-Hippie-Wannabe.

Anything but my real name, Joy Chappell. I know, it sounds like a holy-roller churchy girl. I guess that's what Mom was going for when she named me. Wanted me to sound all innocent and shit. And maybe I was. In my own way.

How can a car-stealing, pot-smoking, LSD-tripping chick be innocent? If you were born in the 1960s, like me, you'd know. All around, there was this message of optimism and hope saying that soon people were going to come together in love and peace. From the films where smiling hippies lived off the land, to songs like *All You Need is Love*, to news broadcasts about people taking to the streets in brotherhood, the Utopian message rang out.

Even Mom, with her *Vote for Nixon* button, teased beehive hairdo and miniskirts, started to speak of women's rights and stopping the war in Vietnam. But it was the teenagers I met that had the most profound effect on my idealism. They told me that by the time I grew up, the world was going to be a far-out, fantastical planet where all we had to do was sing a few songs and smile for bursting cannon balls to become rainbows.

And I believed every freaking word.

So here I was, a kid certain that someday the light of hippie sun would shine on all our faces as we danced barefoot in meadows. I had so much faith in this dream that I thought, if you can really talk to a person, get them face to face and bare the beauty of your child soul, you could soften the hardest of hearts. When I was really little, I even believed that if I told the President to stop the war, he would. He'd just look in my kid eyes and make peace.

Naïve, I know. But when you're a kid, you see the world through your own eyes. And when you're high to boot, everything is tinged with this soft mist, like an out-of-focus camera, and you trust people, thinking they just want to give you a ride.

Yeah, I never knew people were truly ugly until April 7, 1981. The night I peered into the tunnel of darkness.

You know, I really thought the face inside was just a mask. One I could melt away with my Kodachrome soul.

But I was wrong. And by the time I figured it out, it was too late.

I was seventeen and I was about to die.

TWO

KYLE

My half-sister's an idiot. She says I'm Mom's favorite, which isn't true. I just don't mess up like she does. I mean, if she would just think once in a while, maybe she wouldn't be grounded all the time. Or if she planned, she might have some money, and wouldn't keep begging for me to break into my savings

But I didn't put a Strongbox Secret Cash Box on my Christmas list for its name. I wanted a piggy bank that looked like a vault, so I'd think twice before pulling money out. I'm not inserting coins in the slot for no reason, I have big plans. A Black Knight Sidewalk Skateboard with Cadillac wheels that will make me king of the streets.

And I'm almost there. So far, I've saved $7.43. Just $2.56 more and I'll have the $9.99 I need. Then Kyle Wright will be like one of the skater boys, cruising over sidewalks till I hit Wheeler Hill. I'll be perched at the top waiting for that light to turn green. Then, with a quick kick, I'll jet down that asphalt wave, and the only sound will be the wind whooshing past my face. I won't hear slamming doors or Mom crying.

It's all stupid Joy's fault, anyhow. Stupid head. If she hadn't screeched, "You're not my father, you can't tell me what to do," Dad wouldn't have had to put her in her place. I mean, you just can't have a seventeen-year-old talking like that.

Then Mom wouldn't have tried to get between them. And Dad wouldn't have hit her instead of Joy.

He didn't mean it. I know, 'cause he came back later with a big bouquet of flowers for Mom. Said he was sorry.

Dumb Joy. Dumb name. Doesn't fit her at all, since all she seems to do is tick off everyone, arguing with her stupid hippie stuff. Doesn't she realize the hippies are gone? Move on already and get a brain. And keep your hands off my bank.

THREE

JOY

N ow, I don't want you to get the idea that my life is just one endless suck-fest of green donkey dicks. I had all kinds of happy times. I had grandparents and cousins I got to visit every summer, a field nearby my house for awesome fort building, tons of books and, for a couple of years, a best friend who stood by my side. Until...

Well, we won't talk about that right now.

From fifth grade on, Cheryl Silva and I were like two eggs in a nest; we both loved Donny Osmond, *Tiger Beat* magazine, and rainbow sherbet. Of course, I liked a cherry on top, which Cheryl thought was overkill, ruining the *perfect blend of pastel colors*.

Cheryl talked like that a lot, acting like an expert on art because her mother sometimes took her to the park to paint. But it never bugged me, I liked learning from her.

She was the kind of friend who would tell you when you had chocolate pudding on your face. The kind that finishes your sentences. The kind that makes you giggle until your sides hurt.

And when she listened, she was the kind of friend that looked in your eyes and got you.

Not that I told her everything. I mean, I'd hint at some of the bad stuff but couldn't say *it* out loud. That'd make *it* too real.

So instead, I told her old stories of when I was little. Like one day in sixth grade we were in her room, listening to *Only a Moment Ago* on *The Partridge Family Album* when I got to thinking.

"You know, Cher, only a moment ago we were little kids."

"Yeah, fun times, huh?"

"I don't know. I hated grownups always saying children should be seen but not heard. They told us to sit quietly, hands folded in our laps, while they talked about important things like, like..."

"The electric bill?"

"Exactly. Or if they should buy a new vacuum cleaner or not."

"And," Cheryl giggled, "the perfect way to swish the toilet." She held up a pretend toilet brush. "Sani Clean is the best potty scrubber in the world. Your bowl will sparkle with this amazing brush!"

Chuckling, I nodded. "Adults are boring. I mean, can an adult bike with no hands, steering by sheer will like you do?"

"Or do about a million cartwheels and round-offs on the front lawn?" Cheryl added.

"They sure can't shimmy up a tree in eighteen seconds flat."

"You could before I ever met you."

You should have seen me. I thought I was Tarzan, bare-chested, wearing cut-offs like a loin cloth.

"You still think you are," Cheryl teased.

I made fists and pounded my chest like a gorilla. "Barefoot, I'd dare anyone to go as high as I could."

"Climbing higher than me. That's for sure."

"One day Kyle tried to follow, but I climbed higher, teasing him. *Come on, Ba-by. Can't you even climb a few feet?*"

"I bet your mom didn't like that."

"She was in the house. But I do have to give my little brother

7

props. He stuck his tongue in his cheek and reached for the next branch. But it was too thin and bent."

"Little kids are dumb. Everybody knows you have to have a branch as big as your arm or it'll break."

"That's what I said – 'Pick a thicker one, stupid head' – before I grabbed the next branch. Now I was really high, up where the tree gets skinny and you can see all over the neighborhood."

"Next to that weird singing lady's back yard where she practices opera all the time?"

"Yeah, while my parents roll their eyes. Even a few houses over into Cathy's yard, where they have a wooden hot tub that Mom says people go in nude. Never did see any naked people, though."

"You would look."

"Whatever. From up there, I could see as far as the golf course next to our neighborhood. It looked like a big green ocean."

"And what did my friend with the overactive imagination become then?" Cheryl asked. God, she knew me.

"I was a sailor battling waves in a storm, of course."

"I can just hear you shouting, 'Ahoy matey!'" she said, grinning. "Sounds fun."

"It was until stupid Kyle called up saying he couldn't reach. 'Stop being a little baby', I said. 'Sure, you can. Stretch!'"

"Encouragement. Good."

"I don't know why I was helping him. All I ever hear is how amazing he is. How perfectly clean his room is. Or how great his kindergarten report card was next to mine. How he never spilled his milk during dinner. 'Why don't you act more like your brother, Joy?'"

"Can relate. Why did you?"

"Yeah well, he is kind of adorable, when he isn't being so annoyingly perfect. But don't tell him I said so."

"Never." She jerked her head toward her baby sister's room. "Little brothers or *sisters*, should never know when you think they're cute."

"Totally. They'd use it against you."

"Forever," Cheryl agreed.

"He tried, chanting to stretch over and over again. I watched, cheering him on."

"I'm guessing this doesn't have a happy ending."

"He'd forgotten to leave his toes on a lower branch and reached too far for his stubby little arms. I tried shouting, 'No, not that way, there's no…' But I was too late. He tumbled down and started bawling his head off."

"Did you get in trouble?"

"Mom appeared immediately and scooped him into her arms. 'Joy Marie Chapel, what's wrong with you?' she yelled, rushing my crying brother into the house." I sighed. "Didn't follow."

"You were better off in the tree."

"Yep. Where I wouldn't be seen *or* heard."

FOUR

IRIS

Joy was splayed out in a beanbag, curling her toes as she turned the page of another book. What's she reading this time? Probably another of my horror novels that'll give her nightmares. Hard to believe an eleven-year-old would like such frightening stories.

Silly kid. I should tell her to pick something more innocent and age appropriate, like *Willy Wonka* or *The Wizard of Oz*. Taking her to places where magic still exists. Unlike her home. I started to point that out, but the picture in *Glamour* magazine took me back to my own magical time.

And I remembered the note.

Meet me this afternoon at the Villa Motel, Room 14.

I'd blushed when I read what Mr. Wright had slipped onto my desk. Smoothing my hair, I pulled out my compact and checked my lipstick, feeling warm in a way I hadn't since Alan left.

Stop it now, I thought. *He's married and your boss.*

But he looks like Steve Mc Queen on the screen...

I'd never even called him by his first name, for God's sake. And what about his wife? Isn't she some waif of a thing that's always at his beck and call? Maybe she doesn't love him. She never comes around. But if she does, I'd feel terrible.

A week later, Mr. Wright cornered me in the hall leading to the office's restroom. "Hello, beautiful."

"Excuse me." I dodged right, trying to scoot past.

He extended an arm across the door jamb, blocking my entry. "When are you going to let me take you away for a weekend? We could drive up to Monterey. I know this little motel."

"Mr. Wright," I interrupted.

"Ron."

"Ron, please stop. I can't," I said with my mouth, but my body betrayed me. I leaned forward, feeling the warmth of his chest. It would feel so wonderful to be pressed up against it.

I shook my head. *Think, Iris. Joy's not even two and that asshole Alan is never going to pay child support. You need this job.*

I knew the score. Married men had been hitting on me since I was sixteen and scooping ice cream at the Thrifty Drug Store. All they wanted was to play around, and once they got off, they'd drop you. I'd been smart enough to stay away from the wolves, but I'd had a girlfriend at Thrifty who had to go away and visit her aunt in Idaho for several months after getting involved with one.

And Alan had left a hole so deep, I couldn't find my way out. Only saw the darkness. No sky or clouds, barely took care of Joy. It was like I was dead.

I'd fought to claw my way out of that grave and vowed never to let any man return me to it.

"Never say never," I mumbled.

"What, Mom?"

Did I say that out loud? "Nothing. I just noticed that pants are flaring more now. But I couldn't wear them. They'd make me look fat."

Joy giggled. "You never look fat, Mom. Except when?" She raised her eyebrows twice.

I knew what she wanted. Her favorite face. "I don't know..." I teased. "My hands are tired today."

"Come on. Please?"

I looked at the clock. Ronny wouldn't be home for two hours. I curled a lip and then slowly raised my hands to either side of my head. Pressing my palms against both cheeks to smush my face into a Marshmallow Puff Lady, I said in a clown voice, "My mommy's name is Chubby."

Joy giggled. I deepened my voice.

"My daddy's name is Chubby. And my name is Chubby. And when I smile..." I paused to draw out the part the kids loved best. I smashed my lips together and puckered before saying, "... it goes like this!"

I started to bare my teeth, but it wasn't necessary. Joy was already kicking up her feet and roaring with laughter. Her chubby little toes curled again like when she was little.

God, she's growing up. Starting to get curves. Not as much as I had when I was eleven, but I think she takes after her father's side of the family. All straight edges with flat butts and small chests. Unlike me. I'm a winding road with so many curves, I don't know where one begins and the next ends.

She's worried about growing but I think she's fine. I know the other girls in her class are more developed, but I'm glad that she's late going through puberty. I started at ten and look where that got me. Pregnant at nineteen, married to a gas station attendant who could barely afford our tiny apartment.

When I complained about the mice gnawing on the bread or ruining another box of Corn Flakes, he'd tell me, "Don't worry, baby, I'm going places."

Oh, he went somewhere all right. Straight out the door to his new life.

Thank God for Ronny. I know he has his flaws, but he loves

me. I know it. Look at our house. On a cul-de-sac in The Estates, with all new appliances and shag carpet. Had it built special. Ronny made sure to get the newest and brightest. Nothing used for him.

Alan still can't get his act together enough to pay child support. Or visit Joy. Poor kid. She keeps waiting, thinking he'll come. But the asshole stays away.

Her face is changing, too. She still has baby cheeks that fill up like balloons when she smiles, but there's a hint of cheekbones now. I also noticed a thoughtfulness in her green eyes, like she's taking everything in and analyzing it. More so than I ever did.

And he's missing it all. Idiot.

FIVE

JOY

I know, you're wondering when did the Bong Years start? And I'm getting there. Just let me tell my story in my own time, okay? Catalina comes into it a lot, so you might as well know about my first summer there...

———

"Don't forget to floss," Mom cautioned.

"Yeah, those braces weren't cheap," Ronny grumbled, in that grouchy-grouch voice.

In the middle of a hug, Mom stiffened almost imperceptibly before smoothing my hair, something she hadn't done since I was eight.

"Okay." I started to say 'I love you' but somehow the words got stuck when an older girl, a teenager in a baby-blue Catalina Island Camp t-shirt and white shorts, walked by. I take it back, she didn't walk, she full-on floated out the terminal doors before joining the crowd on the dock.

Mom's gaze followed mine as she led me outside. "Maybe she's one of the counselors."

"Lucky Joy," Ronny said, getting an eyeful.

Take a picture, why don't you? I thought, rolling my eyes.

I'd imagined this island camp to be pretty cool when I opened my *Guess Who's 11?* birthday card and the brochure fell out. But now, looking at the teens with their hair sun-streaked and strong, tanned legs, I started to realize that this was going to be way cooler than playing with my Malibu Barbie set.

"Barbies, for an eleven-year-old?" Cheryl had teased when she saw me pushing my Country Camper over the lawn last week.

"So?" I'd said, parking the van under a rose bush and pulling Barbie out from behind the wheel. I brushed her hair with one finger and held her up to my flat chest. Cheryl was right but, even though she was my best friend, she still didn't understand about becoming. Instead of a stupid shag cut, so short people thought I was a boy, I got to have long, silky hair. My boring green eyes turned aqua behind sunglasses and no pimples stained my smooth, peachy cheeks. I had a great husband, Ken, and we loved our daughter Skipper so much that we took her on all of our camping adventures.

"Joy Chapel?" The pretty blonde counselor called my name off a list.

"No more than two shots of whisky a night, kiddo. They won't let you sail with a hangover," the winking Ronny said, loud enough for others to hear.

"Oh, Ron," Mom giggled, slapping him gently with the back of her hand. She loved his I'm-in-public-so-act-charming voice.

With a half-smile, I looked down at my white legs. *Not even Malibu Skipper* I thought, as Mom gave me a little push toward the gangplank where kids were filing onto the boat.

But in a few minutes, it didn't matter; I was in the bow with the June sun on my face. I placed my hand on the rail feeling the engines hum as a girl around my age came up beside me. "Hey," I said.

"Hi," she replied, in a shy kind of voice. Then she wrinkled up her nose. "San Pedro stinks, huh?"

"Guess it's pollution from all these ships," I said, trying to sound all mature.

She nodded and grabbed the rail next to me as *The Catalina Express* sped up. I noticed her long curls rippling in the wind like the choppy waves below us. *I wish mine did that,* I thought running a hand over where my hair stopped just past my neck. *Definitely growing it out this summer. Don't care what Mom says.*

The thick smell of engine oil soon made way for fresh ocean air. Here, the captain really let it rip. The keel hissed over the water, parting the deep blue behind us in a big, foamy V. I put my hand over my chest in the same shape and felt my heart beating slower and slower. Noticing how it got quieter the further we were from shore.

The spray tickled my skin as the island grew bigger on the horizon. I like that word. *Horizon.* It was on my sixth-grade vocabulary list when we read *The Call of the Wild* and I kept imagining dogs mushing toward a snowy wall that always stayed twenty feet away.

"That's the Isthmus," said the girl, who was named Bethany by the way; Bethany Wallach. She was a real Jewish girl, the first one I'd ever met, or even heard of. My parents didn't do church or talk religion much, so she had to explain to me about the Old Testament and the New and Jesus being a prophet, not God, to the Jews. I didn't really see the difference until she told me about them celebrating Hanukah instead of Christmas and getting presents for eight days.

Now I really was jealous.

I followed the line of her finger to the small bay peppered with all kinds of yachts that probably belonged to TV stars or millionaires. A short pier led to a few buildings on shore.

"That's our camp?" I asked.

"No, silly. We're going to take the shuttles." She jerked her chin toward the pier, where four flat-bottomed boats that looked like the ones on the Jungle Cruise at Disneyland were docked. There, a few men, with deep lines and tanned skin so leathery it could have lined Mom's purse, held out hands to help us board.

When about half an hour later we finally chugged around the bend, my heart just stopped. Here, a row of palm trees skirted blue canvas-roofed cabins in a bay with waters so quiet, the littlest angel must have lived there. Surrounding it all were mountains topped with eucalyptus, ironwood and sage bushes.

Wow!

This paradise was going to be home for a whole month. And Ronny paid for it? Maybe he wasn't such a jerk, after all.

Over the next four weeks I learned to sail, canoe, kayak, and my favorite, rowing, because no matter how many circles you went in, it felt like you were going somewhere.

There were day hikes to the top of Miller Hill and moonlit sneaks to raid the boys' camp. I sang goofy songs in the mess hall and tear-jerkers around the campfire. And of course, I bowed at the feet of my cabin counselor, Gail and the others as they imparted teenaged wisdom on stuff like Vietnam, equal rights, and saving the Earth.

One morning during cabin cleanup, Gail lifted a conspiratorial eyebrow and waved us over to her trunk. Thrilled with the attention, we all gathered round her like little chicks ready to gobble up handfuls of feed. When she held up a tattered scrapbook and warned that the contents were secret, our heads bobbed bird-like as we promised not to tell. She slowly opened it to the first page, where glued-in photos of her marching for Earth Day sat at odd angles with stickers and concert tickets.

On the next page, she unfolded a flyer for a women's march and said, "We stopped traffic for blocks during this one. Cops came, billy clubs raised. Thought I'd get beat but they were just being jerks hoping to scare us off."

My jaw was on the floor, but my mind was on what I'd do later. Just before lights out, when we were supposed to write letters to our parents, I'd pull out the little diary Grandma had given me, unlock it with the tiny key, and pour all these moments onto the page.

By the end of the week, I had filled the diary and started using binder paper, folded in fourths and stuffed inside. When no more fit in the diary, I resorted to hiding these secret scribblings under the flowered panties at the bottom of my trunk, figuring no one would look there.

Not that they were anything too crazy. Just the stuff I dealt with every day. Like how come I looked like a pancake from the side, barely with nubs, and only a few wisps of hair on my privates like the nine-year olds in the gang showers, when most of the other girls in my cabin had a fistful of curling hair and Barbie boobies? Or why did the older counselors laugh when I asked what a tampon was? And how come some of the girls from Palos Verdes whispered that they didn't want Bethany, *a Jew*, to be part of their skit at the Talent Show?

Lots of questions, but no real answers. Except maybe how different I was. How others gabbed and squealed while I struggled to find the words.

I marveled at how easy it was for girls like Sydney and Erin. How witty comebacks and one-liners just rolled off their tongues.

But I couldn't even remember jokes our counselor had just told. Most of the time, I was too lost in dreams to keep up with the other kids. So, I just smiled and pretended to get their jokes. All the while wondering, what the heck did I just miss?

Still, I managed to change a bit in that month at camp. And it wasn't just how my shag cut now touched my shoulders, or how the blonde forearm hair showed against my tan like wisps of cotton. I'd memorized protest and peace songs that I mimicked in poetry that I shyly shared with my counselor, Gail.

She later took me up to the boar pits to tell me how mature she thought it was. That I should keep writing because I had some real talent. I thought she was just being nice, but nonetheless I stood taller when she said it.

In those four weeks, I began to see the life beyond pretending. In those four weeks I started to *become*.

And some things just didn't feel right anymore.

I knew just what I'd do when I got home. I would pull out each one of my Barbies and seat them in their Country Camper, making sure to stroke Skipper's hair one last time before sliding the little plastic door closed. Then I'd give the RV one big push and watched it roll to a stop.

Before putting it all into the Good Will box. And walking away.

SIX

IRIS

I hardly recognized the girl that stepped off the boat. Could that tanned kid twittering away with other girls, wide grin showing the gap between her teeth, be my daughter?

Not trusting my own eyes, I raised my hand in a tentative wave.

"Stop making a spectacle of yourself," Ron hissed under his breath. He wrapped an arm around my waist and dug his fingers into the soft flesh under my blouse.

Immediately, I lowered my arm and clasped my hands in front me to look like the well-trained wife Ron demands. Wincing as his pinch tightened down like pliers and bowing my head, I peeked through my false eyelashes to see if anyone who's important in Ron's eyes had noticed my faux pas.

Nouveau riche mothers with flared jeans and glam tops flicked cigarette ash from their manicured nails, while the Beverly Hills elite in Perry Ellis skirt suits rolled their *House Beautiful* magazines into canvas bags.

But the only person that I noticed was Joy, whose high-stepping filly gait sunk to a slow shuffle. With every step, her wide smile folded deeper into a scowl.

I wanted to run to her, take her in my arms like when she was five and spin her around, but Ron's hand was there. If I dared move, it would tighten on my waist like a spring-loaded clamp. I put on my half-smile placid mask.

"Hi, Mom. Hi Ronny," Joy said, giving me a dutiful peck on the cheek before copying my clasped hand pose.

Ron greeted her with a grunt and had started to turn toward the exit when that actor from the Mary Tyler Moore show walked by, arm slung over his son's shoulder.

Suddenly, the Ron that wooed me all those years ago appeared. Pivoting on his Ferragamo loafers, he lifted a rakish brow and trumpeted, "Who took my daughter and replaced her with a tan goddess?"

When the actor, Ted Kite, glanced our way, Ron squeezed Joy so tight I thought he might break her ribs. She stood there, arms stiff at her sides, lips pressed into a smile that never reached her eyes.

The next thing I knew, Ron was shaking hands with Ted Kite. After a boisterous joke or two about sending kids to camp, he swept an arm in our direction.

"My wife, Iris and this tanned goddess is my daughter, Joy."
He didn't say stepdaughter.

While Joy stared at her shoes, I nodded politely and gushed how I was a huge fan. Ted's chortling was cut short when Ron shoved a business card into his hand.

"If you are ever looking for real estate in Santa Juana, give me a call."

Ted held it up like a mini-flag and said he had to go.

Ron shook his hand heartily and led us out of the terminal. Once we were all buckled into the Lincoln, he rolled up the windows and turned on the AC. But that cold air did nothing to dim the rage in his face.

"Did you have to fucking embarrass me?"

"What?"

21

"Your head bobbing like a plastic Jesus in a Spic's low rider."

"I was only trying to act how you want me to."

"Looked like an idiot. You could have said something about my listings, but I should have known when I met you, you were just white trash. Take her out of the sewer, she's still covered in shit."

"I never was trailer trash," I retorted.

I felt the heat before the sound. It spiced the cool air, a flashing palm burning skin with brutal piquancy.

My husband, father of the year.

SEVEN

JOY

I can't remember when Mom married Ronald, I was only two. But I do remember my real dad coming around. And how he used to set me on his knee and start bouncing while singing, "She'll be coming round the mountain" in a Johnny Cash voice. Imagining I was riding six white horses, I'd cry, "Faster, Daddy, faster." And his leg would jiggle so much, I'd teeter before falling off in a heap of giggles.

Once, while rolling around in a fit of laughter, I looked past Dad at the popcorn ceiling and noticed a long crack from one side to the next. "Look, Daddy, a river."

His tickle hands halted, and he froze, staring at that crack for the longest time. Then he lifted me off his knee, stood, and walked away. Kept right on going out the front door.

Pretty soon after that, I started riding a stick horse.

Dad sang, "We'll all go out to greet her when she comes," but he hasn't greeted me in so long I can't remember.

I wonder what I did wrong.

Anyhow, once, during a visit to Aunt Kay's when I was supposed to be sleeping, I crept down the hall to listen to her and Uncle Mike rant about Ronald and Mom.

"Just call me Ronny, like Governor Reagan," Kay mocked.

"Ronny, my ass. He thinks he's hot shit because he drives a Lincoln and lives in The Estates," Mike said.

"Did you see her face?"

"Again?"

"She tries to cover it up with make-up, but I know."

"Asshole," Mike said.

I knew what the make-up was covering. The same thing our perfectly mowed lawn and etched concrete patio did. The same thing shrouding our windows. Mom was just as skilled at curtaining her face in Cover Girl beige as she was in sewing flawless window coverings.

And we all pretended to believe that the marks beneath the foundation were just smears, places she hadn't expertly applied the make-up.

Like today, when I got back from camp.

Yeah, if my real dad was here, he'd kick Ronny's ass. Lay him flat. Wrap Mom up in his strong arms, (they were strong, weren't they?) and whisk us away to a place beyond the mountain.

EIGHT

JOY

S o, you might be asking how a girl like me could go from
being a bare-chested little kid climbing trees on the golf
course and screaming Tarzan, to smoking so many bowls her
green eyes turned red? I don't really know. It just sort of
happened.

Well, that's not exactly true. I did have a plan in mind before
I started getting high. And it made perfect sense in my idealistic
brain. Or so I thought.

It all started on the first day of junior high. My stomach was
doing full-on flips as I combed my hair over to one side; it was
then even longer than after camp, almost long enough to look
like one of those movie stars in black and white movies.
Veronica Lake or Lauren Bacall.

"You do know how to whistle, don't you?" I said, making a
kissy face into the mirror. "You just put your lips together and
blow."

"Joy!" Kyle's voice seeped through the bathroom door into
my movie dream. "Mom says you gotta hurry up or you're going
to miss the bus. And I need the bathroom. You're not the only
one who has school, you know!"

"Okay!" I started to call him a brat but then, remembering that I was now in junior high, decided to act more mature. I shoved the barrette haphazardly above my right ear and swept the door open. "You may enter, younger brother. And I bid you a glorious day."

Rolling his eyes, Kyle shoved past me. With a low bow, he thrust his Mickey Mouse toothbrush in his mouth, flicked on the switch, and said, "Gwoorius day to joo," between vibrating pulses.

"So mature," I muttered, picking my new Scooby Doo lunchbox and Trapper Keeper binder up off the floor.

Nothing was going to get in the way of this day, not even annoying Kyle.

Mom sat at the kitchen table smoking a Virginia Slims while thumbing through a magazine. Their slogan was *You've come a long way, baby*, with pictures of the olden days when ladies wore long dresses. set next to today's stylish tool-carrying women.

It reminded of the day I saw her open the latest *Cosmo* and whisper, "You've come a long way, Iris," over and over. Her eyes had been fixed on the glossy page like one of the undead in the movies I'm not supposed to watch.

I'd tiptoed back down the hall and sat on my bed, rubbing my knotted stomach. My favorite book, *The Call of the Wild*, was lying open on the floral comforter to the chapter where Buck battles all odds in a frozen land. I tried to focus on the words, but my mind kept returning to Mom. In my imagination, she became Buck escaping a cruel master and trotting unbound in the Alaskan wilderness.

I wonder what she would look like with her teased hair flowing free, the snow lighting up her pretty face? She has the nose I wish I'd inherited and a wide smile that doesn't come out much. She's already one of the pretty mothers about the youngest of all my friends' moms. But she'd be even prettier if she didn't have that empty stare all the time. That I'm-somewhere-else look that makes me want to wave a hand in front of her and shout, "Wake up!"

Sometimes, when Ronny is going through a good phase and sales are up, he stops being like the master in *The Call of the Wild* and is actually pretty cool. Making jokes, slapping Mom on the butt, and kissing the top of her head.

Then I get to see her eyes light up like Christmas. That's when I see the power her beauty has, why all the men in the stores are nice, and why some rumpled mothers make *harrumph* sounds when she walks by.

"Do you have everything?" she asked, never looking up from the page.

I waved my cool Scooby Doo lunch box. "Yep, made PB & J, got chips, milk in the thermos."

She blew out a long column of smoke and watched it dissipate in the air. "Okay, get going or you'll miss the bus."

A dutiful kiss and a wave later, I was skipping down my street swinging Scooby's gang in one hand. Right before the bus stop, I caught myself. "You're in seventh grade. Be cool."

A few kids had already gathered in front of mean old Mrs. Barton's house, who throws rocks at you if you step on her lawn. I looked for my best friend Cheryl and when I didn't see her, the butterflies in my stomach started to do loop-da-loops. I didn't want to face those popular kids who sniggered when Shelly Mc Cormack played tag or when Cheryl and I wore matching rainbow socks. Not to mention those eighth graders I'd seen smoking in the park.

Scooby Dooby Doo, I almost said out loud, trying to remind myself how far I'd come this summer, growing my hair out, getting everyone to crack up during that Talent Show skit, and turning deep songs we sang around the campfire into poems in my journal.

The loop-da-loops became knots, so I bent down and pretended to rebuckle my Buster Browns. Chewing on my lower lip, I tried to look like I was concentrating on a crooked clasp but, after doing this five times, I thought it might look weird so I stood up.

Hugging my folder and lunchbox to my chest, I shuffled over to the end of the line. Thought about removing my barrette to hide behind my hair. Maybe if I acted invisible, they'd ignore me.

And it worked, for most of the day. Except when I got lost on the way to First Period and an eighth grader had to show me the way to English. Switching classes. Argh! Why couldn't it be more like Sixth when we had nice Mrs. Wagner?

It was at lunch when it happened. After trying my locker combination seventeen times, I finally was able to put my books away and pull out my shining Scooby Doo lunch box.

I loved that thing. On the front, the Headless Horseman was chasing Scooby and Shaggy off a cliff under a spooky moon. The sides had the Mystery Machine, mummies, and even an escaped circus lion. And on the back, the gang stood facing a haunted house behind a wrought iron fence with a *Danger Keep Out* sign. Inside, the orange thermos was held in place by a piece of metal so your sandwich and corn chips didn't get smooshed.

Neat-o.

Grabbing it by the handle, I swung it in a circle as I bounced down the halls.

"Joy! Over here!" Cheryl called, waving me over to her empty table.

"I looked for you at the bus, but you never came." I sat down and positioned my lunch box on the long grey tabletop so that Cheryl, or anyone else who might be passing by, could admire it.

"Yeah, my dad gave me a ride." She paused and stared at me with horror before pointing. "What is that?"

"It's my new lunch box. Pretty neat, huh? See how it's just like the cartoo—"

"Put it away. Now!"

"Why? It's Scooby Doo."

"People are going to think you're a baby. Look around. No one brings lunch boxes to junior high."

That's when I finally noticed. Brown bag, hot lunch, white bag, plastic bag. Oh no! I was the only kid in the cafeteria with a lunch box.

And I'd wanted to look so cool. It was bad enough being the youngest in my grade, thanks to my December birthday, and usually the smallest. Now they were going to think I was an absolute infant.

I snatched the food and threw it on the table. Gulping down my milk, I shoved the thermos inside and had just slid the lunchbox under my bench when Angie Van Gorman and her flock of nose-in-the-air brats swanned up.

"What's this?" Angie sneered, picking up my lunchbox.

The blood drained from my face.

"Aw, how adorable. A cartoon lunchbox. Just like my preschool brother has." She held it up for everyone to see.

I opened my mouth to protest but nothing came out.

"Give it back, Angie," Cheryl said.

This villain ignored her. And now she started to wave my lunchbox like a baton. The girls behind her started to snigger.

The red crept up my cheeks into my scalp where my barrette hung limply by my ear. I raised a hand to it while Cheryl looked at me with an exasperated shrug.

The next thing I knew, Angie marched her line of populos between the tables as if she were the lead majorette in the Fourth of July parade. "Wook at me. I'm Joy Chapel and I bwought my Scooby Doo lunch box to school."

I didn't know what to do. At home, when Ron was on one of his fist-flyers, I either hid or, if it was real bad, ran all the way to the oak tree in the park, scrambling up those big branches as high as I could.

Nothing to climb here.

"Let's go," Cheryl said, scooping up what was left of her meatloaf sandwich.

All I could do was mumble "Yes." My heart pounded so loud it hurt my brain.

I know. I should have done something, like demand it back. Slap it out of that brat's hand. Or at least tell a teacher.

Instead, I followed Cheryl out of there and let them have their parade, trying to tell myself that I didn't care about that stupid lunch box anyhow.

Cheryl gave me a sympathetic pat before heading to Fifth Period. Alone, the halls loomed but at least I was rid of that humiliating lunch pail. Then I stopped dead in my tracks. If I came home without it and Ronny found out... He was always going off about how I should take care of my stuff, turn off the lights and water since money didn't grow on trees.

Which is a weird idea. I always imagined Dr. Seuss-y trees with dollar bills instead of leaves. I even put a penny in the ground when I was four to see if it'd grow. Used to pour my bedside water on it every morning and when nothing popped up, I figured it was probably because a penny isn't enough. If I'd put in a quarter, a tree would've grown.

I ducked in the bathroom and sat in a stall, praying that it'd still be there. As soon as the bell rang, I sprinted back into the cafeteria where a few hall monitors still patrolled.

"Hey, lunch is over. Get to class," said a girl in a brown jumper and long brown braids.

"Lost something," I mumbled. It wasn't too hard to find. I scanned the food-littered tables for just a few seconds before finding it in the grey trash barrel, perched atop all of the apple cores, brown bags and banana peels. Without checking to make sure nothing was clinging to it, I snatched the handle, lifted it and splattered bright red Kool-Aid all over the front of my dress.

Now, not only did I have to carry this embarrassing thing to Fifth Period but I also had a blood red stain right in center of my chest, on the one outfit Mom said to be careful with because it came from Robinsons.

Looking like the Sundance Kid after the big shoot-out, I slunk toward science class. God, I hoped there was an open desk in the back of the room. But when I tried the handle, it wouldn't budge.

Please, no!

Maybe if I did a mouse knock, the teacher would be nice. Timidly, I curled my hand into a fist.

The door didn't open.

I tried a slightly louder knock, rat-sized.

No one came.

Finally, in frustration, I started slamming my lunchbox against the wood and was mid-swing when the door flew open.

"What is it?" a tall man shouted.

"S-sorry. I-uh, umm, it..."

"You're late."

"Sorry," I said but thought, *I know that, but can you cut me some slack?*

Of course, the only seat left in this huge class was in the first row facing the teacher's desk. Hiding my lunch box behind my back, I scuffled to my seat.

"Rah roh," said somebody in the back.

As soon as Mr. Gomez turned to write on the chalkboard, it started. Whispers. Snickers. Then passing a sketch of a dress-wearing Scooby from desk to desk.

It didn't end there. Oh no. All afternoon, kids jeered. "Scooby Doo, where are you?" This quickly devolved into, "Rah roh, want a Scooby snack?" And "Zoinks, it's a dog!"

By Sixth Period it was just, "Dog."

Even though I ran to get in line for the bus so I could sit at the front, about a million kids were already there when I arrived. Making me the third person on the seat.

Do you know what that's like, to ride a full bus when you

have officially become the school geek? If not, let me tell you. First, you'll have one butt cheek barely poised on the vinyl, your leg braced in the aisle for the impending shove that's supposed to knock you on the floor. Then, a crumpled paper hits you on the head. Next, it's every cuss word your parents ever shouted, with a few you don't even know the meaning of, followed by spit wads in your hair and finger flicks from behind.

Don't tell me I should have stood up to them. Don't tell me I should have fought back. Because it never works. The best thing to do is to pretend it isn't real, ignore it and stare out the window. Or go in your mind to another place.

If you squint hard enough, you might start to see in technicolor like in movies or TV. Once everything is blurry, you can leave your body and become a cartoon detective unmasking a crook who says, "I would have gotten away with it if it weren't for those meddling kids."

For precious seconds, time will stop and you'll be in that bright place where heroes win and shame-faced villains go to jail.

Anyhow, that's what I did, until the rubber band welt started rising on my arm. As the sneering boy crowed his victory over me, I suddenly realized why Scooby Doo cartoons were so popular.

Every episode ends the same, showing us that the monster behind the mask is a person. Just like in real life.

————

I know what you're thinking. One day of teasing does not turn someone into a stoner. You might even think it's kind of funny for a junior high kid to bring a Scooby Doo lunchbox to school. And I'd agree with you, *now*.

But back then I wasn't very good at laughing at myself or standing up to others. Hours later, I might invent witty retorts that'd shut those bullies down but, in the moment, I was too friggin' scared to even think.

I took things all seriously and shit.

Then there was this belief in the peace I always heard about. I knew that someday hippie truth would rain down from every mountain as the tortured danced in circles with the bullies. I had so much faith in this that I refused to say anything mean to anyone. Pretty soon, all hearts were going to soften and open to the free love I heard on the radio.

Man, was I stupid.

Because that incident was just the beginning.

NINE

JOY

If you've never tried it, you might wonder how someone makes a conscious decision to smoke pot. Do they get tricked into it? Is it slipped to them in some brownie? Or what?

I know lots of experts call marijuana the 'gateway' drug and they may be right. I don't know the motivations of all partiers. But for me, pot wasn't the gateway to everything else.

Torture was.

Seventh Grade.

From the second I got on the bus in the morning to the drop-off in the afternoon, every day was the same. Angie Van Gorman and her crew would surround me and begin their torments.

Angie must have carried a *How to Abuse 12-year-olds* guide in her purse because she knew every mean way to make kids quiver and cry. Since I had the distinct honor of being her favorite, she saved the most brutal attacks for me. "Dog, 'tard, freak, troll," she'd bay, while her pack threw their heads back and howled. Even if I could have escaped, it only took seconds for the wolves to draw a tight circle around me, leaving me outnumbered. Trapped.

I know. I should have run, and I did try shoving through

34

once, only to be met with, like, a million hands. They pushed back so friggin' hard, I ended up on my rear.

Humiliating.

That Friday, in history, Angie strolled by my desk and snatched my lunch bag. Staring me down, she waved it in front of my face before turning away and doing something to it. I had resigned myself to going hungry that day when it plopped back down now, sporting a crude Scooby sketch with a long you-know-what hanging down. Then she said loudly, "Mr. Cavalli, Joy's drawing nasty things!"

Next thing I knew, a detention slip was in my hand and my bag was in the trash. I had to charge that day. And it was Stew Surprise, a meat slop that strangely resembled the Alpo Grandma fed Toby. Yuck!

You'd think by the afternoon bus Angie would be tired, but by then she'd be so gorged on power, her brown eyes had a *Night of the Living Dead* sheen. When I saw her coming, I'd slink down on an empty seat, hoping to take cover before she found me.

As if there was anywhere to hide.

She plunked down in the seat behind me, rasping how ugly I was over and over again. Her words carved away pieces of me as if I were some fatted calf. But I was not about to completely go to slaughter. As soon as the bus doors opened, I ran. And ran, putting as much space between that yellow corral and myself as my skinny legs would allow.

One Sunday, as I was listening to deep songs like *Wildfire* and *Seasons in the Sun*, dreaming of how Samuel Garcia would brush the hair back from my face before he kissed me, I had an idea. A brainwave, actually. It was inspired and might just be a way to stop the mean words.

Now, I wasn't totally inexperienced. I'd played doctor with my cousins when I was five and had watched plenty of *Love, American Style* episodes, but all of my experiences were more theoretical, not practical, if you know what I mean. And I'd heard Angie's clique talk about making out, or razzing each other about French kisses and hickeys.

"What is that on your neck?" Laurel Wilson squealed last week in the cafeteria, her eyes peeled for whoever was listening.

"Nothing," Angie replied, lifting up her collar with a cat-lapping smile.

"You and Craig Armstrong? Going?"

Angie raised her eyebrows and shrugged as *The Clique* fawned all over her.

Making out, it seemed, made you cool. But it wasn't like I had any boys who I could ask, and to beg Cheryl for help would be gross. So, this one morning, after practicing nonchalant shrugs in the mirror, I decided that if there wasn't anyone around to give me a hickey, I'd give myself one. How hard could it be?

I tried to bend my neck this way and that, only to discover that my lips could only reach as far as my shoulder. And even then, they were so slobbery I could barely bite down. Still, after twisting my neck this way and that and trying to suck as hard as I imagined *The Crowd* did, I had a red mark an eighth-grader would be proud of.

"Oh, this?" I said into the mirror, dropping the corner of my nightgown. "It's nothing."

"Joy, get dressed. I need you to vacuum the living room. The cushions, too. Quickly, before Ronny gets home," Mom called through the bathroom door.

When I slipped my t-shirt over my head, I realized that no one would be able to see my wondrous monkey bite. I could have made another one on my hand, but that somehow didn't seem very sexy. Another plan to escape geekdom destroyed.

A few minutes later, as I was using the hose attachment to get all of the gook out of the couch cracks, I noticed a round mark in the vinyl. With a blink, I stepped back and stared.

Smiling, I tried to recreate it on the orange throw pillow. Just about the right size.

I nodded. It just might work.

With a quick glance down the hall to make sure Mom was still in her room, I sat down. Then I aimed the screaming tube at my neck, and thrust.

The engine revved and cold metal dug into my throat. "Ow! Ow!" I cried, tugging on a machine that seemed to have a hold of me like skin-sucking aliens.

I stood up and yanked. The whirring creature wouldn't let go.

I know. Why didn't I turn it off? It's so easy to flip a switch. Well, if you've ever had a vacuum hose attached to your neck sucking your skin off, you'd know that logical thinking goes out the window. You grab that metal snake, straining against its power. Tugging. Pulling. Battling.

Until finally, there's a loud pop and you know you're free. You heave a sigh of relief and run down the hall to escape.

Or maybe look in the bathroom mirror.

I brushed my hair out of the way. There on the side of my neck was a perfect red circle. Yeah, it looked more like an extraterrestrial squid's kiss than a love bite, but I didn't care. I now had my first official, okay fake, hickey.

The next morning, I put on a scoop neck t-shirt and snapped my barrette extra high before making sure my choker was placed to hide the hickey from Mom and Ronny. With one last nonchalant eyebrow-raise, I headed out.

Wielding my angry red key of escape, the mark that would forever deliver me from freak prison, I marched down the street.

As I approached the bus stop, the usual jailers were there. Angie, Laurel, and eighth grade Mike Widdle. I'd already unsnapped my choker, bunched it into my leather purse and brushed my hair back. Now, all I had to do was wait for them to notice my glorious monkey bite.

But for once, they ignored me. Even Angie wasn't turning her mouth into a head-crushing torture device.

I stepped a little closer, but not too close; I didn't want to be full-on obvious. I heard a few snatches of the conversation they were into, something about Angie's dad not coming home.

I don't like to be mean, I full-on believe that kindness opens hearts like keys. But there's an evil part of me that would like nothing more than to see Angie Van Gorman getting a little payback. I'll admit it; I couldn't help but gloat when I heard her agonizing over her dad storming out the night before.

I'm not always the hippie I want to be.

Okay, this group was busy. But the day had just begun, and I was brandishing the royal mark that was going to change everything.

Thinking my best friend was sure to be astounded and hoping to catch her before first period, I made a beeline for her locker as soon as I got off the bus.

"Notice anything about me?" I asked her, flipping my hair back with one hand.

She looked me up and down. "No."

"Look closer." I stretched my neck and raised my eyebrows knowingly, like I'd been practicing.

"Umm, new barrette?"

"Oh, Cheryl Silva, if you weren't my best friend..." I shook my head and pointed.

She gasped and covered her mouth in horror. "You burned yourself?"

"No! It's a hickey."

"Doesn't look like one. Looks like a curling iron burn. Anyhow, I happen to know that you are not that type." She jerked her thumb toward the tough chicks down the hall.

My shoulders slumped. If it didn't fool Cheryl, who was as gullible as a first grader, it wouldn't fool anyone. My groaning explanation of how I'd used the vacuum cleaner only made her crack up, and then she said how someday, those mean girls were going to get theirs, so why try to impress them?

I wish I had her confidence. And invisibility power. For some reason, she never got teased like I did. It was as if Morgan le Fey had cast a spell, hiding Cheryl from invading eyes.

Shrugging, I shuffled off to first period, hoping that maybe someone would detect my majestic flag. But no dice in that class. Or the next.

Maybe at lunch? Head tilted to display my standard, I walked past Samuel Garcia. Even tried scratching my neck in a big motion to get his attention. He was too absorbed in his Twinkie to look my way. Not that I could blame him. That creamy filling is pretty delicious.

All afternoon my hands smoothed, wriggled and flapped. With as much spectacle as I could muster, I became a knight brandishing a sword, a prince wielding a rampant shield, and a dragon in mid-flight. Still, no amount of flourishes got a single kid to even jerk a thumb in my direction.

The bus ride home was the final hope of my noble quest. But even there no one noticed.

That's when I realized.

Hickeys are completely overrated.

———

8th Grade.

I'm going to be popular, I'd decided. I'd had it with being a dog and a freak. No more Angie Van Gormans teasing me from the bus. Eighth grade was going to be different. I'd been planning it all summer. I grew my hair out and it got nice highlights from the summer at camp.

But to do this I had to make some changes. And some were freaking hard. I knew where to start, and which girls on the fringe of popularity might accept me. But to go forward, I had to leave some things, and maybe some people, behind. Unless I could get them to advance, too. Although I knew it was hopeless, I tried one more time to convince Cheryl.

"If we get some make-up, blue eye shadow and eyeliner, then we offer to share it with Lisa W—"

"I don't want to wear eye shadow. Anyhow, it's against the rules. If my mom found out, she'd ground me for a month," Cheryl protested, closing the door to her room.

"But she'll never know. We'll be sneaky and put it on in the bathroom by the gym."

She shook her head. "Why do you even care what those dummies think? They were *soooo* mean last year. Or have you forgotten?"

As if I'd ever forget the hours of torture. "That's just the point. If we were popular, it would all stop."

"Not interested. Hey, I have the new David Cassidy album. It's a live concert. Want to listen?"

I nodded and Cheryl opened the clasp on her Crosley portable record player, the kind that looked like a little suitcase, and propped the lid up against her frilly bed. Like most of her room, which was either newborn pink or other layette shades, it was baby blue with a shining white handle.

She lifted the needle onto the vinyl LP. First, there were just scratches but after a few seconds, there was a susurrating hush that transported us to a real concert. The rotating record bobbed over the turntable as screaming girls nearly drowned out David's foxy voice. Cheryl propped the album cover against her bed and the two of us lay on our tummies, chins in hands, gazing at his handsome face. I was soon lost in the reverie of what it would be like to be *his* girlfriend.

In sixth grade, we'd imagined marrying Donny or Marco or David. But now that we were more mature and almost ready for eighth grade, we realized how silly that was. Rock stars like them would want girlfriends. Anyhow, twelve, almost thirteen, was too young to get married.

But girls ready to be teenagers should make major changes. And I didn't care what it took, I was going to escape freakdom. If Cheryl wouldn't listen, I'd find someone else who would. Someone with similar ambitions. (Like that phrase? I read it in a Stephen King book my Mom has.)

As Cheryl chattered on about her imaginary date with Bobby Sherman, I realized what I was going to have to do. And how hard it would be.

I knew it'd take time. The road to popularity couldn't be built in a day. But I had a plan. In the first weeks of school, I'd hang with Cheryl, David and Wanda at the cafeteria table in the far corner. I'd lie low and try a few more times to get one of them to change with me, knowing its futility all the while. Because at the same time, I'd be keeping a lookout, seeking some seventh graders who might be willing to take this upward ride.

When I saw her with her arms crossed over her chest, I knew. She had my same look. Hiding behind her hair but all the while wishing the *special* people would accept her.

"Hi, I'm Joy. Eighth grade wannabe."

She looked at me as if I was crazy. Stepped back and drew her brows together. "Huh?"

"Your name?"

"Oh, Vickie." She paused and narrowed her eyes. "Why are you talking to me?"

"You reminded me of someone."

She tilted her head to one side.

"Someone that is going to disappear pretty soon, I think, with your help."

Now she seemed intrigued. But I didn't tell her my entire plan just then. Just that I wanted to be friends. Didn't want to scare her away just yet.

Over the next few weeks, Vickie and I started hanging out more and more. As I got to know her, I could see why things were tough for her. She'd gone to some Christian private school up until sixth grade, so didn't really know anyone at the junior high. Plus, her parents were mega strict and made her dress all churchy, in long jumpers and knee sox. Maybe she didn't finish my sentences or understand why I dreamed of a different world, but she was pliable.

And that was what I needed.

At lunch, Cheryl had stopped waving me over. I guess she knew the score. I could see it in the way her face fell the last time I'd ignored that brace-faced smile.

One thing I'll say about her is, she's smart. Not only book-smart, but people-smart. Great grades, good flute player, even the ins and outs of popularity. But while she accepted things as they are, shrugging off the cruel comments, I wanted to change the whole friggin' world. Including my status in it.

I did get a twinge of guilt when I passed by, and almost stopped to say hi. Until I heard the hiss of "Freak" from the popular table. That set my shoulders in determination. And the mask on my face.

Anyhow, today was the day. I was armed with an arsenal of blue eyeshadow, crème blush, and strawberry lip gloss. Vickie and I would eat fast and then head to the bathroom, where we'd slowly apply frosted blue to each other's eyes and wait.

I was smearing a fourth coat on Vickie's lids when Maria Wood and Karen Alanson walked in. Cool. These girls weren't part of Angie's mean crowd. They hung out with the popular kids, true, but never joined in when Angie started her taunts.

"Hi," Karen said, approaching the mirror to scratch at a zit on her cheek.

I tried to act nonchalant as I said "Hey" back.

She started to ask about our make-up, so I offered to share. Lifting the wand, I said, "I think this color is perfect for you."

42

And so it began. First with Maria and Karen. Then more girls. I was starting to be accepted. But for some reason, Angie's crowd persisted in their mean words. God, I hated the bus!

One afternoon, still panting from running away from her and Shawn's torment, I stared into the mirror, seeing green eyes so pale they nearly faded into my eye sockets. Two new pimples were threatening to erupt in the middle of my forehead and my frizzed hair was going in so many directions, it could have been used as a compass. I could see why they called me a dog.

I *was* one.

I started to remove the make-up still coloring my face when something stopped me. Instead, I applied a large swath of icy frost to each lid and rubbed a circle of rouge into each cheek.

No better.

Dejected, I picked up the soap and washcloth and began to lather my face. I scrubbed. Rub off those zits! Harder. Get rid of those stupid pale cheeks! I tugged at my mousy hair that now was losing its summer highlights. "Ugly dog." I dug deeper into my skin with the washcloth. God, I hated that face! If I could have ripped it off, I would have.

Bang! Bang! Bang! Fists pounded on the door. "Hey, Joy, hurry up in there. You're not the only one in the family, you know!"

"Shut up! I'm busy!" I cried.

When I looked back at the mirror, a macabre stranger with dripping soap on a bright red face stared back. She could have been one of those weird creatures in a Sunday afternoon horror movie.

"Full-on dog," I said, wiping away the soap with a towel.

A few moments later, all traces of makeup and soap were gone. But my ugliness? That remained, hanging on like the string unraveling at the bottom of my fringed towel. Even if you pulled, the splitting weft would only get longer until finally ending up in tatters.

The only solution was to cut it all off.

I looked around. But I didn't have any scissors. Or even a knife.

———

Hardened faces flash in and out.
  While concrete barriers
  Encase me

Well, my great plan isn't turning out all that great. Some popular girls on the fringe are accepting Vickie and me but *The Crowd* is still as mean as ever. I don't get it. What am I doing wrong? I've tried sharing my make-up, signed up for guitar class, and even put a little hydrogen peroxide in my hair to lighten it. But still it's "dog" and "frr-eak" every day.

I tried going to the Winter Formal last month, but it was just like seventh grade. No one asked me to dance. And I was ready. Had been watching *American Bandstand* and *Soul Train* for moves. Learned this cool backbend floor slap, too.

Christmas was… just like last year. Oh, sure, I got what I asked for, a new Yamaha guitar with a black case, and we ate a lot yummy treats and, as usual, visited Grandma. I even made Dad a special present, a collage of places we'd visit together. I spent hours combing through magazines to find the right ones. Just like the Brady Bunch did, we'd go to all kinds of places— Hawaii, the Grand Canyon, maybe even New York City. I wrapped it carefully, too, tucking in the edges so the corners were smooth like Mom showed me. Best job ever.

Then I waited and waited.

Well, it's good that I have a big closet.

I asked Mom why he didn't come when he wrote he was going to. She said, "He's just an asshole, a big asshole." But I don't agree. I think it's me. Something repels people. Maybe it's because I'm not adorable like Dad's new kids. They're little and cute. Or so he told me on the phone back in October when he said he might visit this Christmas.

I still haven't met them.

Sometimes, I dream I do something so amazing that my homeliness doesn't matter. Like save somebody. Like if I was biking past the park and there was this screech of tires and a crash of metal and I jumped the curb to find the victims inside burning cars and used my super thirteen-year-old strength to pry the doors open and rescue both families before the giant explosion. Then the reporters would come, and I'd be on TV, and the mean girls would stop calling me dog and Dad would have to come visit because parents have to attend the honoring ceremony.

I've biked all over, but in my neighborhood the cars go slow and obey the rules.

"We're going to have to kick it up a notch, Vickie," I said, when she came over to listen to 45's in my room.

"I don't know how. It's like we're locked out."

"I think I have the key." I reached under my bed and pulled out the pack of Virginia Slims I'd stolen from Mom's cigarette case in the garage.

Vickie's brown eyes widened. "I don't know, Joy. If I get caught..."

"We're not going to get caught. And you know it's what *they* do."

"Yeah, saw 'em behind the stall in the bathroom. Sharing one."

"But we'll have to practice first. Come on, we'll go out to the field."

I shoved the pack into the bottom of my purse, and then tried to act all nonchalant when I asked Mom if Vickie and I could go for a walk.

"Thirteen-year-olds do need exercise, Mom," I said, making my eyes so wide you'd think they were fried ostrich eggs.

"Yeah, Mrs. Wright. We are just working on our..." Vickie looked at me.

"Figures. Gotta keep slim, you know."

Mom looked me up and down and tilted her head to one side. "Joy, that's the last thing you have to worry about."

"Actually, it's for me, Mrs. Wright. Been trying to lose a few pounds. Joy's just being nice." *Good save, Vickie.* That was totally believable since she's always complaining about the baby fat around her tummy.

Mom nodded and the two of us marched out the door doing high knee lifts in our best Jack LaLanne exercise show imitation. Thinking we might be watched, we kept it up until rounding the corner. Laughing, I draped an arm over Vickie's shoulder and led her toward the fence edging our tract.

A minute later, were alone in the eucalyptus and oak fields where winter leaves carpeted the ground in brown feathers. Vickie kicked a pile and giggled when they fluttered onto my head.

"Hey, cool it!" I said.

"Like this?" She giggled again and launched a bigger heap my way.

After punting back, I said, "Come on, goof, we're on a mission," and began crunching through the littered branches and leaves. The rhythmic rustling of every step seemed to say, *Soon, Joy, soon.*

I began dreaming of a life beyond geekdom, where popularity's pearly gates opened and shone down on my haloed head. "Oh, this? It's just a cig," I imagined saying to *The Crowd* as I blew a long column of smoke into the air and flicked ash like a glamorous movie star in an old black and white movie.

Meanwhile, all the popular kids would ooh and aah.

"Ready?"

Vickie nodded and leaped into a shallow ravine below. I followed and then we skirted along until we found a couple of trees to hide behind. After crouching down, I pulled out the magical charms that would soon cast our popularity spell.

The matches I'd brought were the kind they give away in restaurants and pretty cheap. I opened the book and tore one out before looking to Vickie for help.

She shrugged. "I don't know."

"Me neither. Even when they were teaching us how to make teepee or log cabin campfires on Catalina, the counselors lit them." I tried scraping the match over the striker, but nothing happened. Pushed harder. Still no spark. Repeated it until the paper was all crinkled and torn. Threw that one in my purse. I am not a litterbug. I did this like seven times, until Vickie finally suggested folding the book in half with the scratch part inside and pulling the match through it.

It worked! She stuck the end of the cigarette into the flame and waited for something to happen. But it didn't really catch. She tilted her head to one side and waved it around.

"I think you have to put it in your mouth and puff on it. That's how my mom does it, anyhow."

"How?"

I reached for the cigarette in her hand and set it on my lips. "Like this." Acting like it was a straw, I sucked in.

"You try," she said.

"'kay." This time, Vickie lit the match and cupped a hand around the flame before lifting it toward me. As soon it reached the end I drew in a long breath. I immediately started coughing and dropped the cigarette.

Vickie picked up the glowing stick. "Ha! Some smoker you are."

I crossed my arms. "You try then."

She lifted it tentatively to her lips and inhaled, not breathing deeply like I had but blowing out a quick puff right away. Vickie gave me a superior look, but she was still choking when she said, "No, *hem*, problem."

When she passed it back to me, I copied her short drag. Sputtered and coughed again. But at least I didn't drop it this time.

Vickie rolled her eyes.

Smoking was definitely going to take some practice.

TEN
KYLE

J oy has been acting weird lately. Well, she's always weird, but since around Christmas she's been certifiable. I mean, why does a thirteen-year-old lock herself in her room so much?

Not that I mind. I kind of like the silence. It's better than hearing her have a cow every time I get the bathroom first. Or the hair torture.

But she at least used to notice when I was popping wheelies. Even gave me advice on how to lean my Schwinn Stingray back so I wouldn't fall over. I pretended to ignore her, of course, but when she was gone, I tried one of her tips. Actually worked.

Now I barely see her. I wonder what she does in there hour after hour. Once, out of curiosity, I knocked and walked in before she could yell "Go away!" I found her curled around one of Mom's books. *The Exorcist*.

"I don't think you're allowed to read that," I said.

"Get out of my room, Kyle!"

"I'm gonna tell Mom."

She sat up and gave me a dirty look. "Is that like your mission in life, or something? To be a tattletale, a narc?"

49

That stung. "No. I don't always tell. Not for you, but because I don't want Dad to—"

"Yeah, *your* Dad might get mad, huh? What about mine?"

I tilted my head, confused. "Yours?"

"You know I have one, right? A real dad. Not some fake one."

I didn't know what to say. Just stared.

"I bet you wanna know about my real dad, don't you? You're so freaking curious. Well, I'll show you my real dad." She sprang up and jerked a thumb at her closet. Joy slid the bypass door open and kicked away some of the shoes and dirty clothes on the floor. Under her pink robe was something shiny with a big silver bow on top. A red and green package. No, not one; actually, a few presents.

I stepped closer and read the tag on the gift. *"To Dad. Love, Joy."* I put my hands on my hips. "Christmas is way over. I don't think Dad would want those now."

"They're not for Ronny, dumb-ass."

"For...?" Then it hit me. That was a present for Joy's real dad. But he hadn't come around this Christmas or for a long time, ever since, I couldn't even remember. Now I noticed the other gifts stacked under that one. I started to count, 2-3-4. Each was a little more faded than the one on top of it.

"Your dad keeps mine away. His stupid temper," Joy's mouth said, but her eyes seemed to know it was a lie.

Joy can be weird, but Christmas... I decided to pretend. "Okay, I won't tell."

"Cool." She didn't look at me before closing the closet door, just slid down the wall and reopened her book. Started reading.

I started to ask more, but her eyes were stuck to that book. I tiptoed out.

Joy may be weird but I guess she knows that it's easier to go into stories that never happened than be part of real Christmases that did.

ELEVEN

JOY

In the quietest moments
Comes the loudest voice of all.

I learned three new chords! D7, A minor, and a barred E. The bar chord was the toughest 'cause you gotta flatten your first finger over all the strings and then get your other fingers all spread out. And since mine are kind of short, it isn't easy to stretch the pinkie all the way to the B string. It sounded a little dull, not ringing like Mr. Curry's chords, but I managed to press down all my fingers at once.

Guitar class is my favorite. An elective I was lucky to get into. In this class, we learn songs they play on the radio, get to go outside on the grass, and even share some things we write. It's all because Mr. Curry is so cool. We call him Furry Curry because he has this big, bushy beard that is so thick, it makes you think of a fuzzy stuffed animal. I bet if you ever touched it, it'd tickle like feathers.

Not that I ever would. Gross.

The kids are pretty cool here, too. The only chick from *The Crowd* is a new girl named Lynette who moved here from way down south, like Oxnard or L.A. or something. Somehow, she immediately got into Angie Van Gorman's favor and everyone else just followed suit. Still, she never calls me names, just tells stories of how it was at her old house, with the station-wagon-driving surfers sporting boards on racks and the big malls and the freeways and stuff.

I liked Lynette. And she was one of the better players in class. Not like me. I didn't exactly suck, but I wasn't the fastest learner, either. My stubby fingers just didn't stretch like some kids.

Now, Kent Freeman could play. I wondered why he was even taking class in junior high, he was so beyond the rest of us. He could play all the bar chords, plus notes, and even songs. Not just the rhythm but the melody. Kent had this ear. He could hear something and then pluck it out note by note, just like the real song.

Once, Mr. Curry challenged Kent to show his stuff. With a smirk that made his fuzzy beard all cockeyed, he put on the song, *Sunshine on my Shoulders*, and asked Kent to memorize it.

While the needle scratched over the black disc, Kent cocked his head to one side and his blond bangs fell over closed eyes. With the guitar cradled in his arms, his silent fingers moved up and down the neck in a quiet dance.

When the record finished, Furry Curry strummed an intro to cue Kent. "Now, together," he said.

What happened next blew us all away. Kent started to play the song note for note!

I gaped as Kent's guitar became a high, clear voice. Our teacher accompanied him in a harmony that was so perfect, I could almost feel the sunshine on my shoulders.

Kent could really make those strings sing.

Sometimes, when I was home alone in my room, just me and

my guitar, I'd try to pluck out a melody as sublime as I'd heard that day. Taking a deep breath, I'd hug the guitar to my chest and clutch the neck as if I could squeeze wonder from the strings. Then, a slightly out of tune rhythm would vibrate off the body and I'd go to a misty place.

But it never quite came out like Kent's.

Although I wished I played better, it didn't matter. When I was alone like this and creating something wonderful, I went to that land of notes where I just became. A place of peace where the mask I had to wear every day slipped off and fell to the floor.

Have you ever experienced that? Found a place where you were one with the moment? Where it was just you and the music?

I hope so, because times like these... well, you know.

TWELVE

JOY

April 22. After guitar class when Lynette asked me for gum! We went to the bathroom and shared spearmint while four of The Crowd came in. Two even talked to me. Tomorrow I'm going to go out to the field when Lynette does.

'Gum' was code for cigarettes in my journal so Mom or Kyle wouldn't know that I was smoking if they read it. Pretty smart, if I do say so.

After Vickie and I got the knack for how to inhale without coughing, our next step was to let everyone know. How? By hanging in the girls' bathroom, of course. There, in the blue mist of Virginia Slims, we could be ready to show any of the popular girls who came in.

The bummer part of this was that it put even more distance between Cheryl and me. She gave me pitying looks from across the cafeteria or in the halls. I tried to tell myself that I was better off without a goody-goody judging me, but deep down I missed my best friend.

We planned it out for about three weeks. Since Vickie's parents didn't even drink wine at Christmas, much less smoke, it was my job to sneak some cigs from Mom's pack on the coffee table. Not exactly hard, since she left them there half the time and was always pacing from one room to the next in a constant cleaning bustle. Wouldn't want Ronny to come home to a mess.

When the coast was clear, I tapped three out, planting them under the Stay-Free pads in my purse. I figured that even if someone was suspicious, they wouldn't look under girl-stuff but still, the first time was pretty scary. Mom came in just as I was closing my purse. I stumbled back, my heart pounding so hard I thought she might notice it pulsing off my t-shirt and ask me what was up.

Couldn't have been more wrong. She wandered into the living room, picked up the pack, and lit one as usual. Then she glanced at the clock and told me I better get going or I'd miss the bus.

"Oh, okay," I said, grabbing my brown bag on the counter.

Once at school, Vickie acted as look-out while I headed for the girls' bathroom to perch inside the empty stall at the end. Since no one was there yet, I decided to practice how I'd hold the stick between my fingers for the best effect. Then, when I heard two knocks, the signal from Vickie that someone cool was coming, I lit the cigarette and leaned back against the side of the stall. That way, whoever came in would see the smoke but not how hard I was trying.

I was surprised that it actually worked. When Karen Alanson came in, she sniffed loudly and said, "Hey, who's got a cancer stick?"

Slowly, I stuck my head out of the stall and lifted a 'hello' chin her direction. "Want a drag?" I said, as nonchalantly as I could muster. What an act! In truth, I was sure that she'd say, "Who'd want to share a cig with dog-lips like yours?" I was scared totally shitless, but I think my act worked because she reached out a hand and took an expert puff that Greta Garbo would have been proud of.

So that both of us would get to hang with the cool girls, every day either Vickie or I would stand sentinel while the other one went inside to smoke. That way, if a teacher or the principal was cruising the halls, someone could alert everyone inside.

As the weeks went on, things got better. I mean some kids still called me dog, but there were a few who actually passed me notes asking for a cig to share, or if I liked a medium cute boy.

One read, *Do you want to go with Shane? He likes you.* 'Go' was our shorthand for going out. It sounded more modern than going steady and basically meant that you said 'hi' to that boy during every break. Maybe even talked on the phone.

Unless you were like that new girl in school, who came in wearing her bikini top under her shirt. I heard she lifted her tee at the guys and said, "I got a new suit. Do you like it?" before going out to the field behind the trees and, well, making-out. She always had hickeys up and down her neck. Way down, if you know what I mean.

But not me. I still hadn't even been kissed, except like from Mom. But that doesn't count.

I'd been three guys' girlfriend and hadn't even held any of their hands. I heard about it, though; how I was a being a baby for not making out. I thought of creating a fake hickey again but, after the vacuum failure, I decided it wasn't worth it.

Things were going pretty good so I decided to make my move. I knew Lynette hung with Angie Van Gorman's elite crowd at lunch on the field and she usually stopped in for a smoke on the way. My plan was to tell her I had a whole pack to share with everyone and then keep following her as she walked out there.

I gulped down my PB & J as fast as I could and rushed to what I thought of as my bathroom stall now. Didn't even wait for Vickie to be look-out, just lit up as soon as I was there. If I had to wait through two, it was fine.

Lynette came in laughing with Maria, hand ready to reach inside her bag for the cigarette she always carried.

"Hey, I got one lit," I said, motioning them over.

We shared the Virginia Slim and then, before Lynette had a chance to say 'later', I told her how I had enough for everyone.

Unsure, she eyed me up and down and exchanged a glance with Maria, who shrugged.

She said yes!

I felt like a hero just returned from war as we marched toward the field where Angie and her crowd were getting into a comfortable circle. Imagining ticker tape fluttering down from the school roof, I fought the urge to begin parade-waving to the kids in the halls.

When my feet hit the grass, I fell in line behind the two of them. Lynette was so friggin' confident. She walked ahead, her perfectly straight hair bouncing off her shoulders, chin held high like a queen or something. I take it back. She didn't walk. She full-on strutted. And with Maria prancing alongside, you'd think they were on their way to a ceremonial ball.

Was Joy Chapel really going out to the popular part of the field? Fighting the urge to pinch myself, I covered my mouth and giggled.

Cooldom, here I come! A grin as big as the field split my buoyant face. I felt awesome.

For about ten seconds.

Then my heart started pounding and my tongue got all dry. I wanted to say something funny or avant-garde like in one of Mom's books. Cool word, huh? *Avant-garde.* It's French and means like the advanced, artsy group. I looked it up when I was reading a *Cosmo* article about modern styles and had been dying to use it in a sentence. Anyhow, when I opened my mouth nothing avant-garde came out. Instead, the words got all stuck in my throat.

Damn.

"Joy's got a present for everyone," Lynette said, lowering herself into a cross-legged sitting position.

"Yeah," I croaked copying her yoga pose. "One for everyone." While a cramp threatened to move from thigh to hip, I fumbled in my purse for the pack I'd stolen from Mom. Closing one eye, I tossed it across the circle, but it landed in the very center. Missed Jeff Widdle by a mile.

I didn't know what to do. Get up and hand it to Jeff? Ask Lynette to get it? I opened and closed my mouth but didn't move.

No one spoke. Time stretched, an invisible clock ticking each painful second. Meanwhile, that pack sat there like a flashing alarm blaring, *Do something. Do something.* Angie sniggered and I started playing with the buckle on my shoe, wondering how Buster Brown made them so strong.

Maria looked over her shoulder before coming to the rescue. "This is a total bust," she said, hopping to her feet. She snatched the pack and tossed it to Jeff, who passed it to a sneering Angie, who passed it to Mike, who immediately passed it to Cathy. None of them so much as opened the box. You'd think it was that gross Halloween candy that stays in the bottom of your bag for weeks until it's so stale, Mom makes you throw it in the trash.

Finally, one kid took a cig from the pack, passing it back to me almost full. It felt like my dead hamster Scuffles in my limp hand.

"So, Jeff, you still going with Karen?" Cathy asked.

He replied 'yes' while others around the group made jokes about coupling up in the park that I didn't understand. I listened but didn't dare say anything until the bell rang.

Everyone stood, but by now I was quivering so much that I was sure I'd fall over just trying to get up. I couldn't even tell if that was my body or the ground shaking below me. Fearing an earthquake, I got on my hands and knees and took three deep breaths. Lynette raised one eyebrow and then crinkled her nose.

I am an idiot.

Still on all fours, I started to explain, but she'd already strutted ahead. I staggered to my feet and jogged to catch up.

God, I wished I hadn't.

Once in earshot, I heard Maria say, "Looks like Lynette has a shadow."

Lynette glanced from me to the crowd. She flipped her hair. "I do, I do."

Angie smirked. "A shadow shaped like a dog."

"Woof," Jeff said.

"Shadow, shadow, where's my shadow?" Maria sniggered.

The next thing I knew, several of them had linked arms and started chanting, "Shadow, shadow," over and over again.

A distorted silhouette rippled over the grass. I halted and shook my head at the shrunken figure.

Still a freak.

Damn.

THIRTEEN

JOY

The crumbling walls
Fall all around
While men draw
Palaces in the dust

It's been raining all morning. I tried opening *White Fang* but my eyes kept blurring on the page. Guess I've read it too many times. Started looking through some of Mom's books. She's got some spooky ones like *The Little Girl Who Lives Down the Lane*.

In it, there's a girl around my age who lives all alone. She's mega-smart, brave as shit, and independent. When her dad was dying, he said he never wanted her to lose her spirit, so he figured out a way for her to have money and a house until she grew up.

That would be so amazing. To live by yourself. No school. No one telling you what to do. No mean kids on the bus.

So this Saturday, I curled up in one corner of my room with

my giant panda and read how this girl survived. When the lady with the long, cruel fingernails came to take her away, the Little Girl made her a special tea. The kind that tasted of almonds. The kind she had to serve with almond cookies to hide the flavor.

I was just getting to the part when a creepy guy asks her if she has a boyfriend when I heard a soft knock on my door.

"What is it, brat?" I asked when I saw Kyle standing there, hair combed all perfect even though it was Saturday.

He put a finger to his lips. "Can I come in?"

I eyed him for a sec to see if he was messing with me before opening the door all the way. Once inside, he beckoned me to the other side of the room. I closed it quietly and approached. Then he just stood there, searching my face, his long-lashed blue eyes everyone compliments him on blinking.

I raised my arms, exasperated. "What? Just tell me!"

He cocked an ear and let the silence fill the room before whispering, "It's Mom."

"Huh? Did Ronny...?"

"No, no not this time. He's off at the Club. Golf buddies."

I looked out the window at the steady rain. Ronny would not play in that. I gave Kyle a bewildered shrug.

"She is in the living room, just staring at some picture."

"Of what?"

"Not what, who."

"Then who?"

"A lady. With lots of make-up."

"Another magazine? So." Mom often got lost in her glamor mags. She'd thumb through them for hours until the astray was overflowing with cigarettes.

"It's a Polaroid. Has an X O written at the bottom."

Then I knew. It was Ronny. Even when he wasn't there, he still left marks.

I'd seen the way he was at their parties. Telling stories to ladies about the movie stars he met on the golf course. I thought that was pretty cool until he'd lean in close and whisper something in their ears that either made them blush or their faces go white.

And Mom would glance over and then pretend to check a button on her blouse or if her necklace was straight, before going to our glass and chrome bar for another Seven and Seven.

"Is she crying?" I asked.

He shook his head. "Just staring."

Part of me wanted to check on her. Make sure it wasn't too bad. Be the comforting daughter. But another part, the kid one, told me to stay in my room with my book and big panda.

I am only thirteen! I thought, staring at the teddy bear Dad had given me three years before. Then I glanced at my baby brother's face. *And Kyle's only ten so come on. Be brave. Like the Little Girl.*

"You stay here. I'll check."

Kyle nodded, his face suddenly looking exactly like it had when he was three and off to preschool for the first time.

In the living room, Mom was so deep in the suede club chair she'd become a part of it. I mean, if a stranger had walked in at that moment, they might not even have seen her and sat right on her lap. She was slumped over, both hands clutching a photo. I could tell she'd been holding it a long time because the edges were crumpled and her hands white. She didn't seem to hear me when I approached.

For a moment, I wondered if it was real. "Mom?"

She still stared.

"You okay?"

Not even a blink.

"Mom?"

Without removing her gaze, she said, "She's not very pretty, is she?"

I glanced at the Polaroid. "No."

"Kind of cheap. Like K-Mart."

I didn't know exactly what that meant but agreed anyhow. "Not like you. All my friends say so."

Now she slowly looked up. "They do?"

"Yeah, they say you're one of the pretty moms. You know, the kind all the dads smile at."

"Hmm."

"You okay, Mom? You been sitting here a long time."

"I have?"

"Yeah."

"Oh." She returned to the photo.

I didn't ask where it had come from. Or who it was. I knew. Didn't want her to have to say the words. Thought about giving her a hug, but we weren't real big huggers in this family. Searched my brain for something to say.

No words came.

Finally, I just went back to my room where Kyle was waiting with a did-you-find-a-magical-brew-to-fix-it look.

But all my potions were in my mind, so I did what I always do, I lied.

"It was nothing. She's fine."

———

In our home, we had a sacred time every night. No, we didn't bend our heads in prayer or listen to Mom read Psalms from the Bible; my parents thought that stuff was for holy rollers. But as soon as Mom brought Ronny his highball and his feet were propped up on the coffee table, Kyle and I knew to be extra quiet. And listen.

In moments we'd hear, "This is the CBS evening news with Walter Cronkite," and we'd settle down at the edge of the family room, our legs crossed like silent monks.

"You kids pay attention," Ronny would say. "He's not called the most trusted man in America for nothing."

And we'd nod, not really understanding why these newscasts were supposed to be so important. I mean, who cared if Mao Zedong invited the U.S. Ping Pong team to China, or Henry Kissinger got the Nobel prize? We'd rather watch *Star Trek* reruns or cartoons. All these broadcasts were boring lectures to us.

Until I was around ten. That's when the Vietnam broadcasts became more graphic and my cousin Jeffrey from Grants Pass up in Oregon got drafted. Even though it made Ronny mad because the phone bills were going up, Mom started to call Uncle Scott more. I could always tell when she was asking about Jeffrey because she'd turn away, lowering her voice to a whisper.

Around that time, the anti-war songs on the radio really began to make sense and I started to see why the hippies were doing what they were doing. Even though Jeffrey was eight and a half years older, he'd played with me in the pool when we'd visited a couple summers back, even showed me how do that thing with your hand to turn it into a squirt gun. Every time I cleared the surface, he'd squeeze a stream of spray into my face. And, giggling, I'd try to shoot back, but Jeffrey was too fast and ducked down before my stream could connect.

The idea of such a good squirter facing real bullets gave me a bad feeling in the pit of my stomach.

So, instead of wishing for cartoons, I started to look earnestly at the mustached man's face flickering on the screen. And listen as if he had a special message for me, thinking he might help me define who I'd become.

"What does *mired in stalemate* mean?" I asked during the commercial.

Ronny took a long draught and swirled the ice cubes around in his glass. "It means, kiddo, that no one is winning."

"Like tic-tac-toe?"

"Yeah, like that." He emptied the rest of his drink and held it out for Mom to refill.

"Then why don't we leave?"

"I guess we don't know how."

"If I could talk to President Nixon, I'd tell him—" I didn't finish, because the commercials were over and Ronny had already turned the sound back on.

But while Walter Cronkite reported on soldiers the same age as my cousin dying in Vietnam, negotiations coming to a stalemate and protesters getting arrested, I imagined sitting down with the president and telling him that love was the answer. That because he was smart and good, he could find a way to peace. Then he'd look in my child eyes and a revelation would come over him.

Light rays from Heaven would shine down. And the next thing we knew, the war would be over.

But when the newscast ended with, "And that's the way it is, March 6th 1972," the war raged on. Mom still stared into space while Ronny downed another highball. And that conversation with the president? It remained a dream.

FOURTEEN

JOY

September 7. Can't deal. Every day I'm all alone. I dream of friends, but there's no one to hang with.
In the darkness of the pre-dawn
A reflecting pool waits
For dual images to lap at its liquid

Another summer gone by, BFD. Oh, I went to Grandma's, saw the cousins and my sweet aunt who laughs all the time, returned to camp and almost ruled in the second-to-the-oldest cabin. Learned how to sail better, that was cool. Even mastered the double half-hitch. Ronny didn't get mad all July, and only once in August.

But all summer there was this weight pressing on my chest. Like a vice or a *Twilight Zone-y* room squishing you. Why? Because I knew that when summer ended, I was going to high school. And it was going to suck. Whereas in junior high kids called you names and snapped your bra, maybe a rubber band on your arm, I heard that high schoolers threw you in trash cans and beat you up if you so much as looked at them.

I was going to be dead meat.

This time, I'd only bring lunch money; I didn't want to blow it like the first day of junior high. No one can laugh at you for that. Mom had gotten me a few new pairs of jeans and shirts the week before. The Dittos my skinny butt didn't quite fill out and a surfer top would be my first day outfit, topped with a white puka shells necklace to show off my Catalina tan.

I looked almost good.

"Can't you give me a ride?" I asked. "Just for the first day?"

Blowing a cloud of smoke, Mom shook her head. "I have to take Kyle."

"Why does he get a ride when I have to take the bus? It isn't fair," I protested.

"You're older. Anyhow, we took you to orientation. You know where to go."

Just then, Ronny came into the kitchen straightening his tie and Mom handed him the steaming cup of coffee she always had ready. He looked a little cranky, so I returned to slurping up the last of my Frosted Flakes. Kyle, who was sitting across from me, curled a mocking lip as if to say, "Ha! Ha! I got a ride, but you didn't."

I wanted to punch that little creep in the head. Instead, I scooped up my bowl and tossed it in the sink.

At the bus stop, the only other kid was some older boy from over by the park who I'd seen around, but whose name I didn't know. He was huddled inside his black hoodie, which I didn't get because it wasn't that cold; a little foggy, yeah, but not hunch-inside-to-keep-your-breath-from-clouding cold. Two strands of stringy hair that probably were making grease marks on each cheek hung down either side of his face. Didn't anyone tell him that can cause pimples?

I thought of saying 'hi', but he was so far inside his shell, I didn't think he'd hear me. Then a thought occurred to me. Maybe he had drawn inward because kids were so cruel that the only escape was to hide.

Terrified of what tortures awaited me, I started pacing back and forth. A smiling mom in curlers passed by in her blue station wagon, followed by Comb-over Kaminski, on his way to sell used cars. No other kids arrived. I checked to make sure my purse was closed all the way. Just my luck, I'd started the day before and now, in addition to navigating through the land of the giants, I had to deal with stupid tampons that might fall out in front of everyone.

With a whoosh of brakes, the bus pulled up. Empty? Well, there was one saving grace. At least I wouldn't have to beg someone to let me sit next to them.

Letting Lurch go ahead, I tiptoed aboard and plopped into the first seat. Even though we made seven stops, the bus stayed pretty empty. I guess not everyone has a little cute brother who rates so high, he gets the one mom ride. I didn't really see anyone I knew, so I kept my face glued to the window, pretending to be fascinated by the passing trees.

It might have been pretty quiet on the bus, but the school? Oh my God! Have you ever gone to a baseball game at a big stadium? Where there are hordes of people pushing and shoving to be first in line and tons of cars jamming the parking lot? Well, the first day of high school is like that. Tons of people crowding the halls. And I couldn't tell which ones were the teachers and which were the kids. I mean, some boys actually had beards!

Crazy.

Maybe I wouldn't stick out like in junior high and could avoid *The Clique*. Maybe even find one to fit into. I craned my neck, looking for a friendly face, but in this sea of bobbing heads it was impossible.

Homeroom was okay, I guess. The teacher, Mr. Benton, went over the rules, explained how to be successful. Blah. Blah. Blah.

First period was in 417. Now, I got to homeroom in 221 just fine and thought I'd mapped out the school in my head, but when I exited toward what I thought was Algebra, I found myself in the Zero pod.

39, 40, 41.

Wrong way. I jogged in the opposite direction, passed my homeroom, made it to the 300's and then? A parking lot. What the fuck? The 400's should come next. By the time I retraced my steps, the bell had rung, and the halls were empty.

Running a hand along the wall like a blind girl, I counted each door. Got to the end of one hall, turned right, and still didn't find it. Now the tears were threatening to take over. I know, a girl of thirteen, almost fourteen, shouldn't cry like a little kid, but ten minutes had already gone by and I still hadn't found my class.

Just about the time I was ready to duck into the nearest bathroom and sit on a toilet all first period, some giant boy, if you could even call him that since he had full-on sideburns and looked about thirty, passed by.

"Lost?"

I couldn't speak, just nodded.

"Let me see your schedule."

After sniffling twice, I passed him my now crumpled class list. He glanced it over and told me that the 400's were down the hill by the gym.

"Just go down those stairs and you'll find it," he said, pointing.

I croaked out a 'thank you' and then dashed down the stairs two at a time. Maybe I wasn't as late as I thought. Maybe no one would notice if I slunked inside. I could just quietly find a seat in the back and nod at the teacher's first day spiel.

No such luck.

When I arrived at 417, the door was not only closed, but locked. I tried jiggling it a few times, but it wouldn't budge. A timid knock or two, okay seven, later, a strict-looking lady with chained glasses on her nose yanked it open.

"You're late," she stated flatly.

Yeah, as if I didn't know. Tell me something new, I thought, but said, "Sorry, got lost."

She ordered me to the one seat that was left in the class. Was it hidden in the back? The middle? Nope. The only seat left was in the front way off to the right, so I had to pass by the whole class to get to it. And yes, you guessed right. I did trip over one kid's big feet, but you're wrong if you think I fell.

Instead, I grabbed the nearest desk and caught myself just in time. I would have sighed in relief if it hadn't been occupied by one of the scariest looking girls I'd ever seen. She lifted one shaved and painted over eyebrow while glaring at me through thick eyeliner that swept all the way into her hair.

"Sorry," I whispered.

She lifted one corner of her blood red lips in a sneer and scattered sniggers bounced around the room.

Welcome to high school, Joy.

FIFTEEN

JOY

C an't figure out high school. It's so strange. I mean, in junior high there was one group that pretty much controlled everything. They were on Student Council, did cheer and sports, dominated every dance and decreed who was in, who was out, from their fortress in the middle of the soccer field. There they sat, like royals in an elevated castle, while the lowly peasants grouped in clusters around them.

Everyone knew that the closer to them you sat, the higher your station. Lots of kids made it to inner keep, but even though I spent close to a year trying every scheme and strategy I could think of, the closest I ever got was the moat two walls away.

But in high school there wasn't just one preeminent spot. Kids hung out in lots of places, although there were three areas at the top of the amphitheater separated by sloping walkways that certain groups controlled. The ranch kids in their blue FFA jackets and John Deere baseball caps kept vigil over the Aggie Wall. On the Jock Wall next to them lounged the Socials; guys flexing their neck muscles and girls ready to break out into a peppy cheer. *Seriously?* The Chicanos; Pendleton plaid boys and

Count Dracula widow's peaks, coupling with chicks in cat-eye make-up and big, hooped earrings, made up the third area.

Other factions hung out in quiet corners here and there. Band kids, Stoners, Hermits, Book Arms. But where did I fit in? I mean, I was too shy for the Socials. No way was I about to lead an assembly by screaming 'rah rah rah, sis boom bah'. I only played guitar, and never in public. I'd only tried pot once and had never raised a dog, much less a farm animal.

Who was I?

Those first few weeks I just wandered. Barely talking to anyone. I mean, I did say 'hi' if someone I knew passed by, but I didn't stop and shoot the shit. What would I say, anyhow? Agree that high school sucks donkey dicks? Tell her how cute her Dittos were? I didn't know.

I took to hanging out in the library just to avoid having to talk to anyone. Here, I could escape to places like New York in the 1950s or the Alaskan Yukon at the turn of the century. Inside these books, I was no longer a timid girl wandering the halls, but a witty Holden Caulfield off on a party adventure.

Nobody bothered you in the library. No dirty looks. And since you weren't allowed to talk, no one called me 'dog' here. On the way to and from, though, the same mean girls from junior high barked their insults. I tried to keep an eye out for them, lowering my head to hide behind my long hair, or ducking away whenever they approached. Sometimes it worked, but most of the time I was too late. They'd grin, elbow each other, and start to woof.

I hated them.

One day, I was sitting at a corner table of the library when a girl that'd gone to my junior high came in. Her eyes had a hunted look that reminded me of that impala being pursued by lions on the *Wild Kingdom* TV show last week.

Then I remembered that there'd been this rumor about her. Supposedly, she'd ratted out some chick when she'd been caught shoplifting at K-mart, saying the other girl made her do it, or some shit. They'd grabbed the other girl, took her into the manager's office, and called her parents. The next week, a huge group had surrounded her, and called her snitch, narc and other mean stuff. One even slapped her. I didn't see it, but I heard it was gnarly, with Lisa crying rivers while the kids all yelled at her.

Messed-up.

I'd never do that. I believe in peace like the Beatles. I know, they broke up years ago, which is why people at this stupid high school don't have a clue about what they stood for. But my Catalina camp counselor Gail played *Give Peace a Chance* all summer and told me about activism and the protests she'd been in. She even got arrested. Full-on cool!

Someday, I'm going to do important things like that.

Lisa grabbed a random encyclopedia off the shelf and made a beeline for the farthest table. There, she propped up a makeshift screen and dropped her head behind it. Once in a while she'd peer around it, but as soon as someone new entered the library she'd twitch and duck back to safety.

I could totally relate.

I watched her for a while, thinking, debating, ruminating, cogitating, weighing the pros and cons. Like all those synonyms? My English teacher, who says we should build vocabulary, turned me on to *Roget's Thesaurus* and I've been finding all kinds of new words.

Anyhow, if I talked to her, she might just tell me to fuck off. Or call me freak. She did hang out with *them* last year.

Lisa sunk so low into the chair, it seemed like she was molding to it. I wouldn't have been surprised to see her body soften and melt before disappearing into the black plastic. This girl was no threat.

Sucking on that sore part of cheek I seem to bite every other day, I slung my purse over my shoulder and scooped up my books. Then I shuffled toward her and grasped the chair opposite. Being totally obvious, I pressed down while sliding it out. The metal feet scraped loudly over the tile floor.

Lisa didn't look up.

Sliding it out a little more, I cleared my throat. Lifted my eyebrows. No response. She stayed hidden behind *World Book Encyclopedia W X Y Z*. What was so interesting in Z? Was she doing a report on zebras?

I almost bolted, but something made me plop down in that seat. Desperation? Loneliness? I started thumbing through the pages of a paperback, waiting for her to look my way. No dice. Set that one down and flipped through a hardcover. She kept her head down. Man, those kids last year really did a number on her.

Maybe I wasn't going to make any friends in high school after all. I'd wander the halls day after day as unnoticed as a shadow. Unseen, disregarded. An outline of a girl. Gathering my books, I started to rise, but then another part of me said, *try, dammit,* so, pretending to be clumsy, I slid my book into hers.

She peered over the top of her *World Book* shield, gave me a wary look.

"Sorry," I whispered, mustering what I thought was a reassuring smile.

Keeping her chin attached to her chest she whispered, "It's okay,"

I pointed at her encyclopedia, some old, dusty thing from, like, 1943, and raised an eyebrow.

She shrugged an apology.

Holding up my own ridiculously boring book, I nodded in understanding. I got it. We both needed something to pretend we were into, so no one would bother us.

I jerked my thumb toward the door, and she nodded. When we reached the hall, I stumbled on words for a few seconds, but she saved me before I fell flat. Soon, we started to chatter about the meaningless shit, both nodding in understanding. Until the bell rang and lunch was over.

On feet lighter than they'd been for weeks, I glided through the halls toward fifth period. Then I looked over my shoulder at the reflected figure in one of the brown-tinted windows. Not recognizing her at first, I halted dead in my tracks. Long hair hid half a face, while vacant eyes stared out through dull sockets. Was this a shade, a specter?

A ghost?

When I realized who it was, I shook my head. She's a skinny wraith. An ugly phantasm.

Dog. Freak.

Who would want to befriend that?

SIXTEEN

JOY

Sept. 30. Lisa and I decided we would try a new group. They have a different flavor of 'gum'. We like it. Pretty colors.

I 've given up. I was never going to pass that boundary and fit in. The best I could hope for was somewhere on the edge. A place where the lines blurred between popular and not. A place where you didn't have to think of snappy things to say, or strut when you walked.

I heard of a couple of kids on that stood on that border, one foot dangling over *Socials*, the other planted in a country of their own. They hung on vines suspended over no-man's-land, a bunch of Tarzan-teens swinging from one group to the next. Swaying toward an abyss I'd always been told was full-on scary.

It wasn't easy finding any of them at first. I mean if I'd had lots of friends that would have been another story. But I didn't know anyone that had connections. And while you could be open with everyone about cigarettes, pot was a different story.

Some kids might freak out and narc on you. Others might think you were cracked.

Everyone knew there was this one group that liked to smoke bowls sometimes. Kind of a rough crowd. One of the guys used to live in the Northwest, where gang fights and all kinds of shit happened. His old neighborhood was in the newspaper all the time. *Prostitution Ring Broke Up On Fifth Street. Police Raid Home Near Oaktree Plaza and Find Cache of Guns.* Things like that.

My parents stayed away from that part of town.

Anyhow, Chuck had an older brother who was a Stoner; you know, someone that smokes pot? And he could hook me up with a few joints. Only problem was they cost a couple of bucks and, as usual, I was broke. I don't know where my allowance goes. I mean, I try to save it and even put it in my ballerina music box before hiding that in the back of my closet under some dirty clothes, and walk away, thinking I'll forget about it.

I guess I have too good a friggin' memory. Damn.

It's not like joints were all that expensive, only fifty cents apiece, but when all you have is a quarter... well, you get it.

"Hey Mom, need any chores done?" I asked.

She looked at me as if viewing a stranger. I wasn't exactly known for being neat and tidy, unlike Kyle, the midget vacuum cleaner and mop in one. "Are you feeling all right?"

"Yeah, just was wanting to help out and maybe make a little money, saving for a... ahh, new poster. My wall looks boring, don't you think?"

Mom narrowed her eyes and stared. "I suppose you could clean the bathroom."

"Cool. What's that worth?"

Shaking her head, she put her hands on her hips and heaved a sigh.

Uh-oh, Joy. Say something, fast. "I'm going. You can let me know later." To show that I meant business, I rushed down the hall and opened cabinet doors under the sink where the cleaning stuff was. I pulled out the toilet scrubber and waved it like a flag before banging the Ajax down loudly on the gold-flecked counter.

"Be careful, Joy! You'll scratch the Formica."

"Sorry," I called, before getting to work.

The next day, I had seventy-five cents jingling in the bottom of my purse and was ready to buy my first joint. Meeting Chuck made me feel kind of like one of those drug dealers in the cop shows Ronny likes so much. First, you find a shadowy place hidden by the school garbage dumpster and then look both ways five times before ducking behind it. Next, you dig in your purse for the quarters, fisting the money until the guy you're meeting nods that the coast is clear. At the last possible second you open your hand, letting the coins drop into his. Finally, Chuck passes you a lumpy envelope containing this weird-shaped cigarette with twisted paper on both ends and you tuck it inside your training bra. *I'm not growing yet, so, yes, I still wear them if you must know.*

After my super-villain triumph, I dashed back to the girl's bathroom where Lisa waited, her brown eyes wide and expectant. "You got it?"

"Shh!" I hissed, putting a finger to my lips. Leading her toward the last stall with a beckoning hand, the two of us then went inside. I closed and double-checked the lock before slowly retrieving the envelope from my bra. With foreheads touching, we peered at the strange-looking thing inside as if it were some sort of magical talisman.

"So, tomorrow?" Lisa asked, referring to our plan to go out in the field by my house on Saturday.

"Yeah, come over around one." I shoved the envelope back down my shirt, hoping no one would say anything like, "Stuffing your bra now, Joy?"

No, I don't! Really. You don't believe me? Okay, there was that one time in eighth grade when Vickie and I were going to walk past some high school boys in the park, but that's all, I swear.

Even though the next day was Saturday, I got up early and only watched two cartoons before making my bed, shoving the dirty clothes into the closet, stacking my books up in the corner, and doing the dishes. With Ronny off golfing and the house clean, there was no reason for Mom to keep me at home.

I finished up a little before one and was about to start reading *The Stand* when Lisa showed up. Right on time for once. Surprise.

When I opened the front door, my mouth dropped to the floor. "What are you wearing?"

"My in-case outfit," she replied.

"In case what?"

"We are followed. I don't want to be recognized."

"No chance of that." Shaking my head, I gaped at her ridiculous outfit.

Lisa's long brown hair was pulled up and tucked inside a... what do you call those French hats? Oh yeah, a beret. Her hair was hidden inside a beret while the rest of her was buried under a long black raincoat that was five sizes too big. It must have been her dad's, because the sleeves hung way past her fingers, and it dragged on the floor. You could just barely make out her hiking boots under all that dark material.

"We aren't spies passing secrets to the commies."

"I know, but if someone smells the..." she glanced around and lowered her voice, "... pot, and calls the police, they won't be able to describe me."

She made me wonder, *should I change my clothes?* I was wearing my usual jeans and a top so bright, I looked like a Christmas tree compared to her. I started to turn toward my room but stopped. Mom was already suspicious about my cleaning kick and if I added dressing differently to the mix, shit, she might grill me. And I was so nervous, I don't think I could come up with a good lie.

"Fuck it. Let's go."

We walked down the street with a nervous Lisa looking over her shoulder every friggin' three seconds. You'd think she was expecting the CIA, FBI, or a swat team to surround us at any moment. We barely got to the corner when she halted, put a hand on my shoulder, and cocked an ear.

"You hear that?"

"Yeah, it's a car. Driving, even."

Her face turned white and her eyes widened.

"It's coming closer. Be cool," I warned, before pushing her ahead on the sidewalk.

Walking so stiffly she looked like she had a stick up her butt, Lisa stared straight ahead as the silver Cadillac drove by. "Is it gone?" she asked, eyes still facing front.

"Didn't even look our way."

With a shaky nod, Lisa let me lead her past three streets, toward the wooden fence with the Road Ends sign that signaled the barrier between the Country Club and the empty fields.

"Okay, go," I said. Now I was the one glancing over my shoulder. Stupid, since I was constantly heading for this empty field. When Ronny got... you know, I'd run and wouldn't stop until I hit the fort some girls and I had built the summer before.

Lisa shot me one more backwards glance. "You sure it's okay?"

"I told you. I know a place. Deep inside. And we never got caught before, did we?"

"Well, no. I guess you have a point." She started to sling a leg over the short fence like a cowgirl mounting a horse, but jerked to a stop halfway over. Horrified, she looked down. Her trench coat had caught on a nail. "Oh no! If I tear this and Dad notices..."

"Just chill. I'll free it."

I bent down and pushed the fabric to the side. I tried to be as gentle as possible, but the hyperventilating Lisa kept breathing down my neck. It made my skin all sticky and was grossing me out so much that my hand slipped and I tore the coat's lining.

"Hey!"

"Hold still!" Using both hands, I lifted the fabric from around the nail. The tear was only about an inch long. "There. Your dad will never notice."

She nodded and the two of us began trekking into the field where the California poppies and purple lupines that smell like grape Kool-Aid were beginning to bloom. My jeans brushed against lots of sticker weeds and shrubs with little grey leaves I didn't know the name of, so I warned Lisa she should take off her coat.

"You don't want it dragging in the dirt."

"Yeah, that'd be a bust." She plucked out a few stickers before slinging it over her shoulder.

After about a quarter mile, we reached a stand of eucalyptus trees where the remains of the girl fort still stood. Man, I was proud of that thing. We'd taken old limbs and propped them up against two trees to support the walls before leaning leafy branches against them. Next, we threaded kite string in and out of the boughs for strength. Finally, we dragged a few palm fronds from Cindy's backyard all the way out there for the roof. Full-on Gilligan's Island tiki hut. Made completely by and for girls. No boys allowed. Any came around, we threw dirt clods at them.

"Pretty cool, huh?" I asked.

"Yeah. You made this?"

"With Cindy and a few other girls that live around here. Look, you can still come inside. Check it out." I ducked through the leafy doorway.

It wasn't as nice as we'd had it last summer. Some of the branches had fallen over and the floor was littered with leaves.

But the old chair and wooden crate were still there, along with the chalked sign of *Girls Only*. I brushed away some of the spider webs with the corner of my top and asked Lisa to sit down.

She hesitated. "What if I go crazy or something? I've heard people can end up in the mental hospital."

"That's just grown-ups trying to scare us."

Lisa looked at the ground and began chewing on her right ring finger. She always did that when she was nervous, biting her ring and pinkie nail down to the quick but leaving the others intact. "I don't know."

"Remember what those Socials did last week? Calling you freak and narc? Do you want more of that? 'Cause I sure as shit don't."

Lisa hadn't been teased as much as me, since she didn't bring a Scooby Doo lunchbox to school on the first day of junior high, but ever since the shoplifting incident, she'd heard her fair share of 'Freak'. She spat out part of a nail and said, "No."

"Then be cool."

"Okay. I'll try."

After sitting down on a wooden crate next to her, I pulled the envelope and matches from my bra. Then I held up the rolled joint for her to see. "Doesn't look like much, huh?"

Lisa shrugged.

Thankful I'd practiced so much with cigarettes, I handed her the matches and set the joint between two fingers. When I brought it up to my lips, Lisa struck a match and brought it closer to my face.

The paper end burst into flames. "What?" I leaped to my feet up, dropping the joint in the process.

Lisa placed a hand on my shoulder, and we stood over the strange little cigarette as if it were a dead animal we thought we could resuscitate.

"What now?"

"Maybe the paper on the end just had to burn. Try again," Lisa suggested.

With a long sigh I told her to go ahead, this time taking a tentative puff when she lit the match. The end glowed crimson as campfire!

"Yes!" Lisa said, before reaching out a hand. The joint barely touched her lips when she took the smallest drag I'd ever seen. I mean, a leprechaun would have taken in more.

She quickly handed it back to me and I drew in a longer breath and exhaled. Smoke plumed from my mouth, filling the hut. My eyes followed the grey mist, sure that some kind of magic was about to begin. Thought I saw something shimmer, but it was just the wind in the leaves.

"Here." I tried to give it back, but Lisa shook her head.

"I don't want to get too high the first time."

"Come on, just a little more," I coaxed.

We continued to argue back and forth for several moments until I happened to glance down to notice that half of it had burned away on its own. With a groan, I shoved it back at Lisa. "Hurry, before it's all gone."

She filled her cheeks with three tiny puffs that probably never reached her lungs. A few seconds later, the rest of the joint had burned down to nothing. *There goes my allowance*, I thought.

Lisa stared at me intently, like she was expecting a rainbow of psychedelic colors to shoot out of my head. "I think I see something," she said.

"Really? Where?" I glanced around.

"Now I feel something." She started to giggle and pointed at her feet. "Hiking boots?"

"With a Pepe le Peu hat. Stylin'," I guffawed.

"My boots. My boots. My booty, booty boots," she chanted.

"Your hat, your hat, your silly little hat."

"Your bra, you bra, your tiny titty bra."

"Hey!" I threw a few leaves at her before coming back with a ridiculous rhyme about her dad's coat that made no sense. We recited one after another, giggling until we were both in hysterics. Lisa removed the trench coat belt and started waving it in circles like a lasso while I darted under and around it in a cowgirl jig.

When our laughter finally died down, we smiled at each other, deciding it was time to go. Didn't want to get caught. We ducked back outside and buried what was left of the joint under a nearby tree before chasing each other home.

Looking back on it, we weren't high at all. I didn't see colors or feel any different. But man, we sure thought we were.

And in the end, it was enough.

SEVENTEEN

JOY

October 4
I'm going to flip you out and trip you out,
Lock you in a misty haze,
As you see the world through my eyes
Cannabis's mind maze

That's my life right now. Ever since Chuck turned me on to his supplier, I've been smoking a couple of times a day. As soon as I get off the bus, Lisa and I meet in the field across from school, at the bottom of the hill where no one can see you, and strike up a joint.

It only takes a moment or two and everything changes. Like the colors. They're so bright. The grass turns this *Wizard of Oz* green, with everything as sharp as the best TV they sell at Sears.

First period is a trip. I mean, imagine looking at a chalkboard with all these numbers and symbols that would confuse a kid on the best of days. Now add Ms. Glasses-On-Nose droning on in her put-you-to-sleep voice. Mix in a hazy view and you've got abstract art.

I did try to copy the algebraic equations but somehow, what was on the board didn't quite end up on my paper. And solving them? Right. With eighty-seven steps until you isolate the variable.

No way. So, I faked it.

By lunch, our buzz would be fading, so we headed out to the same place. And the rest of the day was this technicolor movie like I always read about.

I know, you're wondering does Angie Van Gorman's crew still say things like, "Where did you get that outfit, Goodwill trash?" or "That girl's so ugly I just threw up in my mouth."

And the answer was yes, they did, but it wasn't so loud anymore, you know?

It's not like their words didn't register any more, it's more like when the volume on the radio is turned down and the song is forgettable. Kind of like that. And I was learning to evade them. I mean, in a school with one thousand four hundred kids, give or take, it's not too hard to find routes to avoid certain people.

The halls were still the worst, but Hillview High was so spread out that if I saw certain people coming, I could go another way.

Usually.

Until yesterday.

Lisa and I had just crossed the street and were approaching the parking lot gate when a car full of Socials pulled over next to us. Even though I'd just smoked half a J, I still recognized that Camaro Z28. Everyone knew it. Light gold with mag wheels, it was the envy of every guy on campus and half the teachers. Brian May, a junior who hung out with both jocks and Aggies, was a richie with a dad that had some cattle yard or something.

Anyhow, just about the time I put one foot on asphalt, Brian slowed his car to a stop and rolled the window down. He looked me up and down like Ronny did when he saw the camp counselors in short shorts.

"Hey, Freshman," he called.

Lisa and I froze. I didn't know what to do so I just stared. Brian May, talking to me?

"Come here."

Lisa looked at me and shrugged. Might as well. He did have a rad car. It wasn't until we drew close that I noticed who was sitting in the back. Yep, you guessed it. Frickin' Angie Van Gorman, sneering with her perfect smile that'd never need braces.

And who was in the front? Her sidekick, Shawn Gill, that freckled, tennis-playing... well, hate to say it but, bitch. Brian's right arm was draped over her shoulder and she was snuggling into his shoulder.

"Hi, Joy," Angie said, when she rolled her window down.

This wasn't good. If my mouth wasn't already so dry you'd think I was in the dentist's chair with one of those suck-your-spit things, it was now. I opened and closed it. Nothing came out.

"Oh, are you hungry?" she asked.

If I'd been straight, I might have run. But I just stood there while Lisa giggled; from the high, or nervousness, I couldn't tell.

"What are you laughing about, narc?" Shawn asked, in a shut-the-fuck-up voice.

"So that's the bitch who got Lynette busted?" Brian asked.

"Yeah, we should teach her about telling on friends," Shawn added.

"I-I..." Lisa stammered.

Angie rifled in her McDonald's bag and pulled out a fry. Biting down on it, she chewed slowly as she said, "She looks hungry, too."

"We can share," Brian said, holding up a half-eaten hamburger.

My mind said *go*, but my legs were all watery and wouldn't cooperate. Lisa giggled again. Next thing I knew, half a Big Mac was stuck to my shirt and fries were peppering Lisa's hair.

"Freaks!" Angie cried, throwing a full ketchup cup.

I watched it sail over my head and land at Lisa's feet with a splat. Coagulated red splattered her flip-flops and toes. She leaped back, in a what looked like a slow-motion *Alice in Wonderland* reflex.

The Camaro trio burst into hysterical laughter that rose so high in volume that I was sure it was coming through a Jensen Coax speakers. Waving two fingers, Brian revved the engine and peeled out, leaving dual black skid marks in the road.

Lisa peeled the burger off my t-shirt and pointed at the greasy spot right between my tiny boobs.

"You've got another tittie," she giggled, shaking the French fries out of her hair.

I tried to join her laughter, but this time the high didn't fade everything to mist. This time, it only magnified every moment, in technicolor slow-motion. This time, I wished the high would end so that the stain didn't look like it was flashing 'freak' over and over.

I untied my sweatshirt from around my waist and wriggled into it.

"Come on," I said. "Let's go to class."

EIGHTEEN

KYLE

Joy has a new friend and then all they do is talk, talk, talk. They sound like elves in Santa's toyshop. *Hee-hee. Did you see the way he looked at me? Ho-ho, he totally was checking you out.*

At least this one is nicer than last year's friend. Vickie used to whisper and roll her eyes at me all the time. This girl, Lisa, actually says 'hi' and asks me about sixth grade.

Which is going amazingly, by the way. I made the basketball team and even got an award from the coach. Most Improved Player. Dad said, "That's my boy," when he saw it.

Joy and Lisa came last week, too. They didn't sit in the bleachers and cheer all that much, but I did hear, "Go Kyle!" once. They mostly giggled. I guess that's the way ninth graders are.

Last weekend, they laughed so much their eyes turned all red. Never saw that happen before. Weird.

Anyhow, I'm playing second base and it's okay. Coach says that the right side of the infield is second base's domain. Anything hit between my base and the foul line is my responsibility. Plus, I have to help the first baseman, David Trundle, every time a ball is hit.

Coach said he chose me because I'm light on my feet and can think fast. Also, I'm good at communicating, so the Short Stop and I never get in each other's way. We've won our first two games and it feels great.

Last night, Lisa stayed the night, the first-time Joy had had a sleepover in—jeez, I don't know how long. I wished her room wasn't right next to mine because all they do is whisper and giggle all night. Mom kept getting up to tell them to go to sleep and they'd be quiet for a while, but then a minute or seven later, they'd be right back at it again.

Finally, Dad got up. And I put my head under my pillow expecting a lot of yelling. Or a slamming door.

What happened next was weird. I kept my head under my pillow, but he didn't yell. I lifted one corner and heard him tell them that Lisa'd have to sleep in the extra bedroom if they weren't quiet.

It worked.

Oh, they still whispered over there, but only like the TV turned most of the way down. Not loud enough for Dad to hear.

In the middle of the night I woke up to a funny smell. Like cooking spaghetti sauce or a weird candle. I got up and felt around for the doorknob. (I'm not a scaredy-cat so I don't need a nightlight.) When I opened the door, the smell was stronger, but it wasn't coming from the bedroom end of the house. More like the kitchen. Sniffing, I followed it down the hall to the kitchen, but even though the stink was strong, no one was there.

I looked in the dining room. The family room. Peered outside, where the empty doghouse we planned to fill still stood. Was our house on fire?

Then my stomach got that bad feeling, like when Joy said

something stupid to Dad and he had to punish her. Maybe something was on fire. Should I wake everyone up?

Don't know why, but something made me open the door to the garage. Here, the smell was *wow*! And in the strange glow, I saw Joy and Lisa, heads bent together like some spooky movie.

"What are you doing?"

Joy jumped up, dropping whatever was glowing. A cigarette? "Nothing," she said.

"You're burning something. What is it?"

"Kyle, it's nothing. Just playing around," Lisa said.

"You shouldn't be burning stuff. Or…" I paused. "Are you smoking?"

"No way," Joy said, then giggled.

"Yeah, it's against the rules," Lisa snorted and then covered her mouth.

Now they both were laughing as if they'd just heard the funniest joke in the world. I eyed them. "I should tell."

"Come on, we're just burning some… some herbs from the kitchen," Lisa said.

"Yeah, just herbs," Joy chimed in, with another snort.

I started to argue, but then I remembered how they'd cheered at my game. Still….

"What'll you give me not to tell?" I asked, arms crossed over my chest.

They looked at each other, shrugging.

"I know, you do my chores for a week and I won't tell."

"But how do I explain that to Mom?"

"That's the deal. Figure it out."

So, for a whole week I didn't have to do the dishes or clean the bathroom. Neat. But I still didn't know what they were burning.

NINETEEN

JOY

After the darkness of the clearing storm
The moon breaks through the parting clouds
And the passing trees sway in silhouette

M om and Ronny are having another party tonight and it's
probably going to go on till late.

Not that that was terrible. Some of the couples were
bringing their kids, so, for once, Kyle and I wouldn't be ordered
to the family room to watch TV. We'd be allowed to hang out.
That is, if we behaved and didn't do anything embarrassing like
chew with our mouths open, or forget to say thank-you. And if I
kept an eye on the little kids.

When Mom first told me about it, I groaned. But then she
added that the Knox's were coming from Santa Barbara with
their sons and my eyes widened. Those boys were older, like
seventeen or eighteen. One might even be in college. Cool!

And terrifying.

I mean, I wasn't even fourteen. What would I have to say to

guys like that? Couldn't exactly ask them if they wanted to get high. They might be straight. They were last time I saw them, when we all met at Stern's Wharf for dinner a couple of years back. And I heard they were jocks, one on the football team or some shit like that. Jocks didn't toke much. At least not at my school.

As usual, we spent all afternoon cleaning the house. "Joy, look at this pigsty! I don't know how you can stand to live like this!" Mom yelled, picking a dirty pair of jeans up off the floor and tossing them at me.

Shrugging, I carried them out to the growing pile next to the washer in the garage.

It didn't stop there, oh no. As soon as the clothes were picked up, there were nightstands to dust, a dresser to straighten up, poems on random slips of paper to shove into the desk, a floral bedspread to smooth out (forty-seven times until Mom was happy).

And that was just my room.

Next, it was the hall bathroom. I didn't mind this so much. It was kind of nice to polish the Formica around the sink. I liked how the sparkling gold specks reminded me of palaces and movie star mansions. The hard part was the faucet; Mom insisted the clear plastic handles be spotless. Using an old toothbrush, it took forever to scrub all the grooves. Once the long mirror was streak-free, I was pretty proud of how nice it looked.

"Okay, Mom?" I asked, waving a hand toward the bathroom.

Hands on her hips, she strolled past me. Bent over, she looked for smudges or lingering mold. Tapped a long nail where I'd missed a spot. Then, after a million years, she finally said, "Fine."

Fine? I mean, compliments didn't come easy from Iris Wright but I'd just spent over an hour breathing bleach fumes.

Whatever. Used to it.

Of course, the first to arrive were the Reneys with their toddler in tow and I became resident babysitter while their folks tossed back a couple of Seven and Sevens.

"Hey, Amber. Want a piggy-back ride?" I said, getting down on all fours so the two-year old could climb on my back.

Once she was safely on, I started galloping up and down the hallway. "Hee-haw!" I whinnied. "I'm a bucking bronco."

"More!" she squealed.

Keeping one hand flat on the floor, I reached up with the other and grabbed her around the waist. With Amber secure, I reared my head and sprung into a little hop. Her infectious giggles spurred my bronco to buck again, this time with an arched back so it'd feel like a real rodeo stallion.

"Yee-ha!" I froze.

Glancing up, I blinked, sure I was watching a hair-blowing-slow-motion shampoo commercial. Standing over me, hands on hips, was a full-on hottie, and not just foxy like a surfer at Jalama, this tawny-haired guy was a total David Cassidy.

"Joy, go!" Amber kicked my side.

My knees started to buckle, and I felt the little girl teeter. Before she could fall and run crying to her mom, I dropped to my belly and gently detached her clinging legs.

"So, resident pony, how much do you charge for a ride?" Mr. Hotness said.

I cocked my head to one side, knowing there was something more to that question than the words. I'd read about exchanges like this in some of Mom's books. But just then, I couldn't think. I mean, those dark green eyes had friggin' sunbursts around his pupils. Not real ones, of course, but wow, the center of each eye looked like a star going supernova.

Beautiful.

"Hello?" he said.

"Oh, hi." Blushing, I stood up, brushed off the front of the split skirt Mom told me to wear. Tried to think of something to say that didn't sound totally idiotic.

Moments passed while Hottie looked me up and down. *He thinks this outfit is juvenile. All baggy.* I tucked in my blouse and stuck out my flat chest so my nubs would show. *I should have stuffed my bra with T.P.*

Opened and closed my mouth. Nothing came out.

The two-year-old saved me. "Want Mommy," she wailed.

"Okay, come on, Amber." Barely able to tear my gaze from Mr. Foxy Guy, I smiled apologetically and pulled her away.

Was it my imagination, or were his eyes boring into my back as I walked down the hallway? Probably shaking his head at what a full-on freak I was. Maybe he saw that zit on my cheek. Shit. Should have put on more tinted Clearasil to hide it.

Ronny was throwing back his third Manhattan about the time I led little Amber into the party room at the back of the house. He'd already gone through Fleetwood Mac's hits and was about to pull out the *Hotel California* album when somebody in the corner shouted, *"Hustle!"*

"You all want to Disco?" Ronny called into the crowd.

"I don't know," said a lady with frosted Farah Fawcett hair, approaching him. "Is it hard?"

"Not yet, but come closer and let's see what happens," Ronny said, draping an arm over her shoulder.

Everyone cracked up. Ronny was always making dirty jokes.

I sucked in a quick breath. That's what that boy had meant about charging for a ride. My face turned red again. God, was I stupid!

Luckily, I didn't have much time to think about it because the next thing I knew, Mom had me pushing furniture out of the way for a dance lesson.

When we were all lined up in the middle of the room, Ronny got in front of us and thrust a finger in the air like John Travolta in *Saturday Night Fever*. More laughing. Even me. Ronny was pretty funny when he had an audience.

With I'm-gonna-work-it flair, he started directing everyone in *The Hustle's* steps. "First forward, four steps. Now back, two, three, four. That's it. Left. Right. Clap. Point up. Oh yeah, Jane, you are hot. Roll and kick. Repeat."

My stepdad looked pretty smooth, while the rest of us bumbling klutzes tried to follow along. For once, Ronny didn't get pissed or impatient. Instead, he re-explained the steps like that nice teacher I had in sixth grade.

I think Ronny being nice had something to do with how tight all the ladies' tops were. That's where his eyes stayed during the lesson, anyhow. I looked down at my chest thinking, *I'm never going to grow.*

We bumped into each other a few more times but pretty soon got it. Then it was *The Bump, Bus Stop* and the *Funky Chicken*, until the Wright house was a full-on disco. Well, maybe not full-on, but still it was pretty cool. Little kids, grown-ups, Mr. Hotness and his younger brother Fox Junior, were all going forward and back, twirling around and pointing at the sky. We were almost in unison.

While we were dancing, I forgot everything for a while. Wasn't afraid of Ronny hurting Mom, or worried about what the mean kids said, or even if Dad would come visit. I was just Joy, regular teenaged kid. Smiling. Without even being high.

Until the little kids got cranky and the Reneys and other families started to leave. Then Mr. Knox looked at his watch saying they had to get going, too and Kyle and I were waved to bed so "the adults could have fun".

I pulled out my journal right away and started to write about that amazing night. I started slowly at first, but then my hand sped up, skipping over the page until it looked like jive feet on that TV show, *Soul Train*. That didn't stop me, though. My pen filled page after page, until my fingers cramped and the last car engine revved away.

Now, with everything so quiet, I went to my window and stared at that big moon hanging over our empty street, recalling how all the cars had lined the curbs when the party was in full swing. Orb images reflecting on polished hoods like a light-up floor in a big city nightclub filled my mind. They grew as a poem took shape.

I'd written lots of poetry before, but most of it sounded like a little kid copying *Mother Goose*. But this time I wanted to sound mature. This time, I'd use the tips my English teacher had given us. "Draw on all five senses," she'd said.

I'd include the pounding rhythms in my brain and the watery waves swishing in my stomach every time I peeked at that foxy guy who I wished I'd had the nerve to talk to again. I'd put in how the sweat on my upper lip beaded sweetly, like misty root beer. Then, I wrote a line describing the rush of warmth, hotter than any oven, that had passed over my chest when he glanced longingly back my way as he exited the front door.

I ended the poem with a heart-shaped period, before closing my journal and hugging it to my chest.

Thought I'd be wiped and ready to crash by then, but my head was still at the party, so, lighting a candle to mask the smell, I pulled out what was left of the joint I'd taken a few hits off the day before. Opening my window as far as it could go, I leaned into the screen and held a burning match to the blackened end. I cupped a hand around the baby flame and inhaled.

A blush of red from the burning joint passed over my moonlit hand. I stared, watching it brighten the pale skin. Like a paused film, time lengthened as the party played out in my mind.

Hands outreached, lips parted for a kiss as twinkling eyes

filled my vision with moonlit dreams. *Oh, a dance, with me?* I imagined saying, while doing a spot-lit twirl.

He takes me in his arms, and we glide.

And for one amazing moment, I am a girl aglow.

TWENTY

JOY

B *rad-ley*. Even his name was foxy. It rolled off the tongue like a bong hit of Thai Stick, curling with sweet resin that fills your mouth as you exhale. And ever since the party, it rocked, rolled, spun and trundled off my tongue. When no one was around, I whispered his name again and again. And when I was in social studies, I wrote *Joy Chapel + Bradley Knox = love*, instead of the notes Mr. Gonzales told us to copy.

The way Mr. Gonzalez fretted about communism, you'd think he was McCarthy in the 1950s. With a waggle of his fat finger, he'd warn us how the commies were winning the Cold War. "Boys and girls, we better do something soon. Those commie pinkos are trying to take over the world! They have a huge arsenal, with enough nuclear bombs to blow us up many times over."

Then he'd bemoan over how we should have fought harder in Vietnam and Korea. Invaded Russia after World War II. Blah. Blah. Blah.

I don't know about all that political stuff, but I figured that when doomsday finally comes and the bombs scorch the world, it's going to be okay. Because Bradley Knox and I are going to gather the last surviving children and take them to our cave high up in the mountains. There, with Yoko and John or some other cool hippies as our mentors, we'll live off the land, have twenty-three beautiful children, and write songs vibrating with love.

That's the sort of stuff I dreamed of every night before drifting off to sleep. I was sure Bradley and I had what it took to restart the world.

If I ever got up the nerve to call him.

But whenever I got close to dialing, I'd start to shake, thinking, *What would he ever see in you? Flat as a pancake. Barely any hair down there. Didn't even start until eighth grade.*

Then my mouth would get so dry, I couldn't even croak hello. So instead, I wrote him another poem I'd never send. They filled the pages of my journal with stanzas about sunburst eyes twinkling, hair like a rockin' lead singer, and broad shoulders I could rest my head on during a slow dance. *His teeth are as white as clouds over Catalina.*

I know what you're wondering. Joy, it's almost the end of ninth grade, don't you have a boyfriend yet? And no, I don't. As if it's any of your business.

Lisa says I'm too shy. That I should just walk up to a boy and say 'hi'. When we were out in the field across from the school at lunch one day, she said, "Why not pick someone from the lower Stoner wall?"

"No way. Too embarrassing."

"But you're fourteen and never even been kissed. That's weird," she said, shaking her head. Lisa had had nine boyfriends so far. Not only has she French-kissed, she also even let two of them touch her boobies. She said it made her tingle down there, but had said no when they wanted to go farther.

"So? I don't want to just get my first kiss over with. I want it to mean something."

"Do you even know how?"

"Kind of."

"You've been practicing like I showed you?"

I put my hand up to my lips to demonstrate how good I was getting. Slobbered all over my knuckles while I moaned and groaned like Lisa had demonstrated the month before. "See? I do know."

"Not terrible."

"Now, light up the doobie before lunch is over. I have to get to class."

TWENTY-ONE

JOY

"Hey Mom?" I asked.

"Hmm?"

"Remember the Knoxes who came to our disco night?"

"Of course."

"Do you think we might be seeing them again soon? Like for another party or something?"

"Oh, I don't know. I'm not ready for a big party right now. Things have been going so well. I..." She trailed off.

I knew what Mom meant without her finishing. Ever since the whole picture thing, Ronny had been nicer. No slamming doors or 'fuck you's' in months. I guessed that maybe he felt guilty for making Mom sad with that other lady. He'd brought her a huge bouquet of flowers the next day and had even taken her out to one of the nicest restaurants in town. That night, they came home late, all giggly and whispery before turning music on in their bedroom.

Maybe this year, I'd leave for camp surrounded by fluorescent colors like in those black light posters at Nirvana's Head Shop. Instead of the black and blue filling my vision, there'd be dayglo turquoise in the shape of peace signs.

I sighed. Then again, this was Ronny, not John Lennon. The best I could hope for were the muted colors we had right then.

"But might we go to Santa Barbara and visit on our way to Long Beach?" I asked, raising both brows hopefully.

"You know we won't have time. Just getting you and Kyle to the boats with all your luggage takes hours." As if to emphasize, Mom folded another pair of Kyle's shorts and put them in the bottom of the trunk next to his snorkel and fins.

"O-kay." I got up from the couch and wandered toward the bar room in the back of the house. Was bored, so tried calling Lisa.

"Hey," I said. "It's me."

"I know. You're the only one that would call at nine am in summer," Lisa said. "So, what's up? You getting all ready for Catalina?"

"Yeah. Mom's packing the trunks. Gonna go tomorrow."

"Cool." She paused. "Got any weed?"

"No." I huffed. "Don't even have enough money for a joint. Shit."

"You're always broke. What's up with that?"

"Your guess is as good as mine. Money just disappears."

"You're spaced. Jelly-brained."

I chuckled. This was a common joke in our crowd. We called people that smoked too much jelly-brained, like Jelly Brain Jeff, who was always so stoned he couldn't even tell you if the sky was blue. We had fun laughing at ourselves and all the silly things we said when we were high.

"Why not come over and help me pick out what to wear on the boat?"

"Sure. See ya."

———

The next day, I felt pretty hot as I walked up the gangplank of the *Catalina Express* in my white shorts and tank top. I searched the upper and lower decks, jazzed to see that some of my bunkmates had returned.

But not my best bud, Erin. I hoped she'd come later but wasn't too worried. Camp was the one place where it was easy to make friends. Even for a shy kid like me.

Later, at the Isthmus, I boarded one of same flat-bottomed boats *à la* the Disneyland Jungle Cruise I'd taken for three summers now. Recognizing a couple of the leathered men who held out their hands to help us board, I nodded hello. Then I shook my little booty, proud of my new curves, even if they were full-on subtle.

Soon, we were chugging around the bend, and I again marveled at this unique bay with the palm trees and our blue tented cabins below a hillside of coreopsis, prickly pear, bush mallow and some manzanita plants. Every time I saw that bay, my heart slowed, and each breath deepened like I was one of those meditating yogis in Nepal.

I glanced up at the mountains topped with eucalyptus, ironwood, and sage bushes, searching for Carl's trailer at the end, wondering if he was still there.

Carl Koski. As permanent a camp fixture as Indian Rock or the Lagoon. A German immigrant, he came to California after the war. He was one of the few people who lived on the island year-round, instead of the summer residents like me who stayed anywhere from two to twelve weeks. No one knew how long he'd been on Catalina, but by the looks of his weather-beaten skin and the age spots on his bald head, it was probably a long freaking time.

His home up on the hill was the last in the row of assorted trailers that the camp provided for the boat drivers, handymen, nurses, and resident doctor. As the caretaker, he kept intruders out in winter and made sure our camp ran smoothly in summer.

Plus, he was an expert shoe repairman. You name it, he could fix it. From high tops, to Zories, to moccasins, this guy knew his stuff. Even if your soles were so loose, they flapped like panting dog tongues with every step, he could put them back on. He could create new sandal straps out of odds and ends around his trailer, and stitch together a pair of tennies that were so long gone, it was a miracle that the kid wearing them could even could walk up the hill to get them repaired.

The strange thing was, Carl never wore shoes himself. Not that I saw, anyhow. Now, I did the barefoot-toughen-your-feet-up every summer and was pretty proud of how I could walk over hot sand, gravel, and even a few prickly weeds, but this dude had feet as thick as stacked steaks ready for the barbecue.

Carl had a ritual that everyone at camp knew about. Every morning around dawn, he'd rise and, with one stiff leg from an old injury he never talked about, would limp down the snaky trail to the beach. Then, in loose shorts that somehow managed to stay on, he'd dive through the waves to begin his swim. I don't know how such an old man could keep going for over an hour, but he did. And he said he did it year-round, in all kinds of weather. No wetsuit or rash guard or anything.

What a badass.

Of course, Carl was more than just the barefoot guy who fixed camper's shoes. He was also the resident guru, spiritual guide, mentor and, for me, a friend.

Day after day, Carl would hand out advice along with mended pairs to the line of kids holding broken shoes in their hands. "Sidney, we discussed about this topic. You speak too fast. You should make a pause before the next sentence." Or, "Gail, activism is good, yes. But you also must work on kindness for yourself. Look!" And he'd sweep an arm in a wide arc, inviting us all to take in the surrounding beauty.

I always let other kids go ahead of me so I could be at the end of the line. More often than not, I brought my journal along with a shoe I'd messed up on purpose. Then I'd share a poem or a paragraph while Carl listened patiently, rubbing his bald head with the palm of his hand. Some of my poems he liked, others he hated. But for some reason his critiques never hurt my feelings.

Carl just made you want to be better.

"Joy Chapel!" a counselor's loud voice called after I got off the boat. "*Clipper.*"

I'd made it to the top cabin! So friggin cool! No more *Dingy* babies like Year One, or *Sloop* tweeners in Year Two. We'd be the oldest just-under-fifteen-year-old counselors-in-training, or C.I.T.'s, as everyone called them

I held my head high as I joined the other girls lined up for our cabin.

Summer, yeah!

TWENTY-TWO

JOY

As I entered the cabin, where the tented roof cast a slight blue tinge on everything, I nodded hello to the other girls, while gauging who would be cool to hang with. Most of my bunkmates looked like Book Arms, prep school brainiacs, or Socials so caught up in their outfits, you'd think this was the Academy Awards instead of camp. Not that I was all judgey and shit, but I hoped there be someone to get high with.

I threw my sleeping bag on a top bunk near the window for dibs. If you didn't do dibs right away, you might end up under a chick who snores Hella loud, or farts so bad you wake choking on the fumes. That'd been my fate two summers before and there was no way I was doing the bottom bunk again. It's better to climb the metal railing to the top, where at least you could breathe.

While unrolling my blue Coleman bag, I heard someone clear their throat behind me. I didn't turn, but kept smoothing the nylon cover until it looked comfy.

"Excuse me, but I think that's my bunk."

"Not," I said, stepping down to the floor. "Bag on bunk equals dibs."

In front of me was a chick with straight blonde hair and brow-skimming bangs. Her hands were on her hips and her staring blue eyes were about as intimidating as the puppy we almost adopted from Pets-R-Us. "I always have the top," she said.

I glanced around at all the taken bunks and shrugged. "Not this year."

The other girls in the cabin grew silent, waiting to see how this would play out. One Social adjusted a braid and stepped closer.

Blue Eyes looked me up and down and gave me a sly smile. "But it's customary for the last girl to enter to get first choice of bunks."

My eyes narrowed. What did she take me for? A little *Dingy* cabin first year? "Yeah, right."

"No, seriously. All the best camps do it. Last year when I was in the Adirondacks, it was part of the camp motto. *Last in always wins.*"

One of the Book Arms piped up. "I've never read that. Where'd it come from?"

"From an ancient Navajo myth about weary travelers seeking shelter in the desert."

"I didn't see you on the boat," I said.

With a dramatic sigh, the girl rounded her eyes. "I had to take a later one. Family issues."

The Social, named Jodi, joined the conversation. "Maybe we should welcome someone who's had a rough time."

I couldn't believe my ears. I'd been coming to CIC for four years and it was always dibs. "No way."

"Come on, Joy. Put your bag on the bottom," Jodi said.

I thought about arguing, but didn't like to look like a bitch in front of all the girls. Anyhow, Blue Eyes didn't look like someone who had digestive problems or snored. Still I couldn't let her just get away with it. Grabbing my bag, I swung it off the bunk with just enough force to whip her shoulders. With my message sent, I gave her a fake smile and shoved my bag on the bottom mattress.

"I'm hitting the head," I said, grabbing my purse with a pack of cigs inside.

Instead of going to gang showers, I stole a quick glance over my shoulder to see if anyone was watching and jogged up to the boar pit. This little gulley was where the kitchen crew dumped table scraps every night. This provided the campers with a unique show. We would sit on the hillside waiting for the wild pigs to arrive and munch out.

I know, seems gross. But we campers really got off on those spotted mammals. In twos and threes, they'd snuffle up the dusty trail, the little piglets struggling to keep up with their mamas as they trotted toward all our stinky garbage. I think they liked the leftover pancakes best; at least they usually ate that first.

Finding a spot hidden from the entrance, I tapped a Marlboro Regular from the pack and rested it on my lips like a gangster in an old black and white move. I'd just lit the end and inhaled when I heard a rustling off to the left. Clutching the cigarette between my thumb and forefinger, I thrust it behind my back.

"You know smoking's against the rules," the voice behind the bushes said.

"I don't know what you're talking about."

Then, Ms. Steal-My-Bunk emerged on the path. "Oh, you usually have smoke coming out of your ass? What are you, part dragon?"

I looked over my shoulder. "That's just dust."

"Sure. Wilderness dust smells just like an ashtray."

"So? What's it to you?"

She shrugged. "Not much. But you could at least share."

I narrowed my eyes. "You smoke?"

"I like tobacco occasionally. Of course, there are sweeter

flavors." She held out her hand and I passed the cig her way. She took a long drag and blew four smoke rings.

Impressive.

"What flavors might you be talking about?"

"You know. The herbal kind. From Thailand. Or Acapulco."

Just because she smoked didn't mean I could trust her. "You a narc? Trying to get me kicked out of camp?"

"Now why would I do that?"

"I don't know. Why would you make a big friggin' deal over getting the top bunk when I had it all set up?"

"That was funny. You should have seen your face. You got so pissed."

"Yeah. So tell me more about this Navajo myth."

"What myth?"

"The one that says to welcome strangers."

"Are you jelly-brained?" She chuckled.

Then it dawned on me. "You made it up!"

"Well, hello. You didn't actually think that there was one?"

"Kind of." I shrugged.

"You're a little naïve, aren't you?"

"No. I'm no goody-goody. I get high and shit." I covered my mouth. *Oh no. Now she's going to narc me out.*

"Don't worry. So do I. Actually, once the mail arrives tomorrow, I should have some sweet Acapulco gold. And I might even share. If you let me keep the top bunk."

I burst out laughing. "Keep it! By the way, what's your name?"

She made a long, sweeping bow. "Gina. Gina Levi. Blonde Jew and stoner at your service."

"Joy. Hey."

TWENTY-THREE
JOY

"Gina, come on. Get up. There's someone I want you to meet." I grabbed her dangling arm and started tugging.

Gina groaned. "Let go, I'm sore." She rubbed her shoulders as if she'd rowed all the way around the island instead of the bay.

"It'll be worth it, believe me." I tucked my journal under an arm and headed for the door.

"Okay, okay. Hold up. I'm coming."

I suppressed a grin. I knew she'd follow.

We trekked up the hill behind our cabin to the row of trailers overlooking camp. I hadn't told her about Carl yet, but since she'd been in camp three days now, I figured it was about time. She'd probably heard about him; all campers had, but since her flip-flops were still in one piece, she probably hadn't thought twice about visiting. She was too busy checking the mail for her special delivery.

"So where are you taking me, anyhow? Up to visit the hot boat drivers?" she asked, raising both eyebrows.

"You'll see. Just be patient." I hopped over a boulder and turned toward the left fork leading to Carl's metal home.

"Joy?"

"Stop stressing. I told you it'll be cool, and it will."

"Is this payback for stealing your bunk?"

I waved a dismissive hand. "Over it."

The gravelly path steepened, and I slowed my pace to avoid sliding. I'd skinned my knees along it more times than I could count, so focused on planting my sandaled feet firmly on the trail until I topped the rise.

"Careful, it's slippery."

"I'm fi—"

Her words were cut short and I heard the grating sound of feet skidding on grit. I turned to see arms flailing as Gina struggled to keep her balance. I reached out a hand, too late.

She went down on one knee and cried out.

"You okay?"

Still down on one knee, she nodded grimly. She stood and saw that her shin was scraped and trickling blood. "Shit."

"Sorry." I climbed the last three yards to the crag and extended a hand to pull her up.

She crossed her arms and faced me. "Now tell me where the fuck are we going? And they better have a Band-Aid."

A few yards ahead, I could see Carl sitting in a folding lawn chair that had seen better days. It must have been left out in the rain because the bent aluminum legs were rusted and the webbing was so faded, you couldn't tell if it'd once been green, blue, or red. When he heard the two of us approaching, he looked up and smiled.

"Joy!" he called in his German accent. "You have returned, with other persons."

Gina gave me a confused look and whispered, "This is who you wanted me to meet?"

With a quick nod, I trotted the final few feet to give Carl a quick hug. "Great to see you!" I jerked a thumb toward Gina.

"We'll catch up in a sec, but right now my friend could use some help."

Noticing Gina's bleeding shin, Carl took her by the arm and helped her into another of the ancient lawn chairs. Then he went inside to fetch his first aid kit.

"Is he the shoe guy everyone talks about?" Gina asked.

"Yep," I replied, pointing behind her at the workbench hosting an assortment of tools, leather pieces, twine and rubber scraps.

"But our shoes are fine."

"You'll see."

Carl's lame leg swung wide as he limped back down the steel steps. He carried the first aid box to the workbench and pulled out some Bactine that he sprayed on Gina's knee. She cringed, but, to her credit, did not cry out. When it had dried, Carl grasped a Band-Aid in his thick fingers and applied it to her shin with surprising skill.

"I sink iz better," Carl said, patting her knee. "Now, Joy. No letters in many monz. Tell me of your life."

In reply, I opened my journal to a dog-eared page and passed it to him. While he silently read, I explained to Gina that Carl and I were penpals and he often critiqued my work. "He is helping me to be a better writer."

"So, you're a Sylvia Plath wannabe?"

"Sort of. Or Timothy Leary." I giggled.

With a palm resting on his mottled head, Carl read the page twice. He rubbed the few remaining grey tufts on his bare scalp and leaned back. Then he said that he liked the imagery, but the emotion was too veiled.

"I seek you in the piece, but it is az if you hide from yourself. Where are you on the page?"

How could he know about my mask? The face I wear for the world? I thought I had a perfect disguise.

I pretended not to know what he was talking about and

changed the subject. We started chatting about our respective schools, boyfriends, or lack thereof, and what subjects we liked.

You know, mundane stuff that keeps the mask in place.

When, about an hour later, Gina and I made our way back down the hill, she turned to me and said, "He's cool. I get it."

TWENTY-FOUR

JOY

My counselor, Jan, shook me. "Joy, wake up. It's time," she whispered.

Nodding slowly, I unzipped my sleeping bag, tucked a towel under my arm, and crawled out of bed to join the other Clippers shuffling sleepily toward the door. No one switched on a light or pulled out a flashlight.

We needed the darkness.

Outside, the crescent moon shone over the Pacific, its points sharp and menacing.

"I don't know about this," Jodi said.

"Shh!" Jan warned.

"But…"

"If you wake anyone up," Gina rasped in her ear, "so help me God, I'll say it was all your idea."

Jodi raised her hands and shut up.

We tiptoed down the path toward the cliff stairs. Every once in a while, a girl would kick a pebble and we'd all freeze, looking back for the inevitable explosion of spotlights. Judging by the hard breathing, I think everyone's hearts were pounding so hard we could have been a conga band. I put a hand on my chest.

Then I tripped and fell against Jodi.

"Oomph!" she said.

"Sorry," I said.

Jan stopped and beckoned the twelve of us to make a circle. "This will work only if we are careful. Come on, girls, be stealthy. You are Clippers, great ships on the sea. And soon your sails will be unfurled."

"Unfurled!" Gina whispered while raising a fist.

With a proud head-bob, I copied her fist pump and looked to see if the others would follow suit. With buoyed confidence, several girls nodded and a few even extended curled hands. Jan gave us two thumbs-up and continued forward.

We approached the cliff's precipice knowing that once we descended, there was no turning back. I gave Gina's shoulder a squeeze and stepped onto the wooden staircase.

The sage brush on the craggy bluff rustled in the wind, making me feel like a sailor in a gale. I held tightly to the railing and took two steps down. Then I heard the clinking of pebbles and glanced over at a scurrying ground squirrel. I wanted to call out that it didn't have to run from us, we weren't hunters. At least not of animals.

We were seeking something altogether different.

A minute later, we were on the beach and the leggy Jan stopped to scan the horizon, cliff face, and sandy shore. When she seemed satisfied that no one had followed, she turned toward the place campers were forbidden to go to.

I don't know if the rocky lagoon was man-made back from when this was a rock quarry, or if it was natural, but it sure as shit held every camper's imagination. Stacked boulders created a curved seawall and a pool, allowing water in but blocking crashing waves. With black rocks and still waters that the sun warmed during the day, this pond supposedly was the island's only warm soak.

Making it perfect for our night's mission.

Jan went first. No one dared look but we all snuck peeks. Not that we hadn't seen it before. There were gang showers, after all.

She stood in the moonlight, a nineteen-year-old goddess with brown areolas wrinkling in the night air, each nipple pointing us toward the water. With a wink, she turned toward the pool. In the dim light, her butt cheeks were so white against her tanned legs and torso that it looked like she was still wearing her panties.

Not a single glance was exchanged as we silently undressed. Then, on feet not yet toughened by summer, we tiptoed to the water's edge. A couple of girls stayed wrapped in towels, too shy to show the sky their skin. Even the outgoing Gina hung back.

Jan took a deep breath and dove, a long, sleek racing dive. The reflected sickle moon rippled on the pool's surface. She emerged, flipped her long blonde hair back and called, "What are you girls waiting for? Morning reveille?"

Surprisingly, Jodi was the first to drop her towel. She started marching forward until the rocks underfoot made her cringe. Resuming a tiptoe trot, she waded in until the water was knee high. Here, she stumbled over something and promptly fell over. Jodi surfaced, sputtering and spitting water.

Giggles filled the air.

This was all the encouragement the rest of us needed. A moment later, the lagoon was filled with splashing, dunking, kicking fifteen-year-olds. Boobies bobbed in the water as we jumped and leapt. We were no longer Clipper Cabin, but a group of fairies, sprites and Narnian dryads out for a night's revelry

The water was surprisingly warm for California, having been heated by a particularly sunny day. And it felt smooth over my skin. As I submerged and swam underwater, it rushed through my privates in a way that exhilarated me like never before.

Now, I know what you're thinking, and don't get gross. I

don't mean anything horny or sexy or stuff like that. Instead, the water over naked skin felt natural, like my body and the sea were melding into one.

I was Joy, nymph of the sea, breathing deeply, trying to capture the moment.

Then Gina splashed me in the face. And of course, I splashed her back.

TWENTY-FIVE

JOY

W ell, it happened. Gina's pot finally arrived. Not on day two like she anticipated, but on day six, leaving us boringly straight for a week. Well, not boring. At camp, you don't notice that you're sober like you do when school is going on. It doesn't seem quite so important. Catalina colors are already vibrant blue and turquoise and the clouds dance without any hallucinogenic filter.

Still, I was missing that sweet flavor and the way my brain hummed after a couple of hits. Maybe that's why they call it buzzed, because your brain buzzes like tingly static. So, when Gina held up the envelope she'd mailed herself and raised two eyebrows, I was ready.

We decided to wait until everyone crashed before sneaking out. Daytime was just too dangerous. Even though most of our counselors were cool and probably got high themselves, there were a couple that I was sure had never even seen a bong. They would make a scene if they saw us with pot, and neither Gina nor I wanted to be sent home.

When the Clipper Cabin's sounds quieted into soft breathing and brace-faced snores, I pressed my cocooned feet into Gina's overhead bunk. The springs creaked and I held my breath, waiting for the inevitable groans and pleas for quiet.

A moment later, Gina was hanging her head over with an upside-down grin. Since she'd made sure to keep her bag unzipped when she crawled in an hour before, she was able to snake out silently before shimmying down the railing to land on cat feet. She jerked her head toward the exit and padded over to the door.

I was next to her in a flash, but now came the rusty screen door that the maintenance guys obviously hadn't oiled in forever. I opened it an inch, two. One more. *Squeak!* I froze, not daring to turn around.

Several seconds passed before Gina nudged me. I still didn't move. Then she poked me, and I remembered our cover story. *I had to pee and didn't want to go alone.*

I pressed the door open, holding it for Gina before inching it shut. We crept down the wooden steps and immediately started running past the gang showers. It was a real mad dash. I guess we both were pretty scared we'd get busted.

Once we reached the playing field, we continued sprinting for the path to the boar pit.

"I think we can slow down now," Gina said, a little out of breath.

We'd made it all the way to the ravine, where the smell of half-eaten burgers, stale fries, and pickles that the wild pigs had ignored filled the air. Wrinkling my nose, I glanced back over my shoulder. "Okay."

Gina pulled a small pipe and a plastic bag out of her sweatshirt pocket. Unzipping the baggie, she grabbed a pinch and pressed it into the bowl. It must have been good weed because an immediate sweet scent, kind of like the spice section of a health food store, met my nose. She tucked the baggie back in her pocket and placed the pipe between her lips.

I fished a book of matches out of my pocket and ran one over the striker. It sparked but didn't flame. Tried another. This one lit up, but the night breeze quickly extinguished it.

"Shit, Joy. Can't you even light a friggin' match?"

"Chill. I got this," I said, cupping my hand around my third try.

Holding the pipe in one hand, Gina lifted the other to screen the wind and guide the baby flame toward the bowl. When fire met herb, it sparked and sizzled, and a grinning Gina sucked the sweet incense into her lungs.

"My turn," I said, reaching for the pipe.

Just then there was a rustling in the bushes. I looked and to my horror saw Jan approaching.

"Shit," Gina said.

"Double shit," I agreed.

Gina looked around for a place to hide the pipe, but it was too late. Jan had already seen it.

"I thought so," she said, shaking her head. "When I saw you two running past the head, I knew you were going to get high."

"No, this is just…" Gina began.

"Don't." Jan held up a hand.

I hung my head. "I'm sorry."

Jan approached and held out a hand. Reluctantly, Gina passed the pipe to her. "And the rest?"

Groaning, Gina tossed the baggie at her.

"Come on, girls."

Our flip-flops snapped against our feet as we shuffled back towards camp. *What is Mom going to say?* I wondered. *Or Ronny?* I gulped, flashing back on how Ronny had reacted when I'd come home from camp the first time. And that was just Mom saying one little thing. What would he do if I got sent home?

My heart pounded harder in my chest. "Jan, can't we handle this here? Not with…" I trailed off when Jan turned toward the lodge instead of the head counselor's cabin. "Huh?"

She opened the door and light flooded the entrance. Keeping

my gaze on my dusty feet, I waited for the impending lecture. When instead I heard soft music, I glanced up and almost fell over.

Inside, several counselors, our boat drivers, Matt and Steve, and the maintenance guy, Gabriel, were standing in groups of twos and threes, sipping something out of paper cups. Their happy conversation quieted when Jan stepped over the threshold.

"What do we have here?" the curly-headed Gail asked with a smirk. "Some campers being naughty?"

Gina and I exchanged a perplexed glance.

"Yep, holding out on us," Jan said, waving the baggie of pot in front of everyone.

"Hey! That's mine. I had to go through hell to get it here," Gina protested.

"But of course, you'll share. Won't you?" Gail said.

"Or if you'd rather have us hand it in, I'm sure the head counselor would have a thing or two to say about it."

Gina spoke quickly. "No, Jan, I'll share."

A minute later, we were all passing around the bowl. I giggled when it came my way, thinking that these counselors were all older than me, some almost twenty, and way cool. I was just fifteen. Well, fifteen and a half; I'd be sixteen in December, and to be included in this group that had shared so much with me over the years was a freaking honor.

Joy Chapel is smoking bowls with Catalina counselors. Radical, I thought, feeling at least two inches taller.

After a couple of hits, Jan handed Gina and me a cup. I sniffed at it. Sweet and sour at the same time.

"Strawberry Hill. Try it," Jan urged.

Gina took a sip and nodded. "Yummy. Like Tang or Hawaiian Punch."

Shrugging, I ventured a taste. She was right. It didn't taste sour and vinegary like the stuff my parents bought. It was way sweeter than any of their wines. I took another gulp and grinned.

"Slow down, you only get one," Jan cautioned.

"Okay. You don't have to freak."

Over by the window, Gail was leaning in real close to Steve who was whispering something in her ear. She tugged on one of her curls then rested a hand on his tanned shoulder. I paused and tilted my head to one side. Wasn't she dating Matt?

Weird.

When everyone cracked up, I turned to ask Gina to repeat what she'd said. She was always saying funny things or telling jokes and even when high, she could remember the whole thing, waiting until the perfect moment to deliver the punch line.

Well, one minute we were all laughing and chugging down Boone's Farm sweet wine and the next, there was this horrific crash. A chair lay overturned and Matt and Steve, the two ski boat drivers, were on the floor, rolling over and over in a vicious brawl.

They rose to their feet and Matt laid into Steve, punching him once, twice, three times, attacking him with a violence my stepfather would have envied.

The tanned dude stumbled back, collided with the door, and then bounced forward like a rebounding racquetball off a court wall.

"Stop!" I cried and leaped out of the way.

Even now, Matt didn't let up, but hit him again and again as Steve tried like hell to block each punch. I watched, horrified, as Steve's face swelled under Matt's bloodying blows. It wasn't fair! Matt was at least four inches taller than Steve and probably outweighed him by, like, thirty pounds. Matt was all muscle and meat while Steve was just sinew. Well, plus some dreamy brown eyes. I could see why Gail had been flirting.

The others shouted, too, but the two men kept up their macabre dance. Feet shuffled over the floor. Steve sputtered and coughed, red drool dripping down the side of his mouth. He wiped it away with the back of his hand, bent down, and head-butted Matt in the gut, forcing them both against the ping pong table.

From his hunched over position, Steve groped upward until he had Matt's t-shirt in his hand. Clutching at the fabric, he yanked, but it didn't bring Matt down. Instead, the hulk jerked away and kicked. Steve's arm snapped back with a horrible sound

Then it hung limply at his side.

"Please, no," I whispered, started to see things that weren't there.

Cruel faces jeering.

Ronny standing over me, fist raised.

Mom dabbing makeup over bruises.

Slamming doors.

Mom crying out in pain. Me unable to do a thing.

Kyle asking to sleep in my bed.

Pulling the covers over my brother and me. But they don't muffle the sounds.

Bitch! Slut! I'll fucking show you.

"No, no, no."

Steve glanced down at his arm, then at Matt, before punching wildly with his left. One jab connected with Matt's jaw and wrenched his head back.

"Stop it!" Jan shouted. "You'll get us busted!"

Retreating, I backed into a corner and sunk down to the ground. *Why won't they stop?*

Matt cuffed Steve's shoulder. Struck his gut, chest, neck.

I drew my knees up to my chest and began to rock back and forth. "You guys p-please, no more. No more. No more..."

More crashes.

"No, no, no."

I guess either my tears finally got through or they were tired, because a moment later the fight was over, and the counselors were gathered around me.

"Hey Joy, you okay?" Gina asked, patting me on the back.

I rocked. "It's so wrong."

"I know," Gail said.

I gazed up at Matt and Steve with gulpy sobs. "You guys should f-forgive each other."

"Grow up, kid."

"Matt!" Gail chastised. "She's fifteen. Give her a break."

"Like you did me? Fuck you." He stormed toward the exit and shoved the door, slamming it against the wall with a bang.

I looked to Steve, hoping my innocent eyes would change his heart. "But we should have peace," I sniffled.

Steve wiped his nose on the back of his forearm, leaving a trail of blood and mucus. "Sorry, kid. That's a dream. A song on the radio."

Gail went to him, a wad of napkins in her hand. He took them but when she tried to touch his shoulder, he jerked away. "Leave me alone." Then he followed Matt out the door.

The room got so quiet you could hear the waves crashing on the beach way below.

I tugged on a stray thread that was hanging from my tank top. The hem started to unravel.

Gail chewed on a fingernail while a crossed-armed Jan shook her head.

Gina broke the silence. "Well, that was a friggin' blast," she said, holding out a hand to help me up.

I took it and we shuffled back to Clipper Cabin.

TWENTY-SIX

JOY

"Carl?" I called approaching his trailer. "You around?"

He wasn't sitting in his usual lawn chair, which looked even more forlorn without leathery legs filling it. I went up to the steel door and knocked.

"Vat is it?"

"Oh, just Joy. I thought..."

"Vait un moment."

Maybe this wasn't a good time. Today, his friendly-as-a-Kindergarten sing-along voice was clipped and angry. He sounded more like the Sex Pistols' Sid Vicious than a German Mr. Rogers. I hung my head and started to turn away when the door flung open.

"Ahh, Joy. For you I visit."

"You sure?" I asked, not wanting to be a bother.

"Of corze." He waved a hand, inviting me to sit on a lawn chair.

I hesitated. His gray-blue eyes weren't sparkling, and no smirk lifted the corner of his mouth.

"Sit!" he insisted.

Nodding quickly, I lowered myself into the chair.

"Zo. How are you?" he asked, taking the seat opposite.

"I don't know." I shrugged.

"Somezing has happened?"

I nodded. "Yeah. It was bad."

"So, tell me."

How could I tell him the previous night's events without talking about weed? Carl was a man I looked up to, a minister, mentor, grandfather, and teacher all rolled into one. If he knew I was getting high, he'd lose respect and might not even talk to me anymore. Couldn't deal with that.

"I saw a fight last night. Steve and Matt," I began. "It was horrible. They really hurt each other. Then I tried to get them to make up, but it didn't work. Why?"

"Humans are complicated, Joy."

"But people should love each other. Make peace. Like John Lennon and the Beatles used to. I read—"

Carl cut me off. "So you sink zat those four men never got angry? Or fought?"

"No way. They sang that we should give peace a chance."

"Just because one sings a song does not change zee fact zat zey are human. With many nuances."

"I know, but when someone hurts someone else, on purpose. It's, it's…" My throat got tight as I struggled to find the words.

Carl patted my knee. "It iz very hard to see the ugly side of man. I, too, have vitnissed such things. That is one of the reasons I am here."

I sniffed and dabbed my nose on the corner of my tank top. "You never told me."

"Why repeat sad stories when such beauty surrounds?" He jerked a chin toward the blue Pacific below.

"Yeah, but still, I'm curious."

"Suffice it to say that I vas married and in love. A father. A husband. And happy once."

"They died?"

"No, no, no. All three are living." He stared at the ocean again. "Far away."

"People go away. I know about that." I paused, trying not to think of Dad. "But you're so nice. Everyone likes you. It doesn't make any sense. Not like me. If I'd been better, Dad would have—"

"Stop now! You are not to talk zis way. You are as beautiful and amazing as the sea around zis island."

"But I make people want to go away."

"You do not. They make their own choices, that have nothing to do with you. As did Matt and Steve. I heard of zee fight and understand. When two men pine for zee same woman, he who loses become very angry."

I nodded, trying to understand. I really didn't get it.

Carl must have known that because he raised a finger and said, "I have something for you. I vas going to wait until your last night, but I believe you need zis now."

He rose from his chair and hobbled inside his trailer. When he returned, he was holding something in his hand. He limped down the steps and turned his fisted hand over. Slowly, he opened his thick fingers.

I gasped.

There in the palm of that wrinkled hand was a piece of abalone shell cut into a perfect teardrop. Its turquoise, pink, and lavender colors swirled around a fingernail-sized nugget of blue sea glass. Combined, the two looked just like the sunrise I'd seen over Empire Landing when our cabin had gone on a pre-dawn hike.

I extended a single finger and touched the smooth shell.

Carl smiled and went over to his workbench where an assortment of rope, plastic tubing and shoelaces hung on pegboard. He ran a finger over the wall and shook his head and then fumbled around in one creaky drawer for a few seconds before drawing out a long string of leather. This he laid flat in front of the yardstick glued into the edge on the bench. As he measured the leather and trimmed it to size, he kept glancing back as if sizing me up.

With the long piece of leather cut, he threaded it through the hole he'd bored into the abalone and looped the cord so it would lie flat. Then he pulled out some needle nose-pliers and attached something to both ends. A few minutes later, he was dangling a beautiful necklace in front of me.

The stone caught the light, reflecting rainbow shades onto Carl's trailer. I blinked and smiled, my eyes brimming with tears.

"Well, stand up zo I may put it on."

Nodding, I turned and lifted my hair.

Carl draped the necklace over my throat and did the clasp. Then he patted my shoulder.

"Zere. Keep this. As a reminder."

I didn't ask him of what. But I knew.

"Thank you," I whispered.

TWENTY-SEVEN

JOY

THE FOLLOWING YEAR

This molded plastic bench below deck sucks. Why can't the people that run the *Catalina Express* make comfortable seats? Probably wouldn't cost much to throw a few cushions down. Jeesh. I know the trip only lasts an hour, but when you have a skinny butt like mine, hard seats dig into your bones.

Especially when you are on a less than triumphant trip home.

Shit. Going home again. And it started off great. I was so jazzed because I'm sixteen and got to be a counselor in training. We called them *CIT's for short*. Sounds cool, huh?

I'd passed sailing, canoeing, and was about to take my kayaking test when I got caught with a pipe. This time, it wasn't a cool counselor wanting a hit who found it, but some straight-edge named Martha, who wore shorts so long you'd think she was living back before women could vote. She marched me double-quick up to the camp director, who said she wouldn't send me home, but that I wouldn't be welcome back.

Ever.

I couldn't tell Carl. No way. Instead, I pretend-strutted up to his trailer, hoping my shining pendant would keep him from noticing the fake smile on my face. It must have worked, because as soon as I topped the rise, he limped toward me saying he was glad to see me still wearing it but that it was time to make a new chain. Since I never took it off, a year of swimming showering, and sweat had pretty much worn the leather out.

"Joy. You look better zis year," he commented.

It was true. Things have been better. Two whole years without Ronny's fists; well, except for those couple of times when I got in trouble. Then it happened again. Not that I explained *it* to Carl. I never told anyone about *it*.

I undid the clasp at the back of my neck and passed him the necklace. He carried it over to his workbench and began measuring a new piece of leather. A little thicker this time.

"Yep. I sent some of my poems to the school paper. They even published two. I'm thinking of joining."

Carl looked at my necklace. "As you should. Just like zis abalone shell, you are many colors, Joy. Make zem shine." He finished attaching the new clasp and fitted the pendant around my neck.

I made sure to visit every day but that last one was hellish hard. After packing and making sure my campers were all set to board the boats, I made an excuse to Martha and stole up to Carl's trailer. We chatted for a minute or two before the conversation lagged and the sound of the ferry boats arriving told me it was time to leave.

Tell him the truth, I thought.

I rose from the faded lawn chair like I always did, ready to say goodbye with a nod. But that didn't feel right. With a rush of emotion choking my throat, I reached out both arms to give my mentor a first, and last, hug. I expected that leathery skin to be soft and supple like a well-worn wallet, but instead I was met with a skeletal back barely covering his bones.

Tell him, I thought, as I clung to him like a reluctant toddler resisting going to preschool.

As if not knowing how to respond, Carl patted me on the back and I finally let go.

You're such a wuss, Joy. And a fuck-up

I swallowed hard to hide my tears. "'Bye, Carl." I turned quickly, blinking them away.

"Zee you next year!" he called.

No, you won't.

With a final wave, I walked down the steps into the fog, toward the waiting ferries that would take us to the Isthmus. For the next half hour I kept busy, herding my campers onto the gangplank, telling my fellow counselors that I would write, and smoothing little Heather and Sydney's hair. All of Dinghy Cabin squeezed my waist before boarding the *Catalina Express* for Long Beach.

And my counselor-in-training job was done.

I staggered up the tilted deck toward the bow and looked down at the waves lapping against the hull. Thought about how different this day was from that first twenty-nine-mile trip, when I'd watched shining waters meld with an azurine sky.

Today there was no sun.

Only fog misting my cheeks and an ink-black sea reflecting shadows.

TWENTY-EIGHT

JOY

I'll be a senior in a couple of weeks, and you know what? The colors are better right now. Not from being high, but from two whole years with hardly any black and blue. No Mom buying four jars of Cover Girl Camouflage or wearing long, dark sleeves. Instead, she's sporting flouncy sun dresses and her glowing skin shines pink.

Not that the last two years have been all rainbows. I'm not an idiot. That horrible fistfight on Catalina last year wasn't the only one I wished I could hide in a puff of grey smoke. One race war between Stoners and Cholos made me wish I had superpowers to stop it.

I was at the fair with Lisa. We were laughing and shaking our skinny butts for every fox that walked by when this crowd started to gather near the Flying Bobs. When we trotted over to see what was happening, we found a group of chest-thumping Stoners from our school faced off with about eight or nine Chicanos.

Seething anger vibrated the air so much I could feel it pressing against my chest. Clutching my t-shirt, I gaped as kids I usually thought were cool struck war stances, as if they were in some friggin' elite squad or something.

Jelly Brain Jeff, usually the campus joke, was about as funny as infanticide when he pulled off his leather belt and snapped it together. "Go back to Mexico, dirty spic!" he shouted.

One of the Cholos smoothed his Pendleton shirt. "Fuck you, white boy."

I grabbed Lisa's arm, praying it would end there. People were massing, and the cops were sure to be called soon. I closed my eyes and made a wish. *Police, please come.*

Wishes don't always come true.

A second later, Chuck, a Stoner I'd actually thought was hot, swung his wallet chain at my friend Gabriel, who grabbed it and pulled. Chuck fell forward and the two hit the ground rolling, clawing, and scratching.

A second later, they all went at each other like a bunch of crazed hornets over spilled Coke. It was chaos. One dude hurdled into the nearest Cholo, who arm-blocked him before crashing into the next guy. Feet kicked as dust rose and swirled. Three more white guys flew at Chicanos, their arms raised like angry wings. It was a friggin' arthropod tornado.

Jelly Brain Jeff approached a junior-higher so tiny he probably didn't even have pit hair yet, and knocked him down. Then the fucking jerk grinned at the audience while raising his belt overhead. He flicked his wrist and the air cracked. Next, he whipped it over the boy's head, taunting, teasing, tormenting.

No! my mind screamed, as time stretched. *He's just a little kid.*

"Spic," Jeff spat, before bringing the belt down like a whip. Its lashing tongue left a tire-track welt across the kid's face. He turned toward the crowd and raised both arms triumphantly.

Asshole.

A tall guy named Beto rushed forward and cried out, "*Hermano!*" Then he knelt by the young kid's side and cradled his face in the crook of his arm.

By now, a swaying Gabriel and Chuck were back up with fists swinging. When one connected, Chuck's head snapped back like an old Bop Bag clown that'd just been punched. He went down with a crash.

A few feet away, Beto's face had turned an angry shade of purple. Jelly Brain had just attacked his baby brother. Never removing his gaze from Jeff's back, Beto rose to his feet.

Then I saw the glint of steel.

"Blade!" somebody cried.

Bile rose in my throat and I covered my mouth. The knife loomed as I waited for the hand of God, or Zeus, or Superman to freeze time.

In that moment, I imagined how every belt, chain and knife would be transformed into a flower. Next, the clouds would part, and a great voice would blare from the heavens. We would hear tales of brotherhood and how color is only skin deep. Then each flying fist would become a high five and each snap-kick a warm embrace.

Of course, none of this happened.

A second later, Jeff fell to his knees clutching his gut. The police whistles sounded. And we all ran.

Lisa and I dashed out the gate toward the parking lot, not stopping until we reached her rusty Volkswagen Beetle. As soon as we hopped inside, I pulled out a doobie and some matches. I didn't know why, but my hand was shaking when I tried to light one. Even though Lisa reached out to steady it, I couldn't stop quivering. I finally gave up and handed both to her. But even Lisa had to try three times before sweet smoke was clouding the car windows.

This was a quiet high and neither one of us said a word. Instead of giggling, we sat in that dirt parking lot looking back at the fair. Earlier, it had been bright and full of color, the most exciting thing to hit our town in months. Now, the gleam had been replaced with the harsh neon of night.

The distant voices sounded less like a summer family than an angry mob. Instead of wafting cotton candy and kettle corn sweetness, an animal manure stench rode toward us on blue smoke and cigarette ash. I took a long hit and the Ferris wheel lights blurred.

Then we got out of there.

———

The world is changing. The war is over, and they say civil rights have been won but I don't believe it. I mean, look at that fight at the fair. You'd think Martin Luther King Jr. had never marched or said "I have a dream". I wonder if that revolutionary flame has been snuffed out.

After years of bong hits and shots and making life the colors of imagination, there's still this barrier, an invisible line dividing kids into whites, Mexicans, and blacks. Oh, sure, we cross over and party with each other, but we all know that there's this glass wall between us.

We all live in separate worlds. And it pisses me off.

Ever since Charles Manson made 'hippie' a symbol of evil, kids have stopped hitting the streets to march for peace. Now we teens steal behind trees in parks or shut ourselves into the back of Chevy Vans, where we pass joints around and listen to Pink Floyd take us to the dark side of the moon.

On that side, no one cares when gang fights break out. Over there, it doesn't matter if we are denying people of color their rights. We breathe in Columbian smoke and the guitar's riffs fill our ears as we listen to Pink Floyd's quiet desperation guiding us ever further from the light.

On the dark side of the moon, we are so high we don't notice the rest of the world. Our vision is blurred and all we see are the twinkling stars in space.

TWENTY-NINE

KYLE

Well, stupid Joy is home again. Making everything all uptight and stuff. And things were going so great while she was at camp. Dad and Mom sat close to each other on the couch and laughed at that funny alien in the *Mork and Mindy* show. One Saturday, we had a party and I got to invite Rick; we hung out in my room and played Dungeons and Dragons all night. It was awesome.

Two days later, we picked up Joy in Long Beach and everything changed. I don't know why I had to come, anyhow. It's not like she was happy to see me or anything. As soon as she got off the boat, her grin froze all weird and whatever she was saying to the girl next to her stopped. She barely said 'hi'. She could have at least asked me what I'd been doing these eight weeks. But no! Ms. I'm-such-a-cool-teenager would never stoop so low as to have a conversation with her thirteen-year-old brother.

Dumb Joy.

The whole drive home, she barely said anything. Just mumbled answers to Mom and kept scratching her pen over that old journal of hers. Every time she looked my way, I thought she might be starting some sort of conversation. But it's like she didn't see me. Her eyes got all glassy like a baby doll's and then she'd write something else.

Curious, I tried to peek over her shoulder.

"Get back on your own side, stupid head," she said, slapping a hand over the page.

"I am." I crossed my arms and looked out the window.

Three days have passed and she still isn't talking to me, or anyone else for that matter. Just stays in her room strumming that guitar, or reading books she's not supposed to, or, I don't know what. Mom hasn't said anything, and Dad says, "Children should be seen but not heard."

Unless adults ask questions. Yesterday, Dad asked me about basketball try-outs. When I told him I made the freshman team, he punched my shoulder and said, "That's my boy."

Even though it hurt a little, I grinned, rubbing at it.

Yeah, maybe it's better with Joy in her room.

THIRTY

JOY

W ell, I started my senior year. BFD. I thought it would be different. You know? Like the grass on the field would look greener than ever before. The sidewalks would be cleaned of the gray and black gum splotches, shining like a *Wizard of Oz* Yellow Brick Road. The gym would have bleachers so smooth you'd think they were made of mahogany. And every foxy guy that walked past would check me out and whistle long and low.

The reality didn't quite match my expectations.

Yeah, it's cool to be the oldest on campus. The sophomores try to sit with you at lunch and the freshmen look up to you with open-mouthed awe. Well, except my stupid little brother, who makes faces when I walk by, but I ignore him.

But Gym still sucks. I mean, why did I have to get a locker next to Barbara Perfect Boobs? Her rack is so big you could rest a whole pie on it. And when we dress out, she doesn't hide it. Oh no. Instead, she slowly takes off her top like she's doing a striptease in Vegas before slipping on a Glamorise sports bra. Then she sticks out her chest, telling us that's how she will never get saggy boobs.

I hated to point out to her that no matter how hard you try, gravity wins.

Anyhow, whenever we change, she just stands there, hands on hips, letting those round D cups shine like headlights at every envious girl in the room. And no, I never grew, thank you very much. I'm still a double A and only wear bras because Ronny would have a tizzy fit if I didn't. But I sure as shit don't take it all off in Gym. Even in the shower, I only undress halfway and rinse off my bottom half before hiding under a towel.

I have to admit that I have okay legs. Not chubby and full of cellulite, but long and skinny like one of the models in Mom's glamour magazines. Everyone says I look nice in shorts, so I'm cool with wearing them in P.E. Just wish I had something on top to match.

Sigh.

I'm trying to up my cool meter, but Angie and some other chicks in Algebra are giving me shit. Why did I have to get a class with that tormentor? She keeps whispering behind me. And it's just loud enough for the kids around to hear but, of course, not quite loud enough for Mr. Welch to tell her to be quiet and pay attention.

"Why do they let such dogs in school?" Angie says, lifting her zitless chin in my direction.

Then some cheerleader princess next to her nods. "Yeah, they should be in the pound."

"Woof," adds a jarhead from the wrestling team.

I hate Algebra.

I was complaining to Lisa about it out on the Quad last week when a freakizoid came up to us. She said she'd overheard my problem and had a plan. We didn't know whether to listen or not, so did a 'talk to the hand'. But after a while, I started thinking about it, wondering if maybe her plan would make them shut up.

I didn't tell Lisa, but I decided to chat up the Weirdo and see what she had to say.

Big mistake, but more about that later.

I made it into Journalism. My one saving grace. Most of my classes are so friggin' boring, you have to be high to stay awake in them, but Journalism is a kick. Here, I get to be just Joy.

Our classroom is way down the hill past the gym, with windows that face the fields so even if Mrs. Plante were a drag, I'd have something pretty to look out at.

But Mrs. Plante is anything but boring. On the first day of school, she met each of us at the door with a dainty handshake, her bracelet-filled wrist tinkling like some sort of fairy in a story book.

"Welcome, writer of the future. What be thy name?"

"Uhh, Joy?"

"Enter a place of wonder and find your seat."

When I walked in, every desk had a name tag just like in elementary school. But these weren't ordinary name tags. Mrs. Plante must have really done her homework because below our calligraphed name was a resume of our English accomplishments. Mine had grades from freshman year, poetry I'd gotten in last year's paper and her own opinion of one piece. *Original similes and good imagery,* she wrote about my *Hills Like Shoulders* poem. At the bottom of the name tag were upcoming months, with blank spaces next to them which she obviously expected us to fill in as the year progressed.

Once we were all settled and had read our name tags, Mrs. Plante walked around the room, silently placing a single sheet of paper in the center of our desks. We looked at each other, perplexed.

Where was the rule lecture? When would she start talking about all of her expectations? How would grades be assigned?

We didn't have long to wonder because a moment later, she

tiptoed to the front of the room on friggin' ballet slippers no less and raised a glass vase overhead.

Then she threw it on the floor.

SLAM! CRASH!

The vase broke into a thousand pieces.

"Now, writers of the future. Tellers of tales. Wordsmiths. And Hunter Thompson wannabes. I want you to describe in as few words as possible what just occurred here. And please remember the 5 W's and the H of journalism."

She pointed at the chalk board where it said: *Who, What, Where, When, Why,* and *How*. Then she folded her hands over her paisley skirt belted with fringed macramé and gave us a nod to begin.

Senior year is going to rock!

THIRTY-ONE

IRIS

I slid the Lincoln into the slot and slammed on the brakes, almost hitting my head on the steering wheel in the process. They're so touchy, it'll take some getting used to. Got out to see if it was okay. Of course, I was crooked, so I tried backing up to straighten it out. It took three tries. Ronny says most women can barely drive but I am so bad, I must have showed someone my tits to get a license. And since the new Lincoln Continental is as big as the boat Ronny wants to buy, parking is a real pain in the ass.

"I won't have my wife driving a crap car," Ronny said, when he brought it home.

I thought the old Plymouth Coupe was fine, but I didn't dare argue. "It's pretty. I like the beige color."

"Not beige, champagne, like my tastes." He paused, shaking his head at me as if I were younger than Kyle. He ran a hand along the sleek exterior. "A vinyl hard top and oval opera windows. Three speed automatic. Rear wheel drive. V-8. A full-size luxury sedan. It's about time you show a little class."

I nodded, making sure to thank Ronny profusely. And vowed to be extra careful when I park.

Flipping the visor down, I checked my lipstick and patted my hair. Trying to come up with a lie to tell Ronny, I walked toward the Hillview High sign with the wildcat on the side. Then, I got a little turned around. But after asking a boy with hair so long, only close inspection would verify his sex, I was pointed in the right direction and managed to find the administration building.

Taking a deep breath, I approached the glass double doors which reflected the parking lot, a couple of shrubs, and a woman approaching behind me. I looked over my shoulder and blinked.

Where did she go?

I stood there for a couple of moments before realizing that I'd been looking at my own reflection. Unclenching my fists, I pulled open the door, which creaked so loudly I thought perhaps the Tin Man was nearby, providing sound effects. The rumpled secretary typing away at the front desk glanced up through cat-eyeglasses. "May I help you?"

I cleared my throat. "Mrs. Wright, here to see, Mr... Mr..." *Why can't I remember the principal's name?*

She looked me over from head to toe, apparently rating me on a respectability scale and finding me severely lacking. "Mayer?" she suggested.

Tucking one unbuttoned placket over the other to hide my cleavage, I nodded.

She picked up a phone and pressed one of the buttons. "Mr. Mayer, Joy Chapel's mother is here," she said in a superior voice, as if she and the principal shared a secret about me.

Even if I live to be a hundred, I do not believe I will ever feel at ease in a principal's office. Too many hours spent there as a kid. Iris was caught cursing again. Iris pushed a girl in line. Iris violated dress code. Back then, they paddled you, which was nothing in comparison to what Dad would do when I got home.

I fought the urge to smooth my hair down again as I extended a shaking hand toward the balding man behind the cheap metal desk. I guess even principals don't get real mahogany.

"Please, have a seat, Mrs. Wright."

Clutching my purse in my lap, I lowered myself onto the wooden chair directly opposite him. I gave him an expectant look that he returned for long moments, before raising my eyebrows in the uncomfortable silence. I had just gotten up the courage to ask him why he'd called me in when he finished my thought.

"Have you noticed any changes in Joy lately?"

"No, not really. Why?"

He picked up a typed spreadsheet and replied, "To begin with, her grades. Her B average has dropped to a D."

"What?"

"She's, let's see what her teachers say..." He scanned the document. "... not completing assignments, late to class on five occasions, passing notes, disrespect, and then yesterday..." He sighed.

"Yesterday?"

"Yesterday, your daughter took another student's purse, smeared red paint all over it, and threw it in the trash."

"Joy? She's got a heart bigger than this whole school. Always bringing home strays, feeling sorry for every sad-faced kid, begs me for money to give to hobos."

"Let's call her in and hear her side of the story." He buzzed his secretary, requesting Joy's presence.

I barely recognized the girl that shuffled through the door. Her hair was lighter than it used to be and hung down over most of her face. *When did she bleach it?* It still didn't hide the heavy make-up on her eyes and cheeks. Where the hell she got that, I don't know. In place of the cute jumper and neat skirt I'd set out for her the night before were an old sweatshirt and low-cut jeans that flared over platform shoes. Those shoes were for special occasions!

Even in the heels she looked smaller, as if she'd been growing backwards in some *Alice in Wonderland* fantasy. She was slumped over and wore the scowl usually reserved for Ronny.

Who was this girl?

"Now Joy," Mr. Mayer began, "why don't you tell us why you decided to deface Kourtney's purse?"

Joy stared at her shoes and shrugged.

"Joy. Answer him."

"She was going to make me do stuff."

"Explain," Mr. Mayer urged.

"She was going to make me join her gang. And I didn't want to."

"Now, no one can make you join a gang."

"He's right, Joy," I added, absolutely perplexed.

"Uh-huh. She said that if I didn't join her gang, she was going to get her boyfriend to beat me up."

Mr. Mayer and I explained how that would never happen, that she should have come to an adult, and how it still didn't give her the right to ruin a girl's purse. All the while, Joy kept shaking her head as if neither of us knew what we were talking about.

"Regardless of your reasons, your actions were against the rules and have consequences." Mr. Mayer turned to me. "Your daughter is going to be suspended for the next three days. During that time, I hope she reflects on her behavior. And if I were you, I'd think of getting her some help. I've seen this before and it's best to nip it in the bud."

Mouth opening and closing, I gaped at the man's head. For some reason, I couldn't help but stare at how the lights made his bald head shine. Almost shooting light beams around the room. Hot lasers that I knew would be coming when Ronny found out. And things have been so much better.

Damn.

Or maybe I could keep it from him.

I must have sat there staring for a long time, because the next thing I knew, Mr. Mayer was waving a pen and asking me to sign the suspension notice. In a fog, I rose from my chair and scribbled my name before leading Joy past the smug-faced secretary.

In my brand-new shiny Lincoln Continental, I placed shaking hands on the steering wheel and rested my head there.

"Why, Joy? Why?" I whispered to the silent sixteen-year-old next to me.

Refusing to answer, Joy crossed her arms and curled up against the door.

While I tried to figure out how to hide this from my husband.

THIRTY-TWO

JOY

The disembodied whisper
Their voices howling whips
And rattling chain mail
Their hearts beat with
The recurring thud
Of stocks encasing
Arms and skulls.

They lie
Shivering beneath
Coverlets
Cupping the ears
That are not there.
They long
To reach for the light
And put to rest
The incessant hauntings
But bedclothes
Hold them fast
In the dungeon

Of an imagined
Damnation

M y parents think I'm nuts. Crazy. Bonkers. Off in La La Land. Fucking certifiable. So, they decided I needed to see some shrink. Well, they can make me go but they can't make me tell him shit.

I was sitting in some stupid office, all dark wood, with a sculpted head of a dead guy and more books than any dude could ever read, while this fatso with thick glasses looked me up and down and wrote notes in a spiral pad. Take a picture, why don't you? Jeesh.

"Now, Joy, your mother shared a few things with me but now I'd like to get your perspective on what might be happening," Dr. Bond, not James superspy, said.

"I don't know." *You're the doctor, figure it out.*

"Let's start with what happened at school."

Oh, you mean that place where I'm humiliated day after day? That torture chamber where kids follow me around and call me dog? Where I get high just to deal? I thought, but said, "I got in trouble."

"Yes, your mother told me that and your initial explanation, but I'd like to hear it in your own words."

"I messed up a girl's purse."

"Go on."

"With blush, red blush."

"I see."

No, he didn't. He didn't know shit. He didn't see how this girl was telling everyone that I was going to be in her gang, but she was more of a freak than I was. So now, in addition to being called dog, I'd also be labeled one of the Weirdos, member of an ostracized gang. I mean she wasn't even Mexican, just some white girl like me, trying to find a way to keep The Crowd from teasing her. Only she really was weird, I mean like dumb, and wore these homemade dresses straight out of 1952. I couldn't let anyone associate me with her.

"And then I got suspended." I shrugged.

"Let's try a different tack." He sighed. "How did that make you feel?"

Fucking awesome. "I don't know. Kind of bad."

"In what way?"

"For Mom, and..." I trailed off, not wanting to remember how Ronny had started yelling and how I'd been quiet at first but then got pissed and shouted how he wasn't my dad and couldn't tell me what to do. How his eyes had turned bong-hit red and he'd chased me down the hall grabbing my hair and whirled me around for the punch to my cheek. He'd said to never talk to him that way again.

"How is your relationship with your mother?"

Epic. Like Carol Brady and the Brady Bunch. "Fine. She's a mom. Does Mom stuff."

"Which is?"

Boy, for having so many framed certificates of all the shit he's done, this guy really is stupid.

"She cooks dinner, tells me to brush my teeth, tells me when to go to bed, tells me to get up, go to school. Stuff like that. You do know what a mother is, right?" I gave him an incredulous look.

He smiled smugly and wrote something in his little pad. I tried peering over the desk to see what it said, but it was too far away and upside down.

I rolled my eyes.

"What are you so angry about, Joy? These are just questions to get to know you."

Maybe I don't want to know you. Maybe I don't want you looking inside my brain and prodding around like some weird Dr. Frankenstein stitching together body parts and shooting electricity through me, I almost retorted. But then I flashed on Mom. After Ronny's fist had bounced off my cheek, he'd turned on her and told her what a shitty mother she was. If she didn't have her head up her ass reading those stupid magazines and had done some mothering, maybe her kid wouldn't be such a fuck-up. Fists still curled, he'd stood over her, ready.

I knew more would happen if I told. And Mom hasn't had to cower for, like, two years. Until I got in trouble, Ronny had actually been pretty fun. I blinked, realizing for the first time what she had to deal with every day.

"I am not angry," I replied, putting on the mask Mom used when people asked what happened to her face.

Dr. Bond, not James, tried to get a rise out of me for the next forty minutes of our session. But I kept the mask up. Pretending to be the girl Mom wished I was.

THIRTY-THREE

JOY

Now that I'm a senior, you'd think my family would acknowledge something good about me, but I've slowly been turning invisible. Not like in comic books or old black and white movies on Sunday afternoon, but the kind where people seem to look through me. When I walk into the living room, Mom doesn't acknowledge my presence but keeps her eyes fixed on that one spot in the wall. The hole we don't talk about.

The one that's all my fault.

Oh, I know. I fucked up. Shouldn't have messed up Kourtney's purse. But imagine what would have happened if she told everyone I was in her gang? Then I'd be beyond outcast, part of a freakizoid group.

Hell, I was barely clinging to Lisa's friendship. She'd already been asked to three parties this year. Once right in front of me. I stared into the chick's back and pulled on a stray thread unraveling from my t-shirt while waiting to hear the words, "Joy, you can go too."

But no. She just walked away.

One late Tuesday, I got back from Lisa's to find Kyle on his belly watching *Super Friends* on TV. Even though I walked right in front of him, half-blocking his view, he kept his jaw in his hands. He didn't even whine to Mom.

She was slumped in the club chair, staring off into space.

I glanced from one to other, before trudging down the hall to drop off my books and binder. When I came in again, both were still transfixed on other places. I opened my mouth to say, "Hello? I'm here. Do you see me?" when I noticed the shattered glass on the kitchen floor. I tiptoed toward it, wondering why Mom hadn't cleaned it up yet.

When anyone dropped something, she usually swept up the broken shards so quickly you'd think a flash of lightning had just passed over the floor. When I say 'anyone', I mean me. As Ronny always pointed out, I'm the clumsy one in the family. As if I didn't know.

The glass was spread all over the floor. The quatrefoil pattern (Mom taught me that phrase for four-leafed when she picked out the avocado-green linoleum) now looked like it was covered with jewels. For a moment, I was transfixed by the beauty of rough-cut diamonds shining on four-leaf clovers.

Then I noticed a ruby amongst all those clear diamonds. I reached down to touch it and realized it wasn't a piece of red glass but a droplet of blood. Recoiling, I pulled my hand back to see three more stains on the beautiful tableau, a trail of red flowers leading to the sink.

Don't look. I curled my hands into fists and stepped closer. There, in the sink Mom scrubs daily until it sparkles like yellow daisies, was a towel blooming blood.

I wasn't high, but my brain felt foggy when I turned back to Mom. She wasn't just slumped but hunched over, clutching her gauze-wrapped forearm.

"Mom, you okay?"

She didn't answer, but kept staring at the hole in the wall. I knelt at her feet and touched her arm just above the bandage. She didn't so much as flinch. Gently placing a hand over hers, I uncurled the clenched fingers from around her arm. A rose stain the size of my fist lay in the center of the cloth.

My heart fluttered. Red was a new color. Black and blue I was used to. Black and blue you could hide with make-up. Black and blue stays beneath. But this...

"Mom?" I waited long seconds, but her eyes remain fixed and staring. After rewrapping her fingers around the bleeding arm, I strode into the living room.

I bent down next to Kyle. "What happened?"

Even at fourteen, he knew enough to put a finger to his lips before pointing toward his room. My head a jumble, I trailed after him, dreading what I'd hear. Once we were safely behind a closed door, he whispered that Ronny's drink tasted bad, so he threw it on the floor.

"Mom didn't make it right," he explained.

I give him an exasperated look but didn't argue. He was always making excuses for his father. "Then what?"

"He told her to clean it up. Well, started to make her..." His voice trailed off.

"With his fists?"

"He didn't mean it. He was just trying to get her to do it right." Kyle jutted out his lower lip and hugged himself.

There was no point explaining. Kyle would make this what he needed to.

With a sigh, I trudged back past my silent Mom toward the kitchen, where I got out the broom and dustbin. Then, using my thumb and forefinger, I picked up four large pieces. Clunk. They thudded against the plastic trash bottom. Now you couldn't even tell what had shattered on the floor. As I grasped the broom handle and dragged it across the floor, I understood why Mom always cleaned so quickly. Every pass of the brush erased some part of the story.

Sweep, sweep. The glass no longer sprawled in rubescent

disarray but sparkled in piles. *Brush. Swish.* More of the quatrefoil pattern returned to its soft green.

The tinkling pieces cascaded into the trash like pebbles in a dying stream, yet the bristles kept seeking more fragments. I swept each corner, once, twice, three times, until every sliver was lying on the bottom of the plastic liner.

Soon, the only reminder was the blood. Fucking smears on the linoleum garden. I ripped off a few paper towels and threw them on the floor. Then I stepped on the pile with both feet, hoping that would soak up the stain. Still there. *Shit.*

With more urgency I grabbed another wad and moistened it. *Get rid of it, now.* I began rubbing like hell to mop it up, but multiple strokes did little more than turn spots into blotches. I tossed a few bloody towels into the trash.

Began again.

Why the fucking stains wouldn't disappear was beyond me. No matter how hard I scrubbed and scoured, the smears remained. Without any help. Cartoons blared. Kyle kept his back to the kitchen. Mom's gaze remained on the hole

Then I realized the stains were gone. Had been for several minutes. I hurled the last of the sopping pink towels into the plastic bag and tied it in a tight knot. This, I carried to the outside bins. Slammed the lid shut.

When I returned to the living room, everyone was gone.

Leaving me to float in silence like the invisible girl I was becoming.

THIRTY-FOUR

JOY

W ell, I thought Mrs. Plante was full-on cool. A teacher that got it. Who let you slide if an assignment was late or you didn't follow directions.

Think again, Joy.

Instead, she is a you-can-do-so-much-better teacher. The 'I see the potential in you' cheerleader with so much enthusiasm you'd think she took a handful of uppers before school.

I mean, handing back my article on marijuana use among teens three times? What was she thinking? I was just a high school kid, not friggin' Edward R. Murrow.

"I have seen the wonder that you can create. Your work has approached the sublime before, and I know that it can again. Rewrite the article until it shines like, like..." She glanced around, then pointed to the abalone necklace around my neck.

She would have to go there. The one place I was vulnerable. I was going to blow her off until she mentioned Carl's pendant.

With a sigh, I said, "Okay, Mrs. Plante. I'll try."

So now I'm sitting in my room, trying to figure out how the fuck to turn a report about weed into a *real* article. But what I'd really like to be doing is figure out how to get tickets to IT.

IT was going to be the most rockin', bitchin', radical event of the decade. And if I went, I just know that I would finally be delivered from geekdom to cool land. Then maybe Paul Janssen would finally notice me. Ask me out. Want to get down with me. And be so enraptured by my expert lovemaking, he would ask me to Prom.

When did I become such an expert on sex, you might ask? Okay, I'm not. Still a virgin, if you must know. But I French-kissed a guy at a party last year and I've been reading lots of *Penthouse* and *Playboy* articles from when I snuck some out of Ronny's porno stash. They taught me plenty, probably all I'll ever need to know about doing it.

With foxy Paul, if he ever says hi.

There's a new chick in our Journalism class, Janice-from-New-York-Rappaport. Short reddish hair, hazel eyes with those lashes that flip up without an eyelash curler, and a full-on rack all the guys stare at.

"Hey, my eyes are up heah," she says, when some buzzed Stoner forgets she has a face.

"Sorry," he retorts, before shuffling away.

She cracks me up.

We've been hanging out at lunch and sometimes after school. She doesn't live in Country Club but in the Development, where a bunch of cookie-cutter houses were built about two years ago. The Rappaports even have a pool and she invites me over to work on our tans, although it's late November and getting cold. But true California girls will suffer through 58-degree weather for bronzed legs.

Or so Janice says.

Janice is Mrs. Plante's pet. Everything she writes is freaking Hemingway to our teacher. Mrs. Plante even reads her essays aloud to the class to show us what we should *strive for*.

But will Janice help me with my article? Fuck no. She is too busy with her boyfriend, Russ.

Russ, Mr. Surfer Hottie. Russ with eyes so blue, the sky hides when he looks up. Russ with a tanned torso all the girls drool over. Russ of the Plymouth Valiant fame—a station wagon topped with a surf rack and a stereo system that blasts so loud, everyone invites him to their keggers in the boonies. The one he parks next to the pony keg, with open doors and tailgate, cranking the tunes.

Rocking!

Russ with the tiny penis Janice makes fun of behind his back. Well and to his face, when I'm in the back seat of her Toyota and they are up front, fighting. Then his foxy smile goes all crumply.

I feel sorry for him.

If I was a slut instead of, like, the oldest virgin in my school, I'd get down with him and tell him what an amazing lover he was. How he could work his just-the-right-size junk like no one's business.

Instead, I wave from the back seat and say, "Hello? Other person here."

More times than not, Janice laughs it off. But one night she argued, "Show Joy your baby dick, Russ. So she'll know."

"Janice! That's mean," I said, proud to finally get the guts up to say something.

She only shrugged and told Russ to take her to 7-11 for a diet Coke.

Yeah, Janice can be mean but she's also popular. The girls like her New York accent and the guys... well, I already talked about that. Ever since I've been hanging out with her, almost no one has called me freak.

Maybe they've moved onto some other non-suspecting soul too shy to say anything back. And finally forgotten what a mutant I am.

A whole glorious month with no taunts. Aside from that bitch Angie in Algebra. But she has, like, Tourette's or something.

Now I have to make this marijuana article better so Mrs. Plante will finally say it's satisfactory and approve it for the school paper.

Get to work, Joy.

THIRTY-FIVE

JOY

W ell, sweet sixteen will soon be coming to an end. I don't why they call it that, because it wasn't exactly an angel food cake with sprinkles on top. Sure, there were a few tasty moments, but I'm not too bummed to put it in the rearview mirror. Maybe it's because most sixteen-year-olds get to drive. Unlike me, who has a stepfather who thinks the female brain can't figure out the difference between stop and go.

I only pressed the gas instead of the brake once! And I didn't hit anything; just bumped over the curb. If Ronny hadn't been yelling about how terrible I was, I probably would have braked just fine. But all that yelling made me nervous and I slammed my foot down on the wrong pedal. After that, he said I'd have to prove I wouldn't wreck the car before getting my license. Whenever the hell that is. Which sucks, because that means I'll still have to bum rides or hitch to go anywhere.

One cool thing is that, since Lisa, Janice and I all have birthdays pretty close to each other, we're planning to honor our mutual passage with a kegger! And not just some flat pony keg left over from last week's party. No siree. We are getting a half-barrel and inviting, like, fifty people. Radical.

It's going to be out by the Oil Piers just north of Ventura. We might even make a bonfire on the beach. If we can keep it on the down low until then.

We've been selling pre-party tickets to the bash. Buy a ticket, get a beer. That's what we're telling everyone, anyhow. Truth be told, we need the money. All three of us are pretty broke and I'm saving my money for my ticket to IT.

Now, there's an idea for a birthday present. Maybe Mom and Ronny could get me a ticket to the World Music Festival! Then I wouldn't have to save all of my babysitting money and could buy some really good dope, not the rag weed I've had to smoke lately.

Maybe even get a cool outfit for the show. Joy Chapel would enter the Los Angeles Coliseum looking like a rock star, or groupie, or maybe even a Woodstock hippie.

Yeah!

I suggested it to Janice, but she said, "Bettuh not ask. If they say no, it's too fah, then you can't make up a lie to sneak out. Bettuh keep it quiet fah now."

———

Mrs. Plante finally approved my article about marijuana use. It isn't exactly what I'd hoped. I mean it's full of statistics and numbers of related deaths and boring shit like that. Not really an homage to the almighty leaf.

Still, it was printed in last week's edition of the *Wildcat Times* and a few kids even gave me high fives for it. Cool.

My glory was short-lived, though. Now, everyone is talking about that girl in the news who was found wandering in the desert missing a hand. She almost died. All of our teachers are giving us lectures about hitchhiking, which is stupid because everyone knows that if you're nice enough to someone, they won't attack you. I mean it even works with Ronny. When Mom does what he says and is really quiet and nice, he doesn't go off on her.

Usually.

Until I got suspended. Why was I such an idiot about that freakizoid's purse? If I hadn't been such a fuck-up, Ronny wouldn't have come after me. That time, I really deserved it.

That's what I told Mrs. Plante when she asked about my black eye. That I had done something wrong and deserved to be punished. She looked at me kind of funny, as if I was kidding. But she must have heard about my suspension because she quickly changed the subject.

"I want you to write an article about rape prevention. With what happened to that poor girl, we need to educate our student body."

"But Mrs. Plante, that would never happen to a kid at our school," I argued.

"I wish that were true, Joy. But the reality is that one in four women will be assaulted at some time in their lives. Maybe your article could help reduce those numbers."

"Oh, come on Mrs. Plante. I can't write an article about *that!*"

My teacher would not let me argue my way out of it. She pointed at my throat and pulled the 'you-shine-like-your-pendant' on me again. And when it comes to anything about Carl's necklace, I'm hopeless.

I went to the public library after school, since the one at Hillview High doesn't have jack shit about any kind of sex, consensual or not. I know, I've looked.

My cheeks were kind of red when I went to the card catalogue to look up 'rape'. I glanced over my shoulder to make sure no one could see what I was searching for, before opening the drawer. There were several books on the subject, but *Against Our Will: Men, Women, and Rape*, by Brownmiller, sounded interesting, so I wrote down the number on the small slip of paper and went over to the 300's for the book.

When I saw that there were at least ten books on rape, my brows shot up. I hadn't imagined there'd be so many. I started to reach for one, but then a lady walked by, so I dropped down and plunged my hand into the bottom shelf, pulling out the first one I touched. With a scrunched-up my face, I pretended to read the back cover of something called *The Prince*. It was by some dead dude named Machiavelli and looked boring as shit, but it'd be a good one to go on the top of my pile.

As soon as the aisle was empty, I turned back to pull a few sexual assault books down from the shelves and immediately hugged them to my chest. I didn't want anyone to see the titles. Then I found a table in the darkest corner of our library and pulled out a chair, which made a fingernails-on-the chalkboard sound.

I froze, thinking the lights had just brightened with a spotlight centered on me. Swallowing hard, I stood there for, like, five seconds, waiting for the whole library to come running and point at the books in my arms.

When none of this happened, I placed the books on the tabletop with Machiavelli strategically set on top. I looked right and left, waiting until the coast was clear.

I finally opened *Against Our Will*. Then I started to read. And read. And read.

I discovered stuff I never imagined, much less knew. Like, for example, how rape initially was barely considered a crime, and then only in terms of the property violations. Weird! Hundreds of years ago, punishment barely happened and then only when irate husbands said the rapist had damaged his property.

Being a man's property? Right.

Long ago, they called raped women adulteresses and then punished them, even if they had been horribly beaten or injured.

In ancient Hebrew times, raped women were considered defiled and often stoned to death. Wow!

I guess it's not that different today. Back when I was in ninth grade, I heard about this chick who was raped and stabbed by some guys that had given her a ride. Ended up in the hospital for a week.

When she came back to school, no one would talk to her. I remember when she walked by, people would give her a wide berth and say, "That's the girl who was raped."

People didn't throw stones, except with their looks. She ended up dropping out of school. I don't know what happened to her after that.

One book said that a lot changed in 1974, after the rape of Joan Little by a jail guard in Beaufort County, North Carolina. She was a black prisoner in the County Jail when a white jailer attacked her. She broke away from her rapist, killed him with an ice pick he had taken into her cell, and then broke out of jail. When she was later caught and charged with murder, there was a national outcry for justice for her, and a jury acquitted her.

When I read what her lawyer, Angela Davis, said, I was blown away. "All people who see themselves as members of the existing community of struggle for justice, equality, and progress have a responsibility to fulfill toward Joan Little."

Fuck, yeah! She should have been protected in jail.

After that and a few cases like it, rape crisis centers, consciousness-raising groups, and protests began to emerge. A friggin' grass roots movement took shape and rocking women offered self-defense classes and broke their silence in 'take back the night' marches.

I wanted to be like them.

Taking notes, I imagined marching for people like Joan Little. We'd take to the streets and demand justice. We'd teach girls self-defense and prevent all kinds of shit.

Yep. Someday.

THIRTY-SIX

JOY

"Come on, Joy! Hurry up. Your hauh looks fine," Janice called from the other side of the bathroom door.

I looked in the mirror. Not really. Little hairs that'd escaped my brush stuck up all over. I turned on the faucet and wet it down. Thought it was working, but pretty quickly it turned into a frizzy mess. Brushed it again and leaned closer.

"Shit!"

"What?" Janice called.

"A zit. A freaking new zit."

"Let me in."

I opened the door and pointed to the center of my forehead, where an angry red pimple had started to grow.

"I'm going to be a cyclops for the party. Man. I shouldn't even go."

"Shut up," Janice said, rummaging in her purse. She pulled out a Cover Stick and twisted it open. "Sit down and I'll fix it."

Not believing it possible to hide the protrusion that seemed to be growing like some sort of alien presence by the second, I plopped down on the closed toilet seat.

"Lean closau," Janice said, holding the make-up stick poised over my head.

Shaking my head, I scooted a little closer. Janice dabbed at my forehead.

I jerked back. "Ouch!"

"Hold still."

"But it hurts." I stuck out my lower lip and tried to keep from wriggling.

Janice's touch was no gentler this time. If anything, rougher. But after a few applications, she managed to hide the alien creature growing in the middle of my forehead. Sort-of.

"Thanks."

"Russ and Lisa are waiting. Let's go."

Outside, Lisa stood next to Russ's Valiant, wearing a skintight tee and a camera hanging from a strap around her neck

"What is that?" Janice asks, pointing.

"A Polaroid One Step. I'm going to document this epic night in full color," Lisa replied, brushing a hand over the camera like some sort of actress in a TV commercial.

"But you look like a tourist."

"I do not care. I am photographer, an *arteest*. Anyhow, it hangs right where I want guys to look." Lisa thrust out her chest, which had grown from A's to D's overnight.

Lucky Joy, surrounded by centerfield potentials, I thought, wondering if Paul Janssen, or any guy for that matter, would want to make out with a senior who still wore training bras. I consider faking sick and going home, until Janice blew a pink bubble that popped in my face.

"Camera, huh? Makes sense. Let's go."

A minute later, all four of us were piled inside Russ's Valiant, headed for the Oil Piers. And our very first kegger!

The music of Van Halen might have blasted up the beach, but I wasn't rocking out. Nor dancing with a fox so hot his hands were bonfire coals. Passing a joint to a few Hillview High stoners? Nope.

Instead, I stood next to Russ's car while five pimply freshmen challenged each other to chug-a-lug and spilled half their beer before chasing each other down the beach for a game of tag.

Tag?

I thought this party would be the event of the century; an epic kegger for the books. Long after I'd left my teens behind me, people would be talking about it. Writing songs, even. Future rock stars would get a dreamy look in their eyes as they told of Joy's Oil Pier Party.

The reality didn't quite match my vision. Oh sure, Janice's brother, Keith, got the horse keg. Tapped and ready. We had the plastic cups stacked up in neat rows on a folding table. The music was cranked. Then we waited.

And waited.

Lisa paced back and forth from the near empty dirt parking lot to Russ's car. "Are we too early?"

I looked at my watch. It said 10:23. "I don't think so." I glanced up at the highway, waiting for the stream of headlights to shine down on us like a presidential motorcade. A distant pair grew, and I held my breath.

They passed right by.

"You did tell people tonight, right?" Janice asked. Her voice was accusing.

"Cha! You know we did. You helped make the posters yourself."

"Maybe someone heard it got busted." Lisa played with the camera strap on her neck. She'd only taken one picture all night, of Russ and Keith clinking red plastic cups together.

A second later, an already buzzed Russ strolled up, spilling foaming beer onto the sand. He took a long slurp, flicked some foam off his shirt and slung an arm over Janice's shoulder.

Janice snuggled into it and lifted her chin toward Lisa and me. "Maybe no one showed up because they didn't want to hang out with you freaks."

Lisa stepped back and shook her head. "Seriously? You're going to be a bitch now?"

"Yeah, I bet that's it." Janice turned to Russ with a sneer. "Whatya think, babe?"

"I dunno." He shrugged. "But this blows. I'm about ready to bail."

"I know. Let's take the keg to Mike's. He's got a little gathering I heawd about."

"What? You guys are going to kidnap our keg?"

"This ain't exactly rocking, in case you hadn't noticed." Janice jerked a thumb over her shoulder.

I shook my head. "No way. I worked too hard."

"Me too!" Lisa said. "I even friggin' sold some of my albums to raise money."

"Then don't let it go to waste," Janet argued. "Let's take the keg to a *real* party."

I couldn't believe it. We'd been planning this for months and now she just wanted to pack it up.

"But it's our birthday!"

"Stop whining, Joy. And face facts. No one wanted to come, so let's at least salvage the couple of houws we got."

What choice did I have? Russ was my ride. Shrugging, I joined Lisa who was already gathering up the cups and putting them back in the bag.

Russ might have cranked the tunes on the ride to Mike's, but the car seemed as quiet as Sunday morning.

———

Across the crowded room, Lisa giggled at Mike's stupid knock-knock jokes. I rolled my eyes. When she threw her laughing head back, it was so obvious she was faking, I was sure Mike would halt half-sentence and give her a pointed stare. But no. Instead, he raised his voice loud enough for aliens in a distant galaxy to hear and told another.

"Knock-knock."

Lisa smoothed her hair before asking who's there.

"Voodoo." Mike raised caterpillar eyebrows. What a Neanderthal.

Now she was full-on gushing. Over Mike? Yuck! "Voodoo who?"

"Voodoo you think you are, asking me so many questions?"

This time when Lisa giggled, Mike slipped an arm around her shoulder. And she let him. No way! Last week, she told me that he looked like a gorilla and now she's ready to have his children?

Whatever.

I looked around the little house for someone, anyone, to talk to. But Janice was telling tales of New York to a gaggle of populos, Russ was obviously talking surfing as he acted out getting tubed, and Angie was strutting across the room.

I gulped. Angie here? No friggin' way. She wasn't a stoner. From what I heard, the hardest stuff she ever did was Boone's Farm.

Sweat started beading on my forehead. I turned away.

My gaze darted from kitchen to hallway. Why didn't I bring my brown leather jacket with the fuzzy hood? Then I could hide behind the fur. But, after trying on every pair of jeans, Dittos and cords before finally getting a passable look for skinny ass, I wasn't about to mess it up with a coat.

A pit as hard as one of Mr. Kaminski's algebra tests formed in my gut. I had to get out of there fast. Hiding the side of my face with one hand, I rushed across the room.

"Hey, Russ." I tapped him on the shoulder. "Can you give me a ride home?"

"It's only 11:30. The party's just starting."

I raised pitiful eyebrows at each of his surfer friends, who all shook their heads in turn. Couldn't ask Mike. It was his house. And all the populos around Janice usually ignored me, unless they were looking for someone to tie to their whipping post.

I needed someone to take me home. Now.

I darted in the kitchen praying Angie hadn't seen me. Even though I knocked a chair loudly into the Formica table, the entwined couple there didn't even notice. I shook my head. They were so entangled, you'd think they were honeysuckle vines smothering a tree. Not caring if the last person who drank out of it had mono or some other gross disease, I grabbed a half empty Coors bottle off the table and chugged it down. Slammed it on the counter.

Then *she* came in, smiling sweetly, as if someone had just given her a compliment on that hair which always seemed so perfect. As soon as she saw me, her expression changed. Her surprised eyes popped, before narrowing into pit viper slits homing in on prey.

Her lip curled when she said, "Look who we have here. Joy Chapel, Hillview High's dog mascot."

The entwined couple stopped slobbering all over each other and turned to stare. My face got hot. I began backing away.

"Mike has really lowered his standards."

The girl sniggered.

"Why don't you just leave me alone? It's a party."

"It was, until you walked in." She crossed her arms and smiled smugly. "Why the hell you ever leave your house is beyond me."

The kissy girl, who I now recognized as Kimberly-of-the-homecoming-court, giggled. "I know, she's trying to gross the rest of us out."

"What have I ever done to you?" I asked, my throat tighter with every word.

Angie pointed at me as if to say that my mere presence was a bane to her existence.

I blinked, my eyes brimming with tears. Fisted my hands. *Don't you dare let them see you cry. That'll only fuel their asshole remarks.*

Pushing past Kimberly and Mr. Honeysuckle's vine arms, I dashed out of the kitchen and back into the living room. The music was still cranking, with a few people showing their moves, one dude doing a pretty good imitation of the Robot.

If only I were an android, able to wow kids as my limbs jerked in impossible ways like him. Then, not only would I be admired, but also have a steel heart.

Lisa, who loved dancing, gave me a hopeful look and waved me over. Part of me felt bad as I shook my head, but I couldn't hold it together much longer. I was already blinking back tears and had maybe five more seconds before I lost it.

Ignoring the stares from my friends, I raced from one end of the room to the other. Where was the fucking exit in this stupid house, anyhow?

When I finally found the front door and jerked it open, I stumbled down the steps, disorientated. With no idea where I was going, I started to run. And run.

Getting the fuck away from there.

———

The winter stars twinkled above the streetlamps in the midnight sky. Porch lanterns glimmered through the fog. A lone car's headlamp shone in the distance.

But shadows prevailed. Dusky hands swiped from the gloom. A blackness I'd never escape.

I kept running. Rushing forward in a race against no one.

Each breath drew shorter. I started gasping, chest tightening with every stride.

Palm trees swayed overhead, their sharp fronds whispering like necromancers creating curses. Repeatedly, they murmured, "Dog. Freak. Outcast." Meanwhile, wispy clouds became wraiths assaulting the sky.

Praying that speed would shrivel the words, I tried focusing on my feet. And raced on.

If there truly was a fairy godmother, she'd tell me to close my eyes to erase it all. But when I tried, Angie's sneering face remained etched on the back of my lids.

I sprinted up one street. Down another.

Then I turned the corner and flew headlong into the street. Saw the headlights. Too late. A horn blared and tires screeched.

The next thing I knew, I was splayed out in someone's yard, watching a man in a dark Camaro roll down his window.

"Stupid kid! Watch where you're going!" he shouted, before peeling out.

If I'd had any buzz before that, it sure as shit was gone now. Panting, I hugged my knees as the wet grass soaked into my Dittos. The street was quiet now. Shivers tingled my scalp and pulsed down my spine until I was shaking so much, I thought that big earthquake they always talk about had begun.

I want to go home. Sit on Mom's lap like I had when I was little, feeling her stroke my hair as she told me things that weren't true, like sticks and stones will break your bones but names will never hurt you.

Take a deep breath, Joy. Think. You don't know where you are, but you need to find out. It's almost curfew.

My legs tightened as a full-on Charlie horse set in. Standing, I limped over to a nearby street sign, grabbed the pole with both hands, and started to stretch out my right calf.

The sign said Malibu Avenue. Where had I heard that

before? Racking my brain, I tried to remember street names, but everything was fuzzy and mixed up.

Right or left? Both looked pretty much like dead ends, but I either picked one or stayed on this corner shivering all night. *Eeeny meeny miny moe.*

Left it is.

———

By the time I finally found my way home it was real late, probably past two. I thought maybe I could sneak in and my parents wouldn't notice.

Turning the knob as slowly as I could, I slipped inside.

"Where the hell have you been?" Ronny thundered, his eyes red and angry.

"Umm. At Janice's."

He grabbed me by the collar and pulled me closer. I could still smell the Seagram's under the toothpaste on his breath. "Liar. We called. She was with her boyfriend."

"But I was with them. Really."

"You were whoring around, little slut."

"No! I was with Janice and Lisa, I swear."

Mom stepped into the entryway. "Tell us the truth, Joy. Was it a boy?"

"No." I sighed. Busted, I might as well tell the truth. "I was a party, okay? Some kids had a party."

"Whoring around?"

"I don't do that. I just went to a party." Then, under my breath, added, "Nobody'd want me anyhow."

Mom's face fell. "You lied to us?"

"I thought you'd say no. You guys are so strict."

"I'll show you strict, you little slut!" Ronny raised an arm.

"Stop calling me that."

Grabbing a fistful of t-shirt, he said, "Slutty jeans. Whore top."

"Asshole!" I jerked away.

"Why, you fucking little—" His fist recoiled off my face.

For the first time, I ignored the pain and fear. Instead, rage filled me. Every punch Mom and I had ever endured. Every black eye and bruise. Every cruel word of derision. Every time I'd cowered behind my door. All turned to paper-flashing flame.

Crawl in a hole and die.

I swung. Fists curled like he'd shown me. Connected with that fucking red face. Arms burning with rage. Imitating the blows he'd inflicted year after year.

Smack! Rapid fire strikes shot off from two pairs of arms. Child against adult. Girl against man. Victim against perpetrator.

Mom's screams did nothing to stop the conflagration. Too many years of fuel. I punched and punched. Not giving a shit as to how loud she cried or how much my face was swelling.

She got behind me and grabbed my waist. "Stop, now!" she said, dragging me off him.

I stumbled back, raised an arm toward her but then gasped when I realized what I was doing. A tear-stained face looked at me accusingly.

"What's wrong with you?"

Ronny placed a hand on Mom's back. "She's a spoiled bitch, that's what."

Shaking my head, I backed up. Only now feeling the fire on my cheeks, I cupped them and froze. *I hate him, fucking hate him.*

After lowering my hands, I ran to my room. With a loud door slam, I fell onto the bed and buried my face in a Tide-scented pillow. Pounding the mattress, I screamed, "I didn't do anything!"

Asswipe.

And I'd really been trying lately. Not getting high so much.

Working on my grades, friggin' joined the school paper, even wrote two articles that got published. I tried getting home before curfew. Wasn't my fault I couldn't get a ride.

Why do I even try? No matter what I do, things suck.

A smoldering something changed in me that day. It blistered into a scalding char that burned under my skin. And the tears that flooded my pillow did nothing to smother it.

I fucking give up.

THIRTY-SEVEN

JOY

*C*an't take it anymore. I'm leaving.

I slammed my journal shut and reached into the bottom of my jewelry box where I keep my babysitting money. Shoved the few dollars I had into my big suede purse with the fringe, along with a t-shirt, undies, and my diary.

Mom and Ronny were gone, at the Country Club or something like that. No, I wasn't babysitting Kyle, he's fourteen now and doesn't need it. Anyhow, he was staying the night at Rick's.

I thought about calling my real dad. Maybe this time he'd come around. I actually dialed his number. Hung up when *she* answered. *She* wouldn't want me there. No one wanted me.

I did call Lisa to tell her my plan. Her voice got all high and excited as I outlined how I'd do it. She promised to bring me food and shit.

I was shaking by the time I got to the kitchen. Tore the bread trying to spread peanut butter. The sandwiches ended up kind of lumpy by the time I was finished. But I had supplies.

You'd think I'd be too scared to go out into the field at night... that the idea of coyotes or mountain lions would keep me away. It was just the opposite. The further I got from home, the safer I felt. And when I jumped over the barrier bordering our neighborhood at the dead end, a strange calm came over me.

The moon was barely a sliver. A sharp sickle, like a reaper's scythe grabbing branches from the stand of eucalyptus that covered acres near our home. I glanced up, imagining that silvery point grabbing me by the collar and yanking me back.

Like Ronnie had when I'd come out of the bathroom after our fight last night. Jerking me closer as he bunched up the t-shirt fabric in his hand. Then he rasped in my ear, "When you're eighteen, you're out of here."

Keeping my arms crossed over my chest, I swallowed hard and nodded. My swollen face was still tender, so I kept quiet. I didn't want his fist to move off my t-shirt.

Ronnie heaved several breaths. I stared down the hall wishing the darkness would swallow me. Moments passed.

"Get out of here. I don't want to look at you." He released my t-shirt and shoved me toward my room. "Little bitch."

Fine. Then I'll get the fuck out, I thought.

Before starting today's plan.

About a quarter mile into the stand of eucalyptus trees stood the remains of the neighborhood fort we girls had built a few summers before. Knowing that most of it had long since collapsed, I spent the afternoon taking fallen branches and leaning them against a couple of trees, so I'd have walls for my new home. Next, I wove thinner ones into a patchwork pattern to make a new roof and laid it on top. Then, I took some thick branches to reinforce the sides in case the nights got windy.

I pulled the tarp and sleeping bag I'd snuck from the garage out of the black garbage bag. Afraid someone I knew might ask me why I was lugging a sack toward the field, I'd invented a cover story about playing Santa in an early Christmas party. Lame, I know, but luckily no one stopped me to test its feasibility.

After smoothing the blue tarp, I placed a couple of logs in the corners to hold it in place and set up my bed. Pretty cozy, if I did say so.

With my hut ready, I'd gone home and waited for nightfall.

The eucalyptus boughs hung in the night like a drowning woman's hair at sea. Overhead, the crescent moon dipped in and out of wispy clouds, mocking me. A reminder of how light hid in life's mist.

I took three more steps. Broken branches and dead leaves crunched under my feet. I halted, cocking an ear to listen for trailing footsteps.

A slight breeze picked up and the eucalyptus forest creaked and groaned as if saying, *Look at us, Joy.* Heeding the silent message, I noticed how each had its own unique personality. Some were straight and tall, like Kyle after he solved one of those puzzles he loves so much. Another was bent, my mother shrinking from Ronny's blows. Close to the fort was a half-fallen tree that seemed to be fighting to keep its root in the soil.

My voice sounded flat and empty when I said, "That's me."

Hitching the fringed purse back up to my shoulder, I trudged the final yards to the fort. The *Girls Only* chalked sign had long since faded to white, but the old chair and wooden crate were still there.

I reached inside the collar of my jacket and slipped off the abalone pendant which was embedded with a single shard of sea glass. Even in the dim light it sparkled.

In memory, I heard Carl's voice. *You are as amazing as the sea that surrounds this island.*

I smoothed a finger across the seashell, palmed the pendant, and held it tight in my fist.

After a moment, I pocketed the necklace and used a branch to brush away some of the spider webs from the entrance. Then I crawled inside.

THIRTY-EIGHT

KYLE

During our sleepover, Rick's dad came in saying that my mom was on the phone. With shaking hands, I lifted the receiver to my ear. Mom's quivering voice asked where my sister was. When she and Dad got home, Joy wasn't there.

"I dunno. She was home when I left," I said, shrugging. Then a weird shiver went down my back, like when Rick and I'd peeked around the corner to where his parents were watching that scary movie in their bedroom. The psycho murderer holding up a chainsaw on the screen was so real, I almost thought he might jump out of the TV and attack me.

Mom said Joy was probably just pulling one of her stupid pranks and hung up.

Our sleepover kinda went downhill after that. We'd planned on having a pig-out, challenging each other to eat as much junk as we could stuff in our faces and we even started. Rick set out all kinds of chips, cookies, and even a big tub of ice cream. And I started to stuff my face, but that shaky weirdness stopped me mid-munch.

"Kyle!" Rick said, chocolate sauce dripping down his chin. "You're not even trying."

I shook my head. "Just thought I'd give you a head start to even things up."

"Seriously?" Rick pointed both hands at himself and then at me. It was a ridiculous thing to say. He is about a foot taller than me and probably outweighs me by about twenty-three pounds. Plus, he can eat faster than just about anyone I know. Like some sort of cartoon superhero with devour powers.

Hey, I like that. Devour power. I should tell Joy and maybe she'll put it in her journal. I grinned. Then I remembered Mom's call and my smile stopped halfway.

"Okay, it's my stupid sister. She's missing. Probably snuck out to smoke or meet her dumb friends, knowing her."

Rick got kind of quiet just then. Picked a napkin out of the holder. Smeared the chocolate sauce away. "She's done this before?"

"She used to be out late all the time. But this year things got better. Until..." I clamped my mouth shut. I could NEVER tell about last night. It was Joy's fault, anyhow. If she didn't yell so loud, Dad wouldn't have had to punish her.

"I wouldn't worry. My dad says that we high school kids do all kinds of stupid stuff. That's why he wants to keep 'the lines of communication open', whatever that is."

"She is so stupid. If she'd only think once in a while, then maybe she wouldn't get into so much trouble."

Rick nodded, then pointed at the pile of food in front of me. I shrugged. And reached for a spoon.

THIRTY-NINE

JOY

*A*ll *in white she wanders through mist, a wraithlike figure on a rocky shore. She makes her way toward lapping waves but as she reaches foam, her feet remain dry. She steps forward, rising up above the gentle tide. Pedaling on air, she glides further out to sea.*

Seeking succor, the woman lifts her ethereal arms to the sky. Shards of light sprout from the abalone necklace around her throat and rise through clouds toward the obscured orb overhead.

Shivering, I rolled over and squinted. Still in the dream's grasp, I looked for the ocean but only saw midnight blue. I blinked several times and cocooned my head out. A cold breeze rustled leaves and dim light filtered through the branches overhead.

Branches?

For a few moments, I didn't know where I was. Then my cheek brushed against a zipper and it all came back in a flood. The party. Pointing fingers. Running through streets. Trying to find my way home. Ronny's fists meeting mine. They hated me. Packing up. Fixing the fort. Using my jacket as a pillow the night before.

I pulled out my journal and began to write.

December 12, 1979

In the dimness, shadow giants reach long fingers toward me as I wait for the bright orange orb to rise over the horizon. Peering through my wall of green, I rise and peer at the last stars in the westward sky. The rustling leaves remind me of that night when the electricity went out and our only light was a stone-hearth fireplace.

It is so quiet here in my eucalyptus hut. I cock an ear, straining to listen for friendly sounds. Imagining a friend approaching with a warm cup of cocoa and soothing words. For a while, this fantasy takes hold of me and I start to smile.

But then I remember. And sigh.

I set my journal down and rummaged in my purse for something to eat. My peanut butter and grape jelly sandwiches were smooshed under deodorant, tampons and Clearasil, but I didn't care. I gobbled them up anyhow.

I gotta pee. Shit.

Now, I'd been camping and knew how to pop a squat, so number one wouldn't be a problem. But number two in the field? No way.

What was I going to do?

Praying no one would come along, I ducked behind a tree for a quick tinkle and then stole back inside my leafy fort. That's when I began to realize that I hadn't really thought this out very well. What would I do if it rained? How was I going to take a shower?

And what about school? Would I become one of those burnouts dealing weed at the park?

I didn't have long to think about it because a few minutes later, there was a shuffling sound. Not knowing what to do, I threw my sleeping bag over my head and crouched down. Maybe whoever it was wouldn't see me if I was hidden.

"Joy?" Kyle's quavering voice came from outside.

Don't do it, I thought, as I burrowed deeper under the fabric.

His voice was so small when he called, "You in there?"

Shit. I threw off the bag. "Come on in. You would, anyhow."

He pulled aside the branches that served as a door and tiptoed inside. His face was pale and his eyes were round and hollow, like skeletons, or those poor kids in the third world countries they try to get you to adopt on TV. Did I cause that? I got a guilt pit in my gut.

"Hey."

"Hey yourself."

"You slept here, huh?"

"Nahh. Up in the tree. I was just hiding from you."

"Really?"

"No! Of course, I was here. Where else would I go?"

He shrugged and drew a circle in the dirt with his left toe.

We both just sort of stared then, not saying anything. Kyle picked a leaf off of the wall and started to tear it into perfect fractional pieces. He never did anything without mathematical precision.

"You need to come home."

"No. I can't. They hate me."

"Don't know about that. But you need to come home. Now."

I shook my head.

"Remember that time Mom made a drink wrong?"

You mean when Ronny cut her arm. Why can't Kyle admit his dad is an asshole? "Yeah."

"It feels like that right now."

I narrowed my eyes. "What do you mean?"

"He picked me up early from Rick's, so mad..."

"You're afraid he might do something, to Mom?"

Something else I hadn't considered in my runaway plan. Ronny hadn't hit Mom in, like, years, until that day. The day red became a new color in our home. When I wasn't there to protect her.

Without an insufferable stepdaughter to focus on, would he

turn on Mom? When I got suspended, he was full-on pissed and took it out on me. Once. But the day I was at Lisa's, Mom bore the brunt.

In some ways, I was her shield, armor and protector. A buffer between Ronny's fists and her face.

I had to go home.

"Joy?"

I knelt down and began to roll up my sleeping bag.

FORTY

JOY

Lisa blew a long wisp of smoke over my head. "Seriously? You did that?"

"Yeah. I'd had it. Ronny and all his bullshit."

"You got cajones, girl. May be a full-on freak, but you got cajones. You sure you're a chick?" She raised an eyebrow and pulled on my collar to look down my shirt. "Hmm. Don't know. Could just be muscle."

"Hey!" I slapped her hand away then stuck out my chest. "I don't know what you're talking about. I say, 'Raquel Welch, watch out because these itty-bitty titties are your new competition'."

"More like Burt Reynolds. Are you getting some hair there?" Lisa reached for my shirt again with a giggle.

I curled a lip. This was an old joke. Lisa was always giving me a hard time about my small boobies.

I peered through the ceanothus branches to make sure the campus police weren't looking our way. Nodding to Lisa, I poured the water out of the bong and shook out the ash. Then I stood and brushed the dirt off of my knees.

Usually, getting high at lunch made the empty field look like something out of a fairy tale. But this December, it just looked grey.

"Are you sure this was Columbian, Lisa?"

"That's what Frankie said."

I opened my dry mouth and ran a tongue over teeth that felt like paper. "Doesn't feel like it."

"You still got cottonmouth?" Lisa asked.

"Yeah. Wish I had a beer."

She giggled. "And you used all our water on the bong."

We started walking back toward the parking lot. It's a good thing Hillview is an open campus. That way, the badge can't harass us for being off it. Our cover story when we steal over to the field to smoke is that we were walking to 7-11 for snacks. And we're always sure to keep a few Snickers and Red Vines wrappers in our purses for proof. Or if we're caught in the parking lot, we say Lisa forgot a book in her car.

And adults buy it. Man, they're stupid.

"The colors are just... dull. No rainbows. Maybe I should try hash."

"Or something better." Lisa raised her eyebrows twice.

"Like what?" I rubbed my forearm where Ronny had grabbed me when I'd gotten home, wishing there was a drug to fade bruises.

"Acid. It's the best."

"When did you, Ms. Goody-Goody-I can't-ditch-class, ever try acid?"

"You don't know everything about me."

I crossed my arms. "Okay, then tell me."

"Last summer, when I was staying a couple days at my cousin's, he had some Orange Sunshine. We took some before going to the pool."

"Weren't you scared?"

"All those stories about kids jumping off buildings thinking they can fly are bullshit. Made up to scare us away." Lisa rolled her eyes.

"Yeah. Like *Reefer Madness*," I agreed, referring to a 1930's anti-drug movie that had a bunch of kids go crazy after smoking pot. "So?"

"At first, I thought maybe he'd played a joke on me, maybe given me candy or something, because nothing happened. Brian is always messing around. But while I was swimming, the water started to change. Like it was freakin' alive! And I was part of it."

"Really?"

"Yeah, like I was liquid. Diving deeper as all these colors flashed around. And the sounds! So trippy. Then I swear I became a mermaid. And not just halfway. I had a bright green tail that propelled me through the water... Man!"

"That sounds so bitchin'."

"It was." Lisa looked off in the distance as if reliving the experience. "I'd score you some but it's not easy to get."

"I know. We live in Smallsville."

"I hear that some of the Cholos had some last week."

"Who, Frankie?"

"You could ask him, but I think he just deals pot."

I rubbed my arm again and looked up at the grey December sky. Nodded. "I will. I full-on will."

FORTY-ONE

JOY

Well, this semester Mrs. Plante's really riding my ass. Giving me shit about my focus in class. Keeps lecturing about how much potential I have as a writer. Blah. Blah. Blah.

She almost busted me yesterday.

I'd done a few bong hits at lunch and had a real sweet high going. Mellow, with nice colors. Then I went to class and sat near the window so I could watch the trees sway in the winter wind. I loved the way they bent with every gust and the high made the greens really pop.

"Joy."

I kept staring.

"Joy?"

Janice kicked my chair and I sat upright.

"W-what?"

One kid sucked in a breath, imitating a toke on a joint. A few kids in the back snickered.

Mrs. Plante gave me the teacher stare. "Do you have any ideas for new articles?"

I shrugged. "I dunno. Maybe..." I tapped my chin. "Hey, the World Music Fest is coming up. It's going to be rad."

"Good idea," Janice said. "Everyone is talking about it. Yeah, a few articles about the bands or acts."

I nodded. "Like Cheech and Chong. They're a crack-up."

"We are not going to feature drug-using comedians," Mrs. Plante said.

"But they're funny."

"Janice is right. Cheech and Chong are hilarious. Have you ever listened to *Up in Smoke?*" Craig straight-edge said.

"I don't know about this, kids. It's one thing to write about the dangers of marijuana, with statistics. It's a whole other animal to write about people that encourage drug use."

My high had started to wear off by now and I could think. "But Mrs. Plante, aren't Cheech and Chong like the storytellers and poets of long ago? Don't they put a mirror in front of society to help us laugh at ourselves? That's what art is all about. Isn't it?"

"Joy, you never fail to amaze me." Mrs. Plante nodded. "You're right. Comedy is an art form. Shakespeare had comedies. And while I wouldn't call Cheech and Chong Shakespeare, they do reflect on our times. I'll allow you kids to write an article on them or other bands at this music festival, but I reserve the right to reject anything that's inappropriate."

We all nodded, smiling. Mrs. Plante could be pretty cool.

FORTY-TWO

JOY

I got it! I can't believe it, I'm actually going. In six weeks, Joy Chapel will be head-banging to Nugent, Cheap Trick and Toto at the most amazing, rocking, gnarly, friggin' concert in the whole world.

I read the numbers 006239 again, and with tingling hands smoothed the precious paper with the circle and wings over a page in my journal. No, I wasn't high, just blown away. I was the six-thousandth person to hold one of these tan tickets saying *Wolf and Rissmiller Concerts Presents—Califfornia World Music Festival at the Los Angeles Memorial Coliseum*. Two f's in Cali because we are fucking freaks. Oh yeah.

Paid twenty-five bucks. Been saving my money since Christmas. I know, Kyle is the saver in this family; but since this concert is going to be full-on epic, I tucked every spare dollar in my ballerina music box and only pulled out a couple of bucks when Frankie was selling some Thai Stick. Hey! Pot like that doesn't hit our town every day.

Even my parents had noticed the commercials on the radio and TV. Mom said it sounded like Woodstock in the '60's. She never got to do much of that stuff since she'd had me so young, but I knew she dreamed about it. Sometimes, she'd get this wistful look on her face during a TV show about teenage parties or rock concerts. I feel kind of guilty for getting in the way of all the amazing times she could have had. Without me, she might have lived a pretty cool life. Probably never would have married that asshole Ronny.

I think this concert is going to touch on something, beyond. Like there'll be this hippie vibe everywhere and I'll only have to reach out to find kind hands enfolding mine. Smiling eyes are going to look out from John Lennon glasses and sing about giving peace a chance.

For once, I felt a part of something... well, something big and, I don't know, better. I mean, it's all people talked about. While changing for gym or hanging on the Quad or munching out at Mickie D's, everyone jonesed about how amazing it would be. Cruisers up and down Broadway rocked out to Nugent and Cheap Trick, their cranked tunes and sweet-smelling smoke wafting out of open windows.

Bitchin'.

One Friday night, I saw a black Camaro with five dudes all bobbing their heads to *Surrender*. "*Mommy's alright! Daddy's alright! They just seem a little weird!*" they sang, hair flipping back and forth.

Wish Mom was alright, I thought but cried, "Cheap Trick rocks!" from the back seat of Janice's Toyota.

The tickets went on sale at 10 a.m. Saturday, February second. Just in time, I finally had enough money for that beautiful voucher, that flower-power piece of cardstock, that sublime pass to wonder and amazement. Just one problem. We lived in a small town, boring-ville where there were no ticket sales. The closest place was Tower Records in LA. And I didn't have parents that would let me drive their Lincoln anywhere but to my stupid job at Jack in the Crack, much less over the grade to the city.

But I had friends.

"Come on, Janice. Give me a ride so we can go get our tickets," I begged.

"I don't know. What do you ever do for me but smoke my weed, keeping the reefer to yourself forever?"

"I promise I'll never bogart your joints again. You'll get the first hit. Two. Five. Hell, I'll just sit back and get high on the fumes. Please. It's going to be like, like... beyond."

She gave me long stare and argued that I always said shit like that. But we had to get those tickets! Going to that concert was all I thought about. Well, that and foxy Paul Janssen. If I went to the fest, he'd think I was cool and ask me out for sure.

Something deep in my bones told me that this concert was my destiny. That if I missed it, my life would be out of whack. A shakiness, like I got when Ronny's eyes turned red and he raised his fists, settled in my gut.

So, I started to beg. And bargain. Begged some more.

After several minutes of promising to pay for her gas, buy munchies, bring joints, and then give her my first-freakin'-born whenever that happened, she agreed to give me a ride to Tower Records. Since we'd never waited in line to buy tickets before, we decided to leave super early in case they sold out.

I set the alarm on my clock radio, the same black General Electric analog one I'd first heard *Surrender* on a few months before, to go off a little before 5:00 am. The face had only three numbers because the on, off, and wake to music buttons were where the six would be. But you could tune it to umpteen music stations and damn, I'd checked out just about every one. Still I came back to 105.4, KRQK, time and again.

Why? It rocked!

Hair brushed as straight as I could get it, my wait-in-line-blue-Dittos-Zorie-flip-flop-I'm-trying-to-look-like-a-total-Cali-teen ensemble on, I stood on my front porch checking the wad of cash in my wallet. *Yep, got it.* I nodded after the fourth check. But of course, Janice was late, so I made sure that the money I'd saved for so long was still there about eighty more times between brushing the frizz out of my hair, wiping the dust off of my sandals, and reapplying blue eye shadow.

Finally, forty-three minutes after she said she'd come, with my scalp sore from all the times the brush had passed over it, Janice rolled up in her '76 Toyota Corolla. Lime green with bald tires and a scary rattle every time it went over forty, but it was all hers, as she'd proudly defend to anyone who tried to put it down. She'd thrust a hand into her hip and say in her New York accent, "It's paid fah. And not everyone has a tricked-out dash with New Yawk fuzzy dice."

Janice cracked me up, acting like she was cool just because she'd bought car dice while visiting her Grandma in Queens. Always with the accessories. Barrettes. A macramé belt. Hoop earrings. She was constantly building and rebuilding herself, like an ever-evolving android trying to become human. Still, guys thought she was hot, with the clanging bracelets and the way she said her 'R's' all drawn out like a vowel.

When she honked and waved, I didn't wave back but stomped up, arms crossed, showing her my ticked-off body language. But she didn't apologize or even mention being late. Of course, that didn't surprise me. Even though I was paying for everything including gas and grass, she still made sure I knew she was doing *me* a favor.

I thought of saying something. Didn't. Why was I always such a wuss? Freaking terrified that if I said one angry word, she'd hate me forever?

Cause maybe she would.

Even at 9:17 AM, there was already a line down the street waiting for the store to open. Girls in high-waisted jeans and peasant tops. Dudes in rock t-shirts and huarache sandals. One pacing fat guy, old enough to be my stepdad, wore a purple jump suit that made him look like a bunch of cartoon grapes. I giggled at a couple of disco dorks in skintight polyester pants, their silk shirts unbuttoned all the way to hairy navels. Gross.

We drove a little further and turned into the crowded Tower's parking lot where the sea of cars was host to a full-on party. Dudes sat under open hatches smoking bowls, car stereos cranked head-banging tunes, and chicks so gorge you'd think they were out of *Teen* magazine swayed to the rockin' rhythms. Nearby, frisbees flew over hoods and skateboards jumped curbs while bottles and bongs passed from hand to hand.

My jaw dropped all the way to the vinyl seat.

"Where's a fucking spot?" Janice grumbled, cruising up another aisle of filled slots.

Eyes glued to the surrounding spectacle, I pointed to an empty slot in the next row. Janice immediately gunned the rattly engine and zipped around the corner to snake a space before anyone else could get it.

"Got your money?" I asked, after Janice pulled up the squeaking parking brake.

"Don't have enough. I'll get one later."

What? We were going together. That was the plan, I thought, wondering if I should probe further. She'd been bitchy for the whole ride, barely speaking to me, even turning the stereo off when I tried tuning it in to big city FM stations. I decided the less said, the better. "It's cool, I know you'll get one."

I hoped. She was my ride.

Little bubble butt swaying in her tight Calvin Klein's, Janice led the way through the waves of partiers to the end of the line, where she immediately began chatting up a surfer named Chris. Amazing how fast her mood changed with a cute guy around. I swear that girl knows how to flirt; full-on purrs every word while tabby-moving her hips. And Chris obviously wished he had a bag of catnip he could feed her all day.

I just stood there, thumbs tucked in my baggy jean belt loops, wondering why guys didn't give me the sort of attention they did Janice. I mean, I wasn't that bad, was I? Last summer, one counselor named Pete even called me Sister Golden Hair every time we'd had guard duty together. Good call, bleaching it before camp!

Even though my invisibility cloak seemed to stay on the whole time, I didn't mind. Waiting in line was killer! Never seen so many joints passed around. You'd think the cops would be on parade, but I only saw one black and white that morning and so many people were smoking cigs, it masked the other smoke.

Soon, the store opened, and the line was shuffling forward. I didn't know whether to be jazzed to be moving, or bummed to have this party come to an end.

After a surreal hour of watching Janice purr at hottie Chris one moment and then bitch to me about the wait the next, we were inside the biggest music store I'd ever seen. The latest Cars album played in the background, joining the buzz of excited ticket buyers and shuffling feet. Huge rock bands posters plastered the walls above shelves of funny bobblehead toys. A black light room beckoned from the back, with lava lamps and glowing posters of guys on choppers, gorgeous black chicks with perfect bodies and big 'fros, bright peace signs, and of course, huge marijuana leaves.

I love the vinyl and incense smells of record stores, inhaling as soon as I enter to fill my lungs with sandalwood and Arabian Musk. Then I exhale and breathe in the fainter odors; wood of the record bins, Love's Baby Soft perfume lingering over the cassettes, and the dust rising off the tiled floor. There's nothing like strolling between those record bins, finger running over each plastic-sheathed album, where punks mingle with surfers, disco wannabes look through the hits, and a few moms with Farrah-feathered hair try to find that perfect birthday gift.

Paradise.

Today, a red-eyed Stoner obviously just back from a recent bong hit in the parking lot smiled from behind the counter. He took a sip from the Mountain Dew bottle in front of him and asked how many we needed.

I cleared my throat few times and then managed to croak out, "Umm, one ticket. California World Music Festival."

"You sure you don't want the Texas Jam, Farmer girl?"

"W-what?" *Were my pants that baggy? Do I look like an old farmer?*

"Working you." His blue eyes twinkled as he winked. "Fest, should be the shit."

"Totally," I said, staring at all the pipes in the glass display case, imagining how many people could get high with them. Started doing calculations in my head. *If one bong could be shared with six people, and a pipe with two, that'd be…*

Got so lost in the dream, Janice had to answer the next question. "Cash." She nudged me and I shook my head before passing the handful of bills and coins over the counter.

"Not enough," he said, after counting the last few dimes. "Still need $0.47."

I rummaged around in my purse until I found a quarter, a few nickels, and one penny. I looked at him apologetically.

"I'll toss in a penny for a little fox like you," he said, with a smile that made my stomach do a flip-flop.

Back in Janice's car, I pressed that treasured ticket to my chest and gushed, "If that's what the-wait-in-line party is like, just imagine how awesome the concert's gonna be."

"Yeah, awesome," Janice said, not sounding as enthusiastic as I expected.

I turned to look her square in the face. "You're still going, right? We've been planning this for months."

She kept her eyes on the road as she spoke. "Sure, as soon as my shithead of a brother pays me back what he owes me."

"Cool." I leaned back against the seat and hugged that precious slip of paper.

FORTY-THREE

JOY

"Where was that article?" I tapped my chin with a pen and then began to riffle through the magazines splayed out on the kitchen table. After picking up *Rolling Stone* and thumbing through a few pages, I tossed it back in the pile. Then I grabbed a copy of *Creem* and started to read an article on Cheech and Chong.

"People's experiences, man. How can you say they're right or wrong?" Tommy Chong said, when asked about promoting drug use.

Fuck yeah. Experience. Higher than high. Like Music Fest is going to be. I nodded and copied the quote in my Trapper Keeper.

When the front door banged open, followed by a basketball bounce, Mom shouted, "No balls in the house!" from the master bedroom. How she was able to hear it way back there, I didn't know. Must have been a mother-radar thing.

"'kay!" Kyle called back. With admirable skill I'd never give him props for, my junior jock brother spun his ball on one finger and strutted over to stand opposite me.

I ignored him. Copied another quote. That ball had to stop spinning some time.

It did, but now he tossed it from one hand to the other in annoyingly loud slaps. "What are you doing?"

I rolled my eyes.

"Homework? Something for journalism class?"

"No, I'm digging a pit, your grave if you don't shut up."

"Ha-ha." He hugged the basketball. "I hope it's not going to be like your article on marijuana. It sounded like you thought people should smoke."

"Have you ever thought that maybe the world would be a better place if people toked instead of drank? I mean, when was the last time you heard of a high dude killing someone or crashing a car?"

He shrugged.

"Friggin' never. Because people get mellow when they're high. Like this guy, Tommy Chong. Check him out. *'It's what people go through… in order to get some use of living on Earth. So how can you make any judgement? I can't. All we can do is be funny and make people laugh.'"*

"I don't think Dad would want you quoting those druggies."

"Oh, please. You think your perfect father never got high? I bet he and Mom toke up at every party they go to."

"No way," Kyle argued.

"You're so naïve. Even the president's son smoked pot. Got kicked out of the navy for it."

"Mom and Dad drink but—"

"—but nothing. Everyone gets high nowadays. Except maybe boring jocks like you."

"If I start filling my lungs with that crap like *you* do, I'll never make varsity by sophomore year."

"Mwah?" I said, placing a proper hand across my décolletage. "I know not what you speak."

"Whatever. Just keep it hidden. Dad's been stressed…"

That hit home. Ronny had been on the verge for a while now.

Ever since I ran away, things had been as tense as the last three seconds of a tied basketball game.

Ronny moved like Kyle's basketball, spinning one moment with a blind pass the next. Even if we had a ref. blowing the whistle, he wouldn't stop half-court, but body-slam a teammate before basking in the glory of a hook shot.

And I sure as shit didn't want to become part of that kind of game anytime soon.

"Okay, I'll keep my notes to myself. Dork."

FORTY-FOUR

JOY

W hy did I ever say Mrs. Plante was cool? Because she isn't. Instead, she's a disapproving critic who won't cut me any slack. I've rewritten that article on Cheech and Chong five times and she still says, "I'm not feeling it. Something is missing, Joy." Meanwhile, she has accepted all of Janice's essays. And one was about adopting kittens. Kittens! Really? I mean, are we like in second grade here?

I don't get why Mrs. Plante loves everything Janice writes. She's always praising that New Yorker's *'organization'*, *'ability to cite sources'*, and friggin' *'voice'*. Voice? I have a voice, too. But she says I am hiding it somewhere.

She set my essay on my desk, red pen markings all over it and said, "Your writing seems detached, Joy. As if you are outside of yourself, observing. Don't put a wall between the words and your voice. I want to hear *you*, not some robot mimicking what you think sounds intelligent."

I'm not a robot! My problem is I feel too much. The colors of life are so vibrant sometimes that I have to close my eyes to keep them from overwhelming me. And not just when I'm high.

I can be totally straight and see it. I try to explain it to Janice and Lisa, but they don't get it.

I guess I was born too late. The hippies in the '60s understood about seeking the sublime and so have philosophers, rockers and poets in history. Like in English class last year Mr. Ramirez read to us from *Walden Pond*, about a rocking guy who went into the woods and just soaked up all this shit. He really saw it, man; the animals, sky, clouds, reflection on the water, even the veins on leaves in the trees.

I could relate to old Henry David when he said, "A lake is the landscape's most beautiful and expressive feature. It is Earth's eye; looking into which the beholder measures the depth of his own nature."

Every Catalina summer I felt the same way. For me, it wasn't a lake, but the Pacific that whispered things to me that ended up in my journal. I wrote, *Fuck yeah, Joy. There is wonder. Just look!*

I suppose that doesn't sound all profound like Thoreau, but I don't believe that life was meant to be just fine. We were born from love. It should be freaking sublime! Why couldn't Mrs. Plante see that in my article? I was trying to convey it. Henry David Thoreau perceived something about society in the 1800s, but now guys like Cheech and Chong were our philosophers, a couple of the rare ones speaking for a generation.

One guy on TV called them counterculture comedians. I liked that. Maybe I'd include that in the article. Another person I'd been reading a lot about lately was Timothy Leary. He believed that LSD was a way to open the mind, saying, "LSD is a psychedelic drug which occasionally causes psychotic behavior in people who have NOT taken it."

Ha!

Many people throughout the 1960s believed that psychedelics provided glimpses into spirituality and increased connections to the universe. Some even thought taking the drug could reduce violence. One man, who'd robbed a Hollywood producer at gunpoint and then later taken acid, said he'd "renounced violence" and even returned what he stole. Hell, there was even this group called The Brotherhood of Eternal Love that believed LSD could help create a utopia.

Friggin' utopia. A place with no violence. Shit, yeah.

Chewing on one lip, I read over Mrs. Plante's notes, trying to decipher what the f—

she wanted. Lost in thoughts of a world without people like Ronny, I scribbled several ideas in the margin. Then, the bell rang, and I jolted upright. With everyone shuffling toward the exit, I shook my head, and shoved my essay inside of my folder before stumbling out of my chair.

"Hey Janice, wait up."

She was already at the door when she turned. "What?"

"How about, hello Joy, how have you been?"

She flipped her auburn hair and shrugged. "Hey, how awr ya?"

I grinned as we strolled into the hall. "Full-on excited about the concert."

She looked at me as if confused. "Concert?"

Was she kidding? "World Fest. You got your ticket, right? It's only two months away."

Janice held up her hand like a stop sign and pointed down the hall. After pivoting away on one foot, she shouted through cupped hands, "Michelle, I want my sweater back! You've had it two months."

I opened and closed my mouth, but even if something had come out, it would have been too late. She'd already jogged into a clutch of giggling chicks.

FORTY-FIVE

JOY

."Joy, over here!" someone called from across the quad.

I squinted. Was that Lisa? She looked fuzzy and distorted like a messed-up TV. I stumbled toward her, trying to walk in a straight line, but for some reason my zig-zagging feet wouldn't cooperate. They dragged over the concrete until I shoulder-bumped into some lump of a kid, mumbled "Sorry", and then staggered toward the voice.

"Hello." I started to say more but then I noticed how amazing my tongue was. Soft and pliable. Wow! I twisted it from side to side before running it over the roof of my mouth, teeth, and lips.

"Girl," said Lisa, "you are fucked-up. What'd you take?"

"Jus' some Blue Heaven. Like that." I pointed at the sky. "It's beautiful!" I threw my head back and swiped at the diamond clouds that now sparkled overhead. One seemed so close, I tried to snatch it. The swirling gem dissipated into mist and I teetered.

Lisa grabbed my arm. "Careful."

"Hey, wash your hands."

"You mean watch? Shit, we gotta get you outa here. You're a full-on bust." Lisa looked around, then said something over her shoulder. I think she was calling someone, but her voice was all echoey and I couldn't tell what she was saying.

Everything sounded so funny.

I snorted and then started to giggle. Pitched forward. Felt hands under my arms jerking me upright. Next thing I knew, I was hobbling over undulating walkways, past blurry buildings, onto ground so vividly green it could have been a dayglo cartoon. When I bent to look at the amazing texture of each blade, I slipped on a clump, lurched forward and fell to my knees.

I giggled. "My legs are water. Just like you said, Lisa. Look!"

"Get up, idiot!" Lisa said.

Shielding my eyes from the sun, I glanced up at a figure next to her. Dark hair blew back in slow motion like a romantic TV scene. I blinked as it changed into a black stallion with the wind through its mane. "Whoa," I said.

"Come on," the horse said, as it faded into a familiar face.

"Frankie? Zat you?"

"Yes again, Joy. Just like I told you three times before." Frankie and Lisa pulled me to my feet. "Now walk."

I tried but my legs didn't want to cooperate. I shrugged and Frankie and Lisa half-dragged, half pushed me down the sidewalk toward some psychedelic flames.

"Frankie's van! Time to smoke a bowl!" I clapped my hands. Or tried to. For some reason they didn't make a sound. Tried again. They flapped past each other, creating copies of themselves like handprints in air. I giggled again.

"Yeah, as if you need to get higher," said Lisa. She held me up while Frankie unlocked the side door and hopped inside.

When I lifted a leg to get in, my shin bumped against the metal step, knocking me backwards. I would have fallen right onto the concrete if Lisa hadn't had a death grip on me. I grinned. "Thanks."

"Come on. Get in." She pushed from behind while Frankie grabbed my hands and hauled me up.

The year before, Frankie had tricked out his Chevy van with wall-to-wall carpet, a booming sound system, mood lighting, cozy captain's chairs, and a platform bed in the back. I guess he thought the rad interior would get him a lot of action, although I had trouble imagining Frankie naked. He was tiny, maybe five-two and so skinny you'd think he was one of Kyle's friends.

I landed on all fours, to find living shag carpet with undulating and wriggling fuzzy worms looking for a friend. "Hello," I said as I petted the fibers. "Look, Lisa."

"Shh! Joy! You're going to get us busted." She hopped in and Frankie slid the side door closed.

Ignoring her boring advice, I kept on stroking my new friends. They felt wonderful! I ran my hand over the floor three times until it snagged on something lumpy. Pinching it between my thumb and forefinger, I scrutinized my prize, scrunching my face until I realized that I was holding onto the burned end of a joint that someone must have dropped. "A roach! Light it up."

"Yeah, right. Like you need to get higher," Frankie said.

"Higher! Fuck, yeah!"

"Joy, what's up with you? Every week it's something," Lisa said, hitting me with the back of her hand. "From running away to a freaking tree fort, to smoking a bowl in the girls restroom, to now doing acid at school. You're out of control."

"Pretty cool, huh?"

"No!" Frankie and Lisa said in unison.

I cocked my head. Tried to focus, knowing there was a message in there somewhere. *Out of control?* I stared at the walls.

I furrowed my brow and kept staring, but my thoughts were all jumbled and fractured. Then the bubble window caught my attention. Its tinted glass swelled ever larger until light beams like Fourth of July sparklers shot out. They extended past my head, glimmering in shades of silver, pink, and turquoise.

When they began twisting into kaleidoscopic helixes, the forgotten roach fell back into the sea of worms. I reached out to grasp the brilliant shafts and my hands morphed into fractals with doppelganger trails. I swiped at the whirling light beams multiple times, but they all escaped my grasp.

I turned to Lisa. "Aren't they beautiful?"

She patted me on the back.

"Shit," I heard Frankie say. "We're going to be here awhile."

FORTY-SIX

JOY

I can't figure out what's up. It's like I suddenly have the clap or something. Janice just gives me the three-fingered wave whenever I approach. Frankie is totally MIA and Lisa, the one friend I thought I could count on, hasn't returned my calls for eight days.

Okay, Diary. I'll admit it. After my acid trip two weeks ago, I decided to try a few white crosses before school and cruised onto the quad all hyped up, telling five stories at once. It felt so cool! No shyness at all. I was talking so fast, a couple of kids even patted me on the back. Don't know why Lisa acted the way she did, with a head tilt and narrowed eyes. She seemed kind of judgey, and then walked away. But it's not as if I was putting a heroin needle in my arm. Speed is no big deal.

So now I'm hiding out here instead of the amphitheater for the pep rally. Feeling kind of quivery, thinking my personality repels like metal next to a reversed magnet. If I walked out there, my switched polarity might cleave the ra-ra crowds in two. Then I'd be a lone Moses parting a repulsed teenager sea.

I chewed on the end of my ballpoint pen and looked over at the stacks of books in front of me. Déjà vu to freshman year when this was my hangout. Back to seeking something to fill the void. Returning to the emptiness.

Sometimes I'd read for an escape. Go off to some world where heroes kicked butt or philosophers guided me toward the sublime. But I've been cruising the shelves for fifteen minute and none of the books have sparked the slightest interest. Anyhow, the crowd's roar makes it hard to focus.

"Go, Warriors! Fight, Warriors! Go fight, team!"

I sighed. Thought about going out there and looking for Lisa. For all of five seconds. Then imagined her holding up her talk-to-the-hand gesture and turning away. It was hard enough dealing with the shit storms at home; I didn't know if I could handle her rejection, too.

Fucking Ronny.

I shook my head and rubbed my hairline where a hidden bruise from four nights ago kept me from brushing too vigorously. Closed my eyes, trying to erase the image of his approaching fists. Hell of a lot of good that did. Instead, I saw it all etched on my lids.

Shit.

With a curt nod, I started to rummage in my purse. I knew the tiny yellow tablets were in here somewhere. Yesterday, I'd grabbed them from the master bathroom's medicine cabinet and shoved them inside while Mom was getting laundry from the garage. Almost got busted, emerging from their bedroom only seconds before she returned with the laundry basket tucked under one arm.

I'd planned to wait until Friday night to take them, but what the fuck. Anything is better that this suck-fest. Might as well.

My fingers found a couple in the folds of the purse's lining and I tossed them into my mouth. They tasted like bitter aspirin dissolving on my tongue, but I knew that in a few seconds, that sharp flavor would dull everything else.

The Rolling Stones called them 'Mother's Little Helper' and man, that's the truth. Just like in their song, my mom goes running for the shelter of her little helper when things get too intense. I know Ronny is due home soon when she heads to her bathroom and I hear the medicine cabinet creak open. That same sound fills the silence after... Well, I don't want to talk about that right now.

I kept journaling.

I just ate a couple. Waiting for the sugar change and a sweetened soft-focus world. Soon to blur into an old-fashioned photo.

I paused, expecting honey-dripping light everywhere. Instead, the near empty room still had harsh fluorescents hanging over a few nose-booked kids, behaving for the grouchy librarian who was ready to shush them at any moment.

Ignoring them, I started to fill more pages and was actually getting some pretty cool stuff when, a few minutes later, a strange thing happened. The air in the silent library changed. It grew heavier and thicker. Then the ticking wall clock's second hand paused.

"Huh?" Gaping, I dropped my pen. It rolled across the table and headed for the edge. My lids blinked slowly as a distant brain told me to grab it. But something seemed to be wrong with my muscles because, even though I was sure that I'd told my hand to reach out, it didn't move for long moments. The pen tumbled off the table and fell on the tiled floor with a plastic clatter.

The librarian looked my way and lifted an accusing eyebrow. With an apologetic wave, I bent down to pick it up and shove it in my bag. *Better go.* I thought. I gathered up my journal, hugged it to my chest, and slung a purse over my shoulder.

Standing in the hallway, I looked right. I considered heading for the lockers and doing my usual 'early to class and avoid people' thing. But then I heard the crowd's roar and glanced left, so instead made a beeline for the amphitheater.

Big mistake.

By now, my fuzzy head wasn't communicating very well with the rest of me. Even though I ordered my legs to walk in a straight line, they didn't cooperate very well. Tripping three times on sidewalk cracks, I weaved toward the pep rally.

An echoey stereo sound filled the sunken arena. I looked down and saw kids up on their feet applauding the cheerleaders on the stage below. And of course, who would be in the front row but Angie, who went from cheering to hugging her boyfriend every two seconds. Angie of the perfect hair and curves in all the right places. Stupid Angie, who has spent the last five years coming up with ever more cruel ways to make my life misery.

Teetering a bit, I stood on the top step and imagined all of the things I'd wished I'd said to Angie over the years. I'd return every barb with a witty comeback worthy of the worst bullies in history. *Bitch.*

I hadn't even stood there for a minute when Paul Janssen, super fox, approached. A spring breeze blew his long, dark hair back from his chiseled face. Then he halted a few feet away.

Paul is half Chumash Indian and half Jewish and is six foot tall at least. He has dark, hooded eyes and a strong jaw topped with pouty lips that I was sure would be kissing heaven. I'd been watching him for years but, truth be told, had never even spoken to him.

I bet he didn't even know I was alive.

"Let's go! Go!" the cheerleaders chanted.

I turned toward Paul and jerked my chin in a 'hello'.

Ignoring me, Paul stared at the perky adorables with a smile even my high brain got. He thought they were hot. And I was invisible.

"Give me a G!"

"G," I muttered, wishing I was one of the girls he was drooling over.

"Give me an O!"

"O!" I chimed in, hopping down two steps. I giggled and covered my mouth.

"What does that spell?"

I joined the crowd. "Go!"

I glanced back. Paul's gaze was still fixed on the stage.

The Paul-hypnotizing beauties cried, "Yes, let's go, go, go!"

He licked his lips.

Go, Joy. Now's your chance.

Suddenly, there was this sensation as if someone had taken over my body. And maybe they did, because my arms lifted and dangled aloft as if a puppeteer had just jerked on attached strings. These invisible cords pulled me forward and, with flapping arms, I bounded down the aisle.

I leapt up on stage. "Go, team!" I cried, with a karate kick.

The cheerleader next to me pushed me and said, "Get off!"

Fighting to stay upright, I fisted my hands and lifted my elbows. "To the G-G!" I slurred.

Now the cheering crowd grew silent. Out of the corner of my eye, I saw two teachers rush toward me. And the next few seconds were kind of blurred.

I remember doing a leap and a twirl while grinning up to what I hoped was Paul Janssen's admiring face. I had started to take a bow when adult hands locked on my arms and hurried me off the concrete stage.

And straight to the principal's office.

FORTY-SEVEN

JOY

Last night, Ronny was the worst I'd ever seen. I mean, he could be bad, a couple of punches here and there, but it was usually over in less than a minute. And in the last year he'd only been really rough with Mom three times, maybe four? I'd got a couple of black eyes, but only after getting in trouble or yelling that he couldn't tell me what to do.

But he'd never gone after all of us like that.

When the sounds woke me around midnight, I knew right away what they were. I'd heard crashes like that ever since Mom had married Ronny. I used to cover my ears, waiting for it to be over so I could steal into the hall bathroom to soak a washcloth with cold water. Then, when Mom came in and closed the door behind her, I could dab at her face or shoulder.

"A call at my office? Why can't you do your fucking job?" Ronny's voice came through the door.

"She's just confused."

"No, she's a drugged-out whore!"

The office school called Ronny about the rally? Shit. Why did I trip at school?

"Shut-up, asshole!

"Don't tell me what to do, you fucking bitch."

I heard muffled rumbling and a slam. Mom's cry. "Fuck you!"

I started to cover my ears, but then a thump and another slam jolted me out of bed. I peeked through the door crack at the darkened hallway. At the end, something was shaking.

I knew what it was. But still headed toward it. Cocked a futile ear. It didn't stop.

My insides turned to water. Swallowing hard, I clutched my gut and inched forward.

Kyle was already in the hallway by the time I got to the master bedroom. With his door right across from theirs, it must have sounded even louder to him. His eyes were *Night of the Living Dead* dark circles, begging me to do something.

"Bitch!" Another crash.

I pushed Kyle behind me and knocked on their door.

Another thud. Followed by a muffled cry. Mom's voice.

Knocked louder.

The door stayed closed.

I glanced back at my baby brother, who was clenching and unclenching his fists. He looked even smaller than he had a moment before. I blinked, wondering if fourteen-year-olds could shrink.

Work, brain!

Setting my jaw, I pounded. Still no response. Kicked at the door. Kyle came up by my side and joined me. We hammered so hard, I was sure we'd soon splinter wood, a desperate rhythm that no composer would ever use.

Another whimper came from inside.

I jiggled the knob. Locked. Yanked harder. Pushed Kyle out of the way and ran for the door.

And fell into Ronnie's gut.

He only stared for a moment before grabbing me by the hair. As he swung me in an arc, he screeched, "Go the fuck to bed!"

My back hit the wall and I fell to my knees.

A screaming Kyle leapt at Ronnie and wrapped both arms and legs around his torso like one of those sad monkeys in science experiments. "Leave-them-alone!" he said, through clenched teeth.

Ronny backed up, smashing Kyle into the wall. My baby brother unclenched his jaw and released his grip.

When he slid down to the floor, I thought Ronnie would stop for sure. He never went after Kyle. It was like Kyle had this special glow to him—heavenly angel or superstar spotlight or something. And he did stop for a sec. Kind of stared confused at his son.

Then his eyes went red. I knew what was coming next and started to crawl forward.

But was too late.

By the time I reached Kyle, Ronnie had already lifted him over his head and tossed him back toward his room. Kyle bounced off the bed, a weird circus act. He landed on the floor with a sickening crunch. And did not move.

"Kyle?" I croaked, pushing past Ronnie toward the crumpled heap that was my brother.

His arm was twisted in a weird position and his breath came in short gasps. It sounded like his lungs had shriveled and now could barely hold air. I reached out and stroked his hair.

"Joy?"

"Yeah."

"It hurts."

I swallowed a big lump in my throat. "Sorry."

"Look at what you did," Ronnie growled. "Should have left well enough alone." He kneeled and reached out, but Kyle shrank from his grasp.

Mom appeared, loose bathrobe belt dragging on the ground. I didn't dare look at her face. "Baby?"

"Mom." Kyle stretched his good hand toward her.

She squeezed it, then ran her fingers over his forearm. He

cried out. "It's broken," she said in a distant voice. "But it'll be okay. We'll get you to the doctor."

Only now did I look at her. Disheveled hair. Split lip. Right eye almost swollen shut. She couldn't go out like that.

"Get your keys, Ronnie. We gotta go to the hospital." The words didn't seem to come from my mouth but from some stranger wearing my face as a mask.

While Mom wrapped Kyle's shoulders in the baby blanket he'd had since he was little, I ran to my room and threw on some jeans and a tee.

Cradling his arm, Mom led my sobbing little brother toward the car and onto the velvet back seat. Then she just stood there, hands extended.

"I'll take care of him. I got this, okay?" I gently unclenched Mom's hand from under Kyle's arm and got in beside him.

Mom's good eye was a hollow socket as she closed the door.

Ronny said nothing, but turned the ignition and pulled out of the garage slower than coagulating blood.

During the silent ride to the hospital, Kyle kept his eyes closed against the pain while I stared at the little trucks and cars on the faded blankie. They dipped and bobbed with each hollow in the road as if trying to drive off the blanket. I watched one and imagined that it escaped the fabric and rolled out the window.

Toward the twinkling lights of some distant and empty street.

FORTY-EIGHT

JOY

Kyle's changed. Not like his hair or anything. More like who he is. I mean, he used to race around from sports to school and then home, doing a million things, a life joined together like one of the trippy little puzzles he loves to do. I don't know how he ever was able to put the pieces together and keep going. If I tried to do half the shit he usually did in a week, I'd be so confused, I wouldn't know which way was up. But he somehow finds the subtle shades, matches them, and locks them all together. Until it's one whole picture.

But now the pieces are all mixed up. More like how I do a puzzle, a few pieces here, a few there, but most of it stays in the box.

His cast has been on for three weeks now and all his buds signed it. Grandma even came to visit; brought him this thousand-piece jigsaw of a winding road twisting off toward a farm. It had pretty trees and looked like a real challenge.

He didn't even open it.

Not that I blame him. I mean, one thousand pieces? That'd take forever. And with so many autumn colors, I don't know how you could ever find the ones that fit together. I wouldn't want to try, but Kyle had been into all kinds of puzzles forever. Rubik's Cube. Those metal twisty ones. Jump the Peg I.Q. tester. And he usually won. He never gave up until he conquered them.

He did look at that box sometimes. Stared at the winding road as if dreaming he was there. Maybe he was in his mind. I can relate. I go to places, too. Catalina. The ocean. Tripping into music. My writing.

Yesterday, he was holding the box in his lap when I glanced over his shoulder. "Gonna give it a try?"

He ran a finger up the road toward the farmhouse. "What would it be like to live there?"

I leaned in. "Probably boring, no TV or anything. But maybe they'd have animals in the barn."

"A hay loft you could sit in. Up away from everything," Kyle said.

"That might be cool." I knew what he really meant, but I didn't say. If you don't talk about *It*, *It's* not so real. It becomes the story you tell the doctors. The story for Grandma. The story for school.

"These damn kids were fighting," Ronnie had told the nurse who'd filled in the paperwork. "Wrestling on the bed. Joy got out of hand. Kyle fell."

The nurse had glared at me like I was some kind of monster. She shook her head. "You are so much bigger than him."

I'd wanted to open my mouth in protest. Tell her it wasn't me, it was Ronnie. But I did what Mom always did; I put on a mask and lied.

I met her gaze with an open stare. "Sorry," I said, before remembering to lower my head in shame.

Of course, everyone believed him. And I became the-girl-who-broke-her-brother's-arm. Somehow it got out. Kids at school started to give me a wide berth. Mrs. Plante pulled me aside and asked if I needed to talk to the school counselor.

Sure, I'll tell her all about MY anger issues. How I have such a terrible temper that I have to beat up my brother in the middle of the night.

Still, if I hadn't fucked up so high on Valium that I jumped on stage, the school wouldn't have called Ronny's office. I was always doing stupid stuff like that. What was wrong with me?

"I got two more signatures," Kyle said, changing the subject. He held up his arm and sure enough, the blank space near his elbow now had two more ninth grade scrawls on it. Two more puzzle pieces over an arm that was trying to knit back together.

"Rad." I looked around his room. Books were strewn about and his blue plaid comforter was all wrinkled, halfway falling on the floor. Since he'd broken his arm, Mom hadn't been so strict about making the bed.

Up on the shelf, the Hulk, Batman and some other superheroes stood guard. They looked so strong, all ready to come to the rescue. I wanted to yell at them, *"Where were your superpowers THAT night?"*

"Come on, let's do this. Then you can show off, make me look like a dork," I suggested, taking the box from his lap and dumping the contents on the floor.

We both stared at all those pieces strewn over the blue carpet. A thousand cuts in a peaceful sky.

And started to put them together.

FORTY-NINE

KYLE

Whut's up with Joy being so nice to me? I'm not a baby. Or crippled. Just got a broken arm. And that's almost better. Going to get my cast off in two weeks.

I hope.

Yeah, she asks me if I want to do something all the time. Along with Mom, who seems to think that Chips Ahoy knit bones.

Although they do taste pretty good dipped in milk.

"Not hungry," I told Mom this afternoon when she shook the cookie bag again.

Then I felt bad because she got that look. You know, the one like a dog gets when you stop playing catch? I almost grabbed one to eat right there in the family room, but Dad walked in and I pulled my hand back.

Dad likes strong boys. Not softies that eat cookies all day.

Dad cleared his throat, ruffled my hair. "Hey, kiddo, almost ready to get back on the court?"

I nodded; told him I was. Waited to answer the next question. Dad cleared his throat again. His eyes fell on Joy, who was on the couch, nose in a book. "What the hell are you wearing?"

"Tube top."

"Iris, what sort of a mother buys slutty clothes for her daughter? Are you trying to turn her into a whore?"

"I-uh, got it for camp. For the beach... it... I mean..."

Ronny turned to Joy. "Change. Now."

"Why? It's not like I have anything to cover up."

Kind of agreed with Joy there. She almost looked like a boy up top.

"I don't care if you have the tiniest titties in town. No one in my family is going to go out of this house dressed like that."

"Try and stop me." She crossed her arms.

Standing over her, Ronny pulled his fist back and held it there. I swallowed hard. Started shaking.

Joy looked like she was ready to fight. But then her eyes landed on my cast. She dropped her book and ran into her room.

Dad turned to Mom. "See what some fucking discipline does? You might try it some time with *your* kid."

Mom nodded super-fast while I reached for the cookie bag. And ate two.

They tasted stale.

FIFTY

JOY

Lisa plopped down next to me on the grass. "Got a cig?" she asked.

I tapped a Marlboro out of the package and handed it to her. She pulled out her steel Zippo, flipped it open, and raised her eyebrows twice, signaling that the trick she'd been working on for months was coming. Next, Lisa raised her hand dramatically and brought it down while snapping her fingers to strike the flint wheel with her middle one. When the wick burst into flame, she grinned like a Kindergartner whose coloring page had just been put up on the fridge.

"You got it," I said. "Props."

"It's nothing." She blew a long column of smoke.

Not to be outdone, I raised my own lit cigarette to my lips and pulled in a long draught. Then I blew a series of smoke rings and am stoked to say I even managed to get two inside another.

"So, seen Janice?" I asked, flicking some ash onto the grass.

"I have and I know what you're going to ask next, so don't even go there because she hasn't said anything to me about getting her ticket."

"Why don't you go, then? It's going to be the most rad concert ever. Like Woodstock."

"You know I can't. That weekend is my parents' twentieth anniversary. Big party. Remember I invited you?"

"Yeah, but this is like a once in a lifetime chance. When else will you be a senior rocking out to the coolest bands of your generation?"

"And this is also the last year I'll be at home and able to spend time with the folks for their special day."

"Just because you're in college doesn't mean that you can't come home."

"But it'll be different. If you had a plan, you'd know."

"I have a plan."

"What?"

"Par-*tay*!"

"You can't do that forever."

"Oh, stop being all Mom on me. One is enough."

"Well, you need to get a clue." She paused. "I hadn't mentioned it before, but since everyone is talking about it... your little brother?"

My nose started to tingle, and my throat grew tight. I crushed my cigarette out and started rolling the butt between my fingers.

"I know."

"I don't get it. He's cool. A dork, but cool."

I nodded quickly. Images of Kyle when he was little came to mind. Chubby little fingers snapping Legos into castles, ships, and houses, building a whole city by the time he was six. Kyle trying to climb trees as high as me, only to fall on his head. Kyle asking me to come home when I ran away. A tear rolled down my cheek.

"Well?"

"I always ruin things."

"No, you don't.

"Yes, I do. I'm such a fuck-up…"

"You might be a little crazy with all of your hippie-peace-love-let's-return-to-the-Sixties stuff, but your heart's in the right place. That's why this makes no sense to me. You told me that you never even hit your brother. That when you fight, all you do is hold him down and smother him with your hair because that's, quote, unquote—" she curled her index and middle fingers into quotation marks, "—non-violent."

I twirled the cigarette butt between my fingers again and shrugged.

"Talk to me, dammit!"

I chewed on my lip and whispered, "It wasn't me."

"What?"

Louder this time. "I didn't do it."

"But everyone says…"

"I lied."

Lisa turned to face me fully. "I don't get it. Why?"

"He gets mad sometimes. When I fuck up. When he's irritated at Mom. He—"

"I know. Have for a long time."

"You have?'

"The stories about your black eyes, then running away last year. It was obvious."

"I didn't think anyone knew." Tears welled up and I picked at a hangnail on my thumb. I lowered my voice. "They can't."

"Hey, it's okay. I won't tell." She put an arm around my shoulder.

I tried to swallow. Couldn't. Looked sideways. Didn't want kids to see me crying. Then the rumor mill could add 'crybaby' to 'brother-beater', 'dog', 'pancake-chest', 'stage freak', and all the other things I knew they said about me behind my back.

"If I wasn't such a-screw-up…"

"Stop. It's not your fault. Ronny is just a dick."

I opened my mouth to argue but then wondered, was Lisa

right? I'd always thought there was something wrong with me that made Ronny the way he was. Lots of times I heard him yelling about what a pain in the ass I was before he went after Mom. I'd often thought that if I wasn't there, it'd be better for everyone. He'd actually gone a couple of years without doing anything and only started up again when I got in trouble.

"I don't know."

"Bullshit. You do know. And it's about time you started seeing how cool you are."

"Me?"

"Yes, you, dumb-ass. Why do you think I'm your friend?"

"Are you still? After the acid and the pep rally..." I trailed off.

"Of course. You are like those psychedelic colors you're always talking about. Intense, but cool to be around."

A sob got stuck in my throat. I sniffled and covered my face. Lisa hugged me and that just made it worse. I buried my face in her shoulder.

She held me until the sobs subsided.

I wiped my cheeks with the back of my hand. "That's why I have to go. Don't you see? To escape and be the colors. Just once."

"I get it and I wish I could go with you, girl. But I can't."

I nodded, imagining that beautiful place where multihued music filled every ear.

FIFTY-ONE

JOY

I've felt different since I told Lisa about Ronny. Like a more ethereal and stronger version of myself. I know it seems weird because I sat there crying like a baby for a friggin' half hour, not giving a shit if anyone saw. And I think a couple of tenth graders did notice. But afterwards, I was like a birthday balloon. You know? How the helium makes it bob in the air?

It's been over a week and it still hasn't popped. In fact, that buoyancy gave me some cajones. Deciding I didn't give a shit what she thought, I finally cornered Janice on the school quad and asked her what the fuck was up. Was she going with me to World Fest or not?

"Can't decide," she replied, smoothing her hair with a hand.

"Come on, I need an answer. Yes or no?"

"Then no. I don't have the money. My cawr barely makes it to school and back. And the idea of crowding in with a bunch of stinking people is gross." She crossed her arms. "And why you want to go and surround yourself with that is beyond me."

"What's your problem?"

"You. Total embarrassment. I mean, freaking on stage one second and beating your baby bro the next? Everyone's talking."

I blinked. "I know. It's just—"

"Whatever. Don't you get it?" She glanced around. "I don't want to be seen with you."

I gaped incredulously. What a bitch!

"You know, I've paid for your gas, given you dope, and said nothing while you ragged on poor Russ."

"My boyfriend is my business." She pointed an index finger. "And I give you fucking rides everywhere. You should be thanking me."

"You hijacked the keg for our birthday party."

"Well, if you and Lisa weren't such freaks, people would have come."

It was like when Ronny had just punched my gut. It contracted and I stepped back, whispering, "How can you say that?"

"What? I can't hear you, Ms. Freak."

Shaking my head, I flipped her off. "Fuck you, Janice." I walked away, keeping my middle finger raised until I turned a corner.

Needless to say, Journalism was pretty awkward that afternoon. I thought of ditching, but the last thing I wanted was to get grounded before the concert. Instead, I sat on the opposite end of the class and ignored her. Or pretended to.

While I kept my head down doing my work, Janice wore her fake smile and chatted up kids she'd made fun of lots of times before. She acted like Kenneth and Wanda were her besties as she complimented them on ideas for articles. "Acid-washed jeans. So stylin'. Great idear!" she exclaimed, giving me a smug look at the word *stylin'*.

At least I'm not a callous, uncaring, bitch who wouldn't know the meaning of loyalty if its definition were plastered on her forehead, I thought.

I spent several minutes dreaming of the concert. Janice might not be going but nothing was going to stop me. I was going to rock out with head-banging kids and dance in swirling friggin' circles. For a whole day I'd be somewhere amazing, where no one went off on you and everyone was grinning. A mind-blowing place.

Suddenly, I remembered something I'd read. *What was it?* It had to be there somewhere. I rifled through my notes, making the crinkled pages from the disorganized folder crease and crumple even more.

Then I saw it. The quote that would become the cornerstone of my article.

And I got to work.

FIFTY-TWO

JOY

S ometimes music vibrates at the oddest frequencies, its molecules of forced air surging into each ear in waves. These ripples move out in concentric circles that hum through a family in new and unfamiliar patterns. Their pulsing tempo never quickens, but maintains a steady rhythm that every member bobs his or her head to.

No, I'm not high. Haven't even taken a hit in four days. Got too much going on. And it might sound all dorky and shit, but I've been getting a sweet buzz on this writing.

Did Mrs. Plante finally approve my finished article? Fuck, yeah. She gave me an A *and* put it on the front page of *Wildcat Times*. A few kids even gave me some props for it. Sweet.

But the pulsation I'm talking about has nothing to do with Journalism class or even school. It came from the most surprising place.

Ronny.

Go figure, huh? Of course, he didn't own up to the Kyle incident; instead, he acted like it was all my fault. Even made sure I knew it could happen again if I didn't avoid the figurative eggshells on the floor. And I usually tread pretty lightly over them, stopping mid-step at the slightest crunch.

One morning, after I left a towel on the bathroom floor, he balled it up in his fist and threw it at me. "Pick up your shit!" he said.

I rolled my eyes. "A towel. BFD."

In two seconds flat he was over me, fist raised, red face contorted and twisted. He drew his arm back and narrowed his gaze. Cringing, I covered my head and waited for the inevitable blow.

Tremulous breath blew in millions of cycles per second, but Ronny didn't strike. Instead, he lowered his arm and said, "Fuck." Then he walked away.

A couple of days later, a quiver of change reverberated through the walls.

"Joy," Mom called down the hall. "Time to set the table."

No way was that lilting voice my mother's. I cocked my head and dropped my notebook on the bed when she called for me again.

I stuck my head through the crack in the doorway. "Coming!" Tentatively, I walked toward the kitchen to find Mom *singing* as she heaped mashed potatoes into a serving bowl.

"Oh, there you are. Hurry up. Ronny will be back from his, uhm, appointment soon."

That was weird. No one had mentioned an appointment. "Is he sick?" I asked.

"No, he's good, healthy, better than…" Her eyes got a misty look. "Well, you wouldn't remember."

Mom wasn't usually so forthcoming about Ronny. In fact, she barely uttered his name when he wasn't around, unless it was to tell us to do some undone chore so he wouldn't get pissed off. I couldn't remember a single time she'd mentioned him with a smile on her face.

Figuring it was some business meeting that was going to

bring in big bucks that Ronny'd announce at dinner, I dropped the subject. He loved bragging to a captive audience about scoring greenbacks. So, I got a fake smile ready and set the table.

A few minutes later, we were all munching down Mom's delicious round steak and gravy.

"Oof, This is goob," Kyle said, with his mouth full of mashed potatoes.

I glanced over at Ronny, sure he was going to slap the back of Kyle's head for talking with his mouth full. Instead, he got this weird look on his face. You know the kind of look you have when a little puppy is tripping over its tail? It was like that. Ronny almost looked buzzed, his eyes all glazed and shit.

Was he on acid?

"Kyle, you know better. Now chew your food first," he said, as gently as Grandma when she hadn't seen us for a long time.

"Sorry," Kyle said quickly and then exchanged a bewildered glance with me.

"It's okay. Just pay more attention. Manners are important, you know."

Who was this stranger talking with Ronny's mouth? Had aliens captured my stepfather and replaced him with a pod person?

Mom didn't seem to think anything was weird. Throughout dinner, she chittered away like some happy chipmunk that'd just found a cache of acorns. "And then I found this great pattern for Kyle's room at the fabric store. I could take you there, sweetheart, if you'd like to see it. It's navy blue and matches your comforter."

"Cool, Mom. And since I'm getting my cast off next week, I was thinking maybe we could look for basketball shoes?"

"That'd be fun." Mom continued her happy babbling, but Ronny didn't tell her to shut up once.

I narrowed my gaze and stared at him. Yep, he was either

one of the pod people or had scored a huge business deal. Thinking it was the latter, I started to ask about his appointment, but then figured being quiet was the best course. I didn't want to do anything to break this magical spell.

With one final bite of pineapple upside-down cake, Ronny patted his tummy. "Iris, that was one hell of a meal."

"It was nothing." Blushing, Mom looked up and batted her eyelashes.

Ronny went over to the opposite side of the table and pulled Mom to a standing position. Then—and no, I'm not lying—he grabbed her other hand and, without music, started to dance her into the living room. After, like, five disco twirls, he bent one knee and dipped my giggling mother. He kissed her on the cheek and said, "Okay. Shower time."

You could have knocked me over with a ninth-grader's joint. My parents, acting like Snow White and the Prince in some Disney cartoon? What the frick?

I exchanged a bewildered glance with Kyle, who shook his head and shrugged. If it was anyone else, we might have joined in, but with Ronny we knew better. Both conditioned to sit at the table until given permission to get up, we sat in silence until Ronny retreated down the hallway.

"Mom, can I be excused?" Kyle asked, when she glided back into the kitchen a few moments later.

A smiling Mom nodded while scooping the leftover mashed potatoes into a Tupperware tub. She closed the lid with a snap, drummed her fingers over the top, and started to hum a soft song before putting it away in the fridge.

Mom humming? What?

After making sure everyone else was out of earshot, I got up to clear the table and pulled Mom aside. "What *is* up with Ronny? Did he inherit a million dollars or something?"

Mom's voice was low, but it still sang when she said, "You have to keep this to yourself. Okay?"

"Sure."

"He's seeing a counselor. And it's helping with... everything." She squeezed my shoulder, with vibrations so hopeful you'd think she was water and a magical pebble had just been dropped in her pond.

"That's great," I said, trying not to shake my head. *Here we go again.* It's what Ronny did. He'd get full-on asshole, a Sex Pistol guitar rift, then promise to be better by vomiting AM radio bullshit into the microphone. And Mom would sway to the rhythm until the beats quickened and turned on her.

She gave me a squeeze.

While I prayed Ronny would keep our radio tuned to the bubblegum sounds of the Bee Gees, Donny Osmond, and the Archies.

FIFTY-THREE

JOY

There's gotta be someone. Think, Joy. Think.

I walked through the halls, scanning faces. Racking my brain to remember if any of them said they were going the fest. Lots of my friends had given me props for my article, saying the concert sounded epic, but when asked if they were going, the answer was always the same.

A big fat no.

"Hey, Frankie!" I waved and jogged to catch up with him.

He turned. "How's it going?"

"Still looking," I said.

He shrugged. "Got nothing, chickee. And I asked. Sorry."

"Aww. It's all good. I'll figure something out."

"Maybe you could sell your ticket."

"To the event of the year? No friggin' way!" I hit him with the back of my hand. "Do you know how long I saved for this? Hell or high water, I'm going."

"Okay." He raised his hands in defeat. "Then you better start walking, or stowaway on some train. 'Cause it's tomorrow and LA is eighty miles away."

"Yeah, right."

Lisa approached. "Friday! Party time."

Frankie did a power-to-the-people air punch and bobbed his head.

She turned to me and scanned my face. "Still no ride, huh?"

"Frankie says I should walk. Or make like a full-on Disney film and ride the rails."

"Boxcar stowaway, huh?" She guffawed and then tilted her head to one side. "Why not hitch?"

I swallowed hard. "Alone?"

"I don't know," said Frankie, shaking his head. "Remember that chick with no hands?"

"Oh yeah, forgot about that." Lisa chewed on one lip. "I think you're just going to have to skip it, Joy."

While my face blanched, I stared at her incredulously. Opened and closed my mouth but nothing came out. How could she say that? She knew how much this meant to me.

"Anniversary party *mañana*," Frankie said, changing the subject.

"Yeah, at the club house. You're still coming, right? Janice, being her usual bitchy self, bailed, so if you don't come, it's just my stupid little sister. And she is such a mini-me, copying everything I do. It drives me nutters."

"I'm there. Bought them a carburetor bong and everything."

"You what?"

"Just working you." He winked and forced out a laugh. "My gift will be appropriate for the older generation."

I knew what the two of them were trying to do. But it didn't work. I gave them a half-hearted smile and waved two fingers. "I'm out."

"Hey Joy, don't go," Lisa said, reaching for my shoulder.

"It's all good. I got some notes to put together before Journalism. Wish your parents happy anniversary for me." I gave her a sideways hug. "Later."

———

When I arrived in class, even Mrs. Plante wasn't there. I plunked down in my seat and rested my chin in my hands as my teacher's inspirational posters shouted clichés from the walls. A kitten held on for dear life with the caption, *Hang in there, baby*, next to a giant foot that said, *Keep on Truckin'*.

I rolled my eyes and sighed, "The only place I'm trucking is this stupid, boring town."

Other posters reviewed the parts of speech and the five W's and H of journalism, but the one that gave me pause featured a gull soaring through clouds with, *You have the freedom, and nothing can stand in your way.*

Mrs. Plante was that in spades. She sure didn't let anything stand in her way, as she'd explained back in October in the story of how she became an English teacher.

"You know, class, I never thought I'd end up here. Wasn't much of a reader as a kid. I actually struggled, barely making it through high school. But I loved stories. All kinds. On film. From my friends. And for some reason in newspapers."

"They had them back then?" Janice quipped.

She winked at Janice. "Yes, even back in the Ice Age." Mrs. Plante got a wistful look on her face and continued. "It started while I was waitressing the graveyard shift at Denny's. Since it was pretty dead when the morning edition arrived, I could grab a cup of coffee and sit in one of the empty booths and read about our amazing world."

She paused here and grabbed the globe. Holding it aloft, she spun it and said, "Think of all the places you can go, kids! The world is waiting for you. I realized that back then. And waitressing was not going to get me there, so I signed up for an English course at the junior college. Reading still was hard and I had to get tutors just to pass. But one course turned into two, and four, and twenty, until I had enough units to transfer to the university."

She spun the world again and smiled lovingly at us. "And I'm so glad I did."

I glanced at the seagull poster again. *Nothing can stand in your way.*

With a nod, it was decided. I would hitch. Alone.

FIFTY-FOUR

JOY

I turned off the alarm as soon as it clicked. Cocked an ear to see if I'd woken anyone. Worried that someone in my family would get up and discover my plan.

I lay there for long moments. After I realized that no one had heard, I started drifting into dancing dreams. Then a bird outside my window twittered. I blinked, confused in the dark.

Then I remembered. This was the day. It was going to be like what I'd read about in *On the Road* and *The Electric Kool-Aid Acid Test*. We'd dance circles in the sun and friggin' transcend.

Fuck yeah.

After a quick shower, I combed my part into a perfect line before running a brush through my hair. Not bad. It'd finally grown to my waist and the blonde highlights were shining like the music I was about to hear. I snuggled into my peasant shirt, slipped on my pale-yellow overalls, and donned my abalone necklace.

I had just grabbed my purse and was about to steal out the back door when a pit in my gut stopped me dead in my tracks. I'd never hitched this far before and even Frankie, who was no paranoid punk, had advised against it. On impulse, I glanced back into the kitchen at the wooden handles in the knife block. As usual, Mom had them all polished and stowed in their slots. Leaving a hole in the bottom row that reminded me oddly of a wound, I wrapped one in a napkin and shoved it in the bottom of my purse.

My stomach's strange twisting continued, but I dismissed it and was soon jogging down the hill toward the freeway. The sun's shoulders still hadn't rounded the hills but there was a faint glow to everything. Orange and surreal.

When I got to the big cross-street, I almost turned toward Janice's house. Maybe if I asked her one more time, she'd drive. I started to push the crosswalk button leading to her neighborhood when I shook my head.

Yeah, right, I thought. *She's barely speaking to you. Probably would narc to your parents about hitching. And Joy Chapel, you are not going to miss the most epic concert of the decade.* I did an about-face and dashed across the opposite street.

I ran my hand over shrubs and tree trunks, the bark rough and comforting under my fingertips. I snapped off an oleander flower and tucked it in the bib pocket of my overalls. I knew it would fade quickly, but the red petals were shaped like dancers and gave me something to dream about while I waited.

A few headlights shone in the distance; beat-up vans heading to the fields, Cadillacs off to business, or Love Bugs chugging south. Maybe one of them would be cool and give me a ride.

Not yet.

At the 101 South onramp, I found an elevated place on the grassy bank, adjusted my purse on my shoulder and stuck out a thumb. The quiet of an early morning was beginning to make way for Saturday's bustle as cars whizzed past. I knew it'd be a while, but I thought at least the surfers with their boards sticking out the back of a station wagon would slow.

No dice. Minutes passed. The sky brightened. Must be close

to six-thirty and the opening band started at noon. If someone didn't give me a ride soon, I might miss it. Shit.

I eyed my spot, wondering if moving further back might make me more visible and had just taken a step when a construction truck stopped. The dad-aged guy in a paint-splattered t-shirt asked where I was going.

"L.A. Coliseum."

"Doing a job in Camarillo. I'll take you that far. Hop in the back."

I swung a leg over the tailgate and found an empty spot between a saw and a pile of lumber. He barely waited for me to settle in before gunning it. If you could call it that. This old Ford had about as much power as Lisa's moped and took almost five minutes to get up to freeway speed.

Hair rose around my head like a storm, whipped at my cheeks, tickled. I smiled, imagining how wild I must look to the passing people. I started to sit up higher to display it like a banner, but then my shirt flapped against my skin and icy wind cut my torso and I huddled down against the cold.

I must have drifted off, because the next thing I knew, we were in a Denny's parking lot and the dad construction worker was sticking his head out the window telling me we'd arrived.

After thanking him, I hopped over the side panel and headed inside. The hostess behind the glass display case looked me up and down and raised an eyebrow. My hand shot to my hair. "Windy truck," I said sheepishly.

"Restroom's that way." She jerked her thumb toward the back.

Keeping my head down, I walked quickly to avoid drawing attention. But when I looked in the mirror, I wondered why the heck I'd bothered. No wonder that girl had stared at me so strangely. My hair was a jumbled mess of tangles and knots. I looked full-on Halloween crazy.

"Some fox you are," I said, attacking the mats on the ends

first. That brush battled bravely, but even after five minutes it was still a frizzy mess. The only way to fix it would be to start all over again.

"Shit." I splashed water on my face and up into where my part should have been, ran my brush under the stream, and kept trying to bring order to those twists and snarls. I had to step back a few times because ladies kept approaching saying, "Excuse me, can I get to the sink?"

Finally, after what seemed like hours, I felt presentable enough to emerge and head over to the counter. When the coffee arrived, I spent a few moments warming my hands around the mug, before glancing up at the *Enjoy Coca Cola* clock on the wall.

Nine-o-clock already! And I still had... gosh, fifty or sixty miles to go? I wasn't sure. I hadn't looked at a map. Just figured whoever gave me a ride would know.

You don't have to tell me. It wasn't much of a plan. But damn, I was a third of the way there and had done it all by myself.

With a satisfied nod, I lifted the mug to my mouth and tried a sip. Shuddered. Took the sugar dispenser, poured a bit, tasted. Still too strong. How could Ronny drink this shit black? Asked the homeless guy next to me to pass the cream dispenser. Milk-chocolate-colored bands swirled in the cup.

I slurped a long draught. Now, *that* was a cup of coffee.

Pancakes appeared in front of me, butter suns melting. When the syrup rained down, I stuck in a finger and watched the yellow pads slide. Cut a nice triangle out of the corner with the edge of my fork. Tasted the maple. Imagined the day.

So sweet.

FIFTY-FIVE

IRIS

I can't believe Joy actually got up before we did. She said she wanted to get an early start, but God, she must have been gone before six. Of course, that concert is all she's been talking about for a month. Telling anyone how she's going to be part of the new Woodstock. Playing her albums so loud, Ronny shouted at her to turn that shit off.

She's been improving these last few weeks. Going to class. Actually called the last time she was going to be late. Then she had a feature in the school paper. Not that I completely approve of how teens emulate those drug-using comedians, but I have to admit that her article was good. Surprised me. Of course, she has been scribbling away in that diary ever since I gave it to her for her ninth birthday. That girl always has her nose in it. I'd wondered what she was saying and tried to respect her privacy, but I'll admit it; after she took the car out without permission, I looked.

It was both better and worse than I imagined. Better in that she wasn't having sex, or at least not writing about it. Worse because pot seemed to be her whole life. Every entry was about getting high. No wonder her grades had been so bad.

I think a lot of that has passed. She seems more... *involved*, I guess the word is. More in life and less in a fog.

Maybe it's because of Ronny. A whole month without an... an incident. I think counseling is helping. And so far, he's agreeable about going. Three appointments and counting.

I know what happened with Kyle rocked him to the core. He may have been in denial at first, but then he became more—oh, how do I explain? More tender. I mean, he's started to ask Kyle how he's feeling. Every day. Plans to buy him a new bike as soon as the cast is off. Even suggested that I take some classes at the college.

Ronny wanting his wife getting smarter? Who was this man?

The only person that didn't get more sympathy was Joy. I think Ronny blamed her for the whole thing. Whenever she was around, his face would cloud over and he'd bark some order at her. Or criticize her as if he believed the lie about her wrestling with Kyle until it got out of hand.

"Would you get up off your skinny butt and do something? You know your mother could use some help around here."

I know I should have come to her defense more often, but arguing with him never works. What's best is to find a chore to get her out of Ronny's sight before things escalate.

Maybe that's why she left so early today. She wanted one day without any yelling, cringing, or darting away. A time where she could escape into music and friends. One perfect day.

I think she's earned it.

FIFTY-SIX

JOY

"Thanks for the ride. I mean, *gracias*," I called, as I flew out of yet another truck, this one driven by a Mexican gardener who spoke no English. Lucky for me that he knew the word 'Coliseum' and was headed that way.

As soon as my feet hit Figueroa Street, I could feel the difference. The hum of thousands of people streaming toward Exposition Park was like an electric current with vibrations so friggin' strong, I wondered if there was a downed power line nearby. I scanned the sidewalk but didn't see any exposed wires shooting electric bolts my way.

Hmm.

A shadow fell across my face and I glanced up at a huge monolith. Mountainous, it towered over me with an elliptical bowl so much like the super old Roman Colosseum, I almost expected to see chariot-riding gladiators with their swords and shields held aloft. Cocking an ear, I listened for the thundering hooves of bridled stallions and the cacophonous roar of lions, leopards and bears ready to battle a bestiarius, like in my tenth grade World History book.

Long lines of morning light stretched through the multiple

244

arches. Was this a building, or a portal to a floating Mount Olympus where gods and goddesses bestowed mystical gifts upon each of us?

"Cool," I whispered, hugging myself.

Up ahead, the iron fencing stood in stark contrast to the mystical structure. Surely something so sublime would need no bars to keep people out? Anyone in such a magnificent place would instantly be so enraptured that they would tread lightly on the inspirational structure.

As I drew closer, the coursing crowd narrowed into a scurrying line, all wanting to be first inside. At first, I thought about pushing with the rest, but when a Goliath in a sleeveless jean jacket started to cut ahead and I saw the Hell's Angels emblem on the back, I deferred. Better to let the multi-pierced punks and leviathan bikers go ahead than risk their wrath.

As I floated closer with the growing throngs, a host of odors filled my lungs. Strong cigars blended with Camel unfiltered tobacco. Freshly washed hair. Old Spice cologne. Smog and mist. Hot dogs grilling. Popcorn. Pretzels. And of course, the sweet smell of burning Thai stick, Columbian, and hash.

Pausing, I inhaled deeply.

"Hey, get going!" some chick with a red 'fro said from behind.

"Sorry." I flashed her a peace sign and toddled forward.

Next, the line passed by the carnival section, where rides like the Tilt a Whirl, Zipper, Loop-a-Plane and Scrambler were already running. With eyes as wide as rock and roll's power, I grinned, imagining the sweet buzz I'd get before heading over to the midway and stepping onto the Ferris Wheel.

After squeezing through the turnstile, the surging crowd started to trot, and jog, then full-on run to grab that primo spot near the stage. With no choice but to go with the flow, I let the current carry me forward

Then we were on the field. If Zeus had looked down from the

clouds, he would have seen ants scurrying toward an egg-shaped bowl where a platform enticed like honey. Behind the stage stood a triumphal arch that was flanked on either side by seven smaller arches. This huge structure was fronted with tall scaffolding, shelving speakers at least five stories high.

Since I let a lot of people go ahead, I didn't exactly score the best spot. It was around the middle of the grassy field, but it didn't dull my spirits. Even if I'd ending up in the nosebleeds, you couldn't have wiped the smile off my face.

"Rock and roll!" a dude from the crowd crowed.

"Right on!" I covered my mouth and glanced around but no one was judging. Instead, people were bobbing their heads in agreement. Cool!

I'd never heard of the first band, some punk one named after dogs or something. When they played a lick or two, I tried swaying and clapping to get into them. But then the lead singer shouted something about how the crowd should cut their hair. In a full-on rude voice, he told them to get in style with a New Wave do like his. Stupid guy.

Next thing I knew, people were booing and throwing shit. Total buzz kill.

"Hey, uncool!" I shouted, wondering if '80s kids even had the chops to peacefully congregate.

"Assholes, huh?" a dark-haired guy around my age said.

"Cha."

He sidled up closer. "Guess *get a haircut* isn't the best way to inspire a crowd."

"Yeah, not exactly a wise move."

He turned to face me. *Not gorgeous, but not bad either.* "I'm Julian."

"Joy." I saluted. "Hey."

"Hey back."

Someone lobbed a hot dog at the stage, followed by the roar of laughter. I took a step back when next, the riled-up crowd started pelting garbage at the band. Two minutes later, the punkers were ankle deep in orange peels, paper cups and pizza crusts. I shook my head and glanced at the exit.

"This blows. Wanna go check out the Rock and Roll Midway?" I asked.

"Sure." As we walked, Julian told me that he was from someplace called La Mirada that is kind of close to Knott's Berry Farm. He was in tenth grade and, like me, decided to come solo because his bud had bailed a couple of weeks before the concert.

"You hitched?"

He nodded. "It's not as easy for a dude to get rides, but I'm not exactly intimidating." He poked a thumb at his narrow chest. True. Rail thin and barely as tall as me, Julian did not evoke images of chainsaw-wielding psychos or switchblade-carrying thugs. He actually was kind of cute, if you're into that squeaky-clean *Tiger Beat Magazine* heartthrob sort of thing.

"Got ya."

Exiting the field, we turned left toward the Midway, which was a full-on county fair with the concession stands and rides I'd seen while in line. We got tickets at the booth and then debated over which attraction to try first.

"Maybe we should save the Zipper for later. I had pancakes earlier. Don't want to hurl."

"Okay, but before anything..." He raised both eyebrows dramatically and paused for long seconds.

After ten seconds passed, I said, "What?"

"First we should get into, shall we say, the spirit of the day."

I grinned. "You holding?"

He reached into the pocket of his faded jeans and pulled out a baggie.

I held up a hand. "Hey, you can't light up here."

"No need." He waved the plastic bag that contained not weed, but a couple of tiny orange tablets.

I squinted at them. "Uppers?"

He shook his head. "Look closer."

I tried but couldn't guess.

"Sunshine. The orange kind." He raised his eyebrows so many times that he started to look like a cartoon character. "I've been saving them for today. Was going to do both and really fly, but for someone..." he cleared his throat, "special, I'll share."

"Really?"

He nodded and repeated that ridiculous eyebrow lift before opening the bag. With a shrug, I reached in, grabbed one tablet between my thumb and forefinger and popped it into my mouth. Bitter on my tongue, it tasted like medicine, which I knew was just temporary.

Because pretty soon everything was going to be full-on candy apple sweet.

FIFTY-SEVEN

JOY

Julian's gift made the next few hours blur into a *Willy Wonka Chocolate Factory* trip. That little pill became a golden ticket, taking me from grey reality to a mystical world of swirling lights, reverberating sounds and cotton candy air. It's hard to remember it all because I was so high, but I do recall midday sitting on the Ferris wheel, taking in the smoggy cityscape of Los Angeles. Julian was next to me, an arm slung over my shoulder while far below, truck-dragons spewed exhaust and cars snaked over ribboned freeways.

Then, one distant building took a deep breath. And blew it out

My eyes widened as this huge skyscraper became a cubist robot just activated by an alien species. This tower swayed, its glass walls bidding steel and concrete neighbors to come alive. One after the other, they began to wobble until every distant building was moving and conversing.

Their animated chatter hummed over the sounds of Ferris wheel gears and laughing people. They seemed to love how elevators tickled their spines, foggy mist sprinkled their reflective skin, and human feet flowed like blood through veins and artery floors.

A cloud passed over the tallest one in the center, its shadow creating a great mouth which spoke to me alone. "The guardians of the city of angels welcome you. We who look over the city open our arms to all who seek."

"Seek what?" I asked.

"Why, the answers. For what *IS*. Here and now. For those who dance in truth."

I nodded slowly. Here was the perfect answer to every question I'd ever asked. It might not make much sense to you, but at this moment everything was so friggin' prophetic, I thought if I could only hold on to it, I'd go to a place beyond sublime. I closed my eyes and squeezed Julian's hand, fighting to capture this moment in time and the back of my lids flashed images of my skyscraper friends rising skyward in a kaleidoscopic embrace.

LSD's mist filled my every cell.

We kept to the Midway that afternoon, breathing in the flashing colors while rippling rides carried us over trippy seas. Neither of us was really into the first few bands, anyhow. But, as the sun sunk lower in the smoggy sky and the high began to wear off, the Outlaws' guitar licks floated toward us with words about some other love song.

I grabbed Julian's hand to pull him away from watching someone lob a baseball at a stack of milk bottles. "Dude! We're missing the show!"

"Let's go." He gave me a sideways hug before letting me lead him toward the music.

My trip had almost dissipated by then, but I did see a few treble and bass clefs float by as we skipped through the crowd. When I turned to smile at Julian trailing behind me, one final psychedelic burst of cranking tunes blew back his hair before turning to mist.

Back on the green, instead of letting go of my hand, Julian gave me an earnest look and grasped the other one. Then he leaned back and spun me in circles like a six-year-old in a gravity game.

I giggled as we twirled ever faster. When the Outlaws played a rocking tune, Julian let go of my hands, stamped his feet, and cried, "Yeehaw!" Like cowboys at a hoedown, we switched to a square dance by linking arms that spun me so fast, I thought I was back on the Scrambler.

"Stop. Stop! I'm going to be sick," I cried.

Laughing all the while, he slowed to a halt and released me. Dizzy, I fell back on the grass and looked up at the sapphire sky. He bent over me. "You okay?"

I sat up and hugged my knees. "Great."

He sat down next to me and we bobbed our heads to the last few songs of the Outlaws' set. Shadows lengthened as they finished their encore, giving the two of us a break from the raucous noise of the day.

Now that the acid had completely worn off and we were straight, we didn't quite know what to say to each other. I suppose, because I was the older one, it was my job to come up with smart quips and stuff. But a sudden attack of shyness robbed me of anything interesting to say.

"That was awesome," I tried.

"Yeah, totally." Julian looked past me at the stage, where the road crew was setting up for Cheap Trick.

"Next band should rock."

"Hmm. Hmm." He glanced around again as if looking for friends he was going to meet.

I desperately tried to think. *Say something, Joy. He's going to bail on you.*

He took one step away. Another. Still nothing.

I heard Janice's voice in my head. *When in doubt, plant one on him.*

So, I grabbed his skinny shoulders, pulled him toward me, and gave him an awkward kiss. He was stiff at first but when he relaxed into it a second later, well, wow!

One kiss led to two and three. Now I knew what those songs were talking about when they said kisses like wine. They really do make you want more.

A few minutes later, Cheap Trick sang, "I want you to want me," and I whispered into his ear, "I do."

He pulled me close after that.

And stayed until the end.

FIFTY-EIGHT

JOY

The next few hours were like something out of a dream. I won't bore you with all the details, but I will tell you that Joy Chapel rocked! Yes, she did. Head-banging, boy-kissing, hippie-swaying rock and roll!

I know, I've bragged about all my 'experience', but the truth is, this was the first time I'd really made out. Not like we were gross in public or anything, but that Julian knew how to kiss! Man, for a sophomore, he had lips.

But all good things must come to an end, and before we knew it, Nugent was finishing

Cat Scratch Fever, with a guitar stroke that had everyone screaming and clapping like crazy. The spotlights dimmed as he exited the stage and for a moment, we were plunged into darkness.

Then the stadium lights were up, casting this harsh glare over everything.

Concert-goers emptied the field as quickly as retreating waves. I kicked at a Styrofoam cup. It bobbed in the garbage sea, where a community unlike any I'd ever experienced had sailed only moments before.

The trash shuffled under my feet. This wasn't good. My palms grew clammy and a shudder passed over my body. It was near on midnight and I was a long way from home. It was one thing to thumb it during the day starting in my small town, but now?

"Hey, Julian," I began. "I noticed that we're in pretty in a poor neighborhood."

"It's a little ghetto, yeah."

"So, I was wondering if maybe you could, you know, hitch me home? I don't want to chance it alone." I swallowed hard and crossed my fingers, praying that after all those 'no's' I'd heard these past few weeks I'd finally hear a 'yes'.

I didn't dare look him in the face as he readied his answer. Instead, I drew a circle in the grass with my toe. My heart pounded.

"Of course, chica," he said. "I'll keep you safe." He put a protective arm over my shoulder, and we stopped at the snack booth for chocolate milk and donuts before heading for the exit.

"Maybe after this, I could call you?" he asked. "I know we live far away from each other, but maybe my dad could bring me up your way sometime."

I smiled shyly. "Maybe," I said, imagining a picnic on a blanket at the park, like in one of those old Gidget movies.

Since we'd waited so long and were walking slowly, enjoying our snack, we were amongst the last to leave. By now, the crowds had thinned until there was just a trickle of kids ahead and behind. We followed these last, scuffling concert-goers down the sidewalk toward the freeway onramp, a couple of streets over.

The two of us chatted about mundane things that I can't quite remember now, like school and annoying siblings and didn't notice the battered Dodge until it slowed and pulled up nearby.

An older guy like, maybe, thirty, with slicked back hair and a cigarette in one hand, leaned out the window. "You kids need a ride?" he asked, flicking ash. It hung for a moment then fell to the street like rain.

I bent over but couldn't make out the face on the bald man next to him because he kept staring straight ahead. He never once turned toward Julian and me.

Why?

Julian started to nod but I shook my head slowly. My entire body tensed and both feet dug into the concrete. I couldn't move. There was something about these guys I didn't trust. "I don't know…" I whispered.

"Well?" The driver blew out a long column of smoke and the burning cigarette flew toward me, landing at my stuck feet. I watched the red end flare and then dim as smoke curled around my legs.

I started to protest again, but Julian must not have heard because the next I knew, he was leading me by the hand toward the strange man sitting shotgun, who went from statue stillness to vaulting out the open door in a flash. Something prickled over my skin when he folded back his seat and upturned a palm for us to get in. Shuddering, I rubbed my arms and tried to search his face, but it stayed averted.

He wouldn't look my way.

Julian didn't seem to notice. He was too busy acting the part of a gentleman. With his head held high, he took hold of my chocolate milk carton and gave a half bow. "Ladies first."

"Don't bump your head," the driver said. "Wouldn't want you to get hurt."

My feet screamed "No", but then Julian pushed me and said, "Go on."

I told myself that everything was fine. I was with a guy. He would protect me. With a nod, I ducked down and eased past the two-door's seat belt to sit in the back.

Julian got in beside me and the front seat snapped into place, locking the two of us behind a vinyl wall. The stony-faced men in front didn't seem to fit in with this battered Dodge. One bald, the other with a military haircut and both wearing button-down shirts and sport coats, they could have just come from a business meeting. But the torn seats, stained carpet, and faded interior of this two-door told a different story.

One that was making my muscles clench tighter by the second.

Then it hit me. *Two doors?* Anyone who hitches knows you should never take rides like this. But it was too late to get out now. The engine was revving, and the car was in drive.

"Where you kids live?" the driver said, pulling away from the curb.

"You'll take us all the way?" I asked incredulously.

His voice was a stone tombstone. "Ya. Sure."

Julian elbowed me and whispered in my ear, "See? I told you I'd get you home safe." Then he raised his eyebrows several times and reached for my hand.

"So where?"

"Well, first we need to go north. Get on the 101 as soon as you can. I think it's… Wait, where am I?"

We were no longer driving along a busy street but were on an empty one, with graffiti-splashed walls. Julian looked a little perplexed but continued talking, while I stared out the back window. "Anyhow, after you drop her off, we could head back south toward my place in—"

Suddenly, the bones in my hand were being crushed.

"What?" I said, turning toward Julian. And gasped.

Inches away from his face was the black barrel of a pistol, its dark cylinder a cavern.

Only now did I see the gunman's face. It was long and stretched out of proportion, with thin lips in a tight line. His reddish-blond brows were drawn together above eyes so cold and menacing, no one would dare to cross him.

The driver turned a corner onto a deserted street, with caged store fronts and discarded blankets so old and tattered even the desperate homeless wouldn't use them. I thought about that knife in the bottom of my purse. Could I stab him?

The bald man's finger rested on the trigger that he would no doubt squeeze before I could strike. The backseat windows? No, they were so tiny that even a toddler couldn't fit through them. I considered grabbing the driver, but I'd be cut down before my hands were around his throat. If Julian went for the gun, he'd be shot down. There was no escape

The knife stayed in my purse.

The driver pulled over to the curb. Keeping the gun trained on both of us with one hand, the gunman used the other to open the door, pull himself to a stand and slide the front seat forward. "Get out," he ordered.

Julian did as he was told, but when I started to follow, the driver said, "Oh no. Not you. You're staying."

As I watched through the open door, the gunman took Julian's wallet, pulled the money from inside and tossed it on the stained sidewalk. The fifteen-year-old shook his head slowly and mouthed, "I'm sorry," with helpless tears in his eyes.

The bald man tucked the money in his jacket pocket and slid back into place. Then he shut the passenger door.

Leaving me alone with the two of them.

As we pulled away from the curb, I stared out the back window at Julian's shrinking figure. *I never gave him my number! I'll never be able to tell him. If...*

Cheap storefronts gave way to X-rated movie houses and slums where whores wouldn't even dare walk. They passed in a blur as I thought of Mom singing at dinner. Kyle putting a puzzle together. Grandma's crackly laugh when she won a game of Yahtzee. Lisa hugging me when I confessed about Ronny. Carl fixing my broken sandal. Catalina Island with dolphins leaping in and out the sapphire blue.

I clutched at my abalone necklace and started to cry.

The gunman shoved the barrel closer to my face. "Shut up. Now."

And I did.

As if a switch had been turned off, my tears immediately dried. My mind clicked into action and I remembered the article on rape Mrs. Plante had made me write. For I knew without a word that this was what they had planned for me.

I reached for the chocolate milk on the floor and took a sip. My tongue tasted no sweetness. I swallowed another mouthful. Chalk.

I don't want to die.

We turned down an alley toward a row of what looked like abandoned shacks and the car slowed. *What did I read?* One book said that you should get rapists on your side, make yourself more human if you want to survive.

Forcing my trembling jaw to form words, I asked, "Oh, is this your house?"

The driver let out a sniggering laugh. "I wouldn't take a disgusting thing like *you* to my house." He put the car into park and turned around to look me full in the face. Staring at me with eyes full of hatred he said, "You're going to act like a freak while my buddy watches."

I took another sip of my chocolate milk. Clung to the carton as if it somehow protected me. A waxy cardboard shield. The other man kept the gun trained on me and got out. He waved it at me.

I shook my head no. *I can't.* I pressed my carton shield to my lips. *No. Please don't.*

The driver reached in and snatched it from my hands. "Get the fuck out. And you fucking better not say anything."

Okay, Joy. You're not here. Go outside yourself. Be strong. You can do this. You have to.

To live.

FIFTY-NINE

JOY

No, I'm not going to tell you about the horrors inside that abandoned shack. I never want to repeat what those men made me do. I will tell you that, in a situation like that, the degradation is nothing in comparison to the fear of dying. All you can think about is survival and you are willing to do anything to keep that finger from pulling the trigger.

So, I did.

When they were done, the driver asked, "Should we let you go or not? Are you going to keep your freak mouth shut?"

I spoke quickly. "I won't tell, I promise."

"I don't know. What do you got to give me?" Those cold eyes looked me up and down.

With a shaking hand, I rubbed one arm. Tried to think. I'd spent all my money. Didn't even have a cheap watch to give him. There was nothing.

Knowing I was about to die, my fingers sought comfort in the abalone pendant at my throat. Grasping the cool shell, I started to close my eyes.

"I asked you a question, bitch."

I opened my eyes. "This is all I got." I undid the clasp and lifted the necklace off my throat. "It was a present from a really nice man, the nicest in the world. He lives out on Catalina and made it for me last year at camp. Carl's awesome. I can talk to him about all kinds of stuff. School. Mom. My stupid brother. I always wear it. It helps me to remember that someone believed in me."

Staring at the gun that still pointed at me, I rambled on. "He says I shine like the colors in the shell. See?"

The driver reached for the pendant, but the other one stayed his hand and lowered the gun to his side. He stared at his scuffed shoes and said, "No, let her keep it."

The driver scoffed and gave him a condescending look. Then he said to me, "Okay, whore. You won't tell?"

I shook my head quickly.

"Because we'll be watching. And if you do..." He pointed at the gun in his partner's limp hand.

"Get out of here," the gunman said flatly.

"But where do I go?"

The driver gave me quick directions to the freeway, and I headed for the doorway and passed over the sagging porch.

I started walking down the deserted alley thinking I'd done it. Maybe my words had made a difference. And they really were letting me go.

A few more steps and I'd be at the corner. Free. Heading home. Open the door and Mom'd smile like she used to when I was little. Before Ronny had turned her face to a mask. Before the blues, blacks, and fading purples. She'd be wearing a dress so bright, you'd think the flowers were blooming right there.

"Mom?" I whispered.

Home. Where Kyle would look up from his puzzle. The mystical castle floating in dream clouds would light up his face. He'd smirk and snap the final piece into place. *Little genius.*

I saw the streetlight at the corner. A beacon shepherding me forward. Started walking faster.

My feet kicked up some dust. I watched the mini-cloud, thinking how like Kyle's mystical puzzle it is.

I'd escaped the monsters. My words had been the key to softening their hearts.

I heard a pop like a balloon. Glanced around

I stumbled. Took another step forward. Heard a second pop. Stumbled again. Weren't my words enough? Hadn't I got through their masks? I thought the less vicious one had lifted his when I told him the story of my necklace.

A third pop.

Now I was sure my words hadn't worked. To them, I wasn't human.

Echoes flashed.

Freak! Slut!

"Mommy..." I called.

And then I thought... *she named me Joy.*

And I remembered why. Catalina. Dad's knee. Giving Kyle a piggy-back ride. The fort where girls ruled. Mom showing me how to crack eggs. Laughing in the jacuzzi room. Discoing to *The Hustle.*

Dog! Echoes tried to smoother smiles. Leering faces cast shadows.

No, my name is Joy. Redwoods in Big Sur. My guitar singing at a campfire. Lisa's arm draped over my shoulder. The poems I'd shared.

Then I looked to the right. Saw the truck spewing exhaust. Two men leered from the cabin and it backfired again.

Screaming, I started run. *No. No. No. Not again.* My feet moved faster. Didn't slow until I'd rounded three corners and could see the freeway onramp straight ahead.

Drawing closer, I noticed that there were still a few stragglers left over from the concert. Or maybe in this part of town there is always someone wandering the trash-littered streets.

A police car was parked nearby. I thought of approaching. Almost did. But then I remembered what they'd said. I glanced over my shoulder, eyes scanning every car, graffiti-sprayed building, and shadow. A homeless man pushing a grocery cart full of stuffed plastic bags looked my way. Was that a pistol bulging beneath that blanket? Then a dark-haired man driving by flipped a U-turn a block away and I halted.

He's watching me.

I stood there on the sidewalk and turned in a circle as every face distorted like some macabre movie. They all shriveled, then stretched into my monsters' allies. An abetting lattice wove throughout the block. *Careful now.* I imagined an enmeshed tangle of predators had suddenly been knit and now multiple barrels were trained on me.

Keep your freak mouth shut.

My thundering chest sent a message to a trapped mind. *Don't tell. Don't tell. Don't tell.*

Only now feeling the pain, I clutched at my gut. Breath caught in my throat and I rocked back and forth. Struggling to breathe, I stayed that way for how long, I don't know.

I want to go home.

Clenching my jaw, I forced a foot forward. Another. Stopped again, sure a bullet would find me.

Go outside yourself. Now.

I began to watch myself as if from a distance.

Cold, stiff fingers comb matted hair across her face. With tears hidden, the fractured seventeen-year-old hobbles over to the 110 onramp and, with a hanging head, sticks out her thumb.

SIXTY

JOY

I know what you're thinking and you're right. I mean, what the fuck? Hitchhiking after what you've just been through! Are you batshit crazy, or what?

The answer is yes, and no. My thoughts were all twisted at the time, so it's hard to explain why I decided to thumb it home instead of heading for the first phone booth in sight. I guess my brain wasn't working right.

I wanted my Mom so much, wishing she'd wrap me up in a tight hug like after I'd gotten lost in that national park when I was little. If only I could feel her hand stroking my cheek, maybe I'd find out that this all was just a bad dream. I'd wake up and there she'd be, standing over me, telling me it was time to go to school. I wanted to hear her voice more than anyone's just then, but things had been better at home. And I had lied about Janice giving me a ride. If Ronny found out, he would start all that shit again.

That's the 'no' part to the are-you-crazy question. The 'yes' part is that reality had twisted, and even though my high had worn off hours before, I was still enmeshed in its distortion. Chlorotic yellow pouring from the streetlights overhead gave

263

every face a death pallor, making me think *they* were close by. Menacing eyes flashed from the shadows while looming specters hovered.

I heard threatening whispers as my fractured brain told me that my captors were part of a gang. Their members made sure no one reported them by following each girl after an attack. They stood guard everywhere, demanding strict obedience. I heard their words repeated. *We will cut you down if you so much as make a move to tell.*

I stayed away from phones and police.

A cold breeze picked up a piece of trash in the center of the street, and it swirled like the harbinger of a coming storm. I rubbed one arm and then the other, trying not to breathe in the malodor that hung in the air. Then I closed my eyes, and the gun flashed on the backs of my lids.

I won't tell. I promise.

Don't you see, hitching was the only way? But this time, I'd be beyond careful. No ride unless they seemed safe.

At first, I didn't even notice the cars driving past. I couldn't stop crying. Between sobs, I told a college couple a few feet up the hill they should never hitchhike again.

"But we need to get home. No other way," the girl replied. Then she gave me a concerned look. "You okay?"

I nodded. Fighting the urge to huddle down inside my peasant shirt, I thrust out an arm. Almost forgot to stick out a thumb until I glanced at my balled fist. I blinked and lifted it off clenched fingers.

A few minutes later, an old man in a battered truck pulled up. I stood back and let the couple take the ride. After wiping my nose on a sleeve, I made myself jut out a thumb again. As cars whizzed by, I thought of home, where I'd burrow under the sheets and shovel the floral comforter over my head until the blackness of sleep buried me.

God, I wanted to escape this place. I kept shaking. But I

shook my head at the next car. Said no to three more. So, don't rag on me. I was being careful.

"Hey, chick! You want a ride or what?" a girl around my age shouted from a Volkswagen van's window.

"Maybe," I shouted back, before stepping closer to peer inside and see if they were from the concert. The orange van was filled with six teenaged gals who told me they were from Santa Barbara and had stayed in the Coliseum parking lot for some zzz's before starting the long drive home.

"So?" she asked.

"Yes please!" I ran to the other side, where another girl with a red 'fro was already sliding the side door open. Seated on the carpeted floor next to two dark-haired chicks, she had a round face and reminded of an Ewok from *Star Wars*. I stood there staring as if she wasn't real.

"Are you getting in, or what?" she asked, bending her legs so I could fit past.

"Yeah. Thanks." I crawled over some Marrakesh-print pillows, through the sea of outstretched and Indian-style bent legs toward an empty spot on the other side. Once there, I leaned up against the wall, avoiding the redhead's gaze.

"Hi, I'm Wendy." She introduced the two dark-haired girls on the floor and then pointed toward the platform bed. "The sleepyhead to your right is Carol. That's our fearless driver, Deb, and the girl who stole shotgun is Andrea."

"Is it my fault that you're so slow, you move backwards?" Andrea said, smiling.

Wendy flipped her off and the two giggled. I pressed my back tighter into the van wall and squeezed my eyes shut.

"Hey, are you all right?" Wendy asked.

"Yeah. I mean..." I paused. "No. No, I'm not..." My voice started breaking.

"It's okay. You don't have to say anything." She scooted up next to me and started to put an arm around my shoulder.

"Don't touch me!" Like a recoiling revolver, I jerked away.

With my lower lip quivering, I crumpled to the floor and pulled my knees toward my chest. My whole body began to shudder, and I curled tighter into a ball. The inside of the heated van suddenly turned to a winter that even a fetal position couldn't warm.

"You're safe now. No one's going to hurt you here."

As my chest heaved and my bruised lips sucked for air, two of the girls pulled a blanket up over me. And we drove toward home.

SIXTY-ONE

JOY

Someone gave my arm a gentle shake. "Hey, we're almost there."

I drew a quick breath and felt fabric rushing into my mouth. *Why is my face covered? A shroud!*

I squirmed and my eyes flew open to find, not a white sheet but geometric patterns. Blinking repeatedly, I pawed at the bunched-up blanket. I had to escape! Panting, I struggled toward the blanket's edge.

I sat up and turned to find Wendy peering at me, concern on her sunburned and freckled face. She went to squeeze my shoulder, but my body curled into itself before I could stop the knee-jerk response to her touch.

"No! Don't—" I began, but then covered my mouth. "Sorry."

"It's okay." She removed her hand and gave me a gentle smile. Then, jerking her head toward the girls who were splayed out in various sleeping positions, she said, "We figured you must have gone through something fucked-up. That's a shit neighborhood down there."

They know? My mouth clamped shut like a hurricane door. Voices in my head shouted, *Freak! Dirty freak!*

267

Now, it was all I'd ever be.

Not daring to look at her or any of the others, I suddenly wanted to escape my own skin. I'd just be met with a mixture of disgust and revulsion.

My gaze fixed on my shaking hands. Dirt was caked under each nail and my shredded cuticles were rimmed with old blood. *When did I rip them?*

"Next exit is your town," the driver said.

"Yeah, get off on that one then you guys can drop me off anywhere. I'll walk," I offered, my voice hoarse and husky, like a stranger's.

"No way."

"I don't want to be a burden. It's late."

"More like early." She jerked a thumb at the window, where black had given way to the grey of dawn. "Oh no, chickee. We're taking you all the way."

"Yep. You're going home," Deb said.

Home. Tears rimmed my swollen eyes with the word. I sniffed and swallowed the hard pit in my throat. Trying like hell to compose my shit, I said, "Okay, go straight ahead, then turn right on Main."

———

"Thank you so much. Maybe sometime we could..." As soon as the words escaped my lips, I stopped, knowing it was a lie. I would never see them again. The last thing I wanted was a reminder of the night I planned to bury forever.

When the van door slid closed, Wendy pressed her face up to the glass and made a silly face. I gave her a half smile, like the one I used to give Dad when he left after one of his rare visits. Deb stuck a hand out the window and waved as the clattering Volkswagen pulled away from the curb and turned a corner. I kept staring at the empty street until the engine was a rattling echo.

The sun's orange head had just topped the rise of the hills when I turned toward home. After fisting my hands, I threw my shoulders back and shuffled toward the third house from the corner.

I climbed two steps and walked up to the heavy wooden door. Now that I was closer, I noticed that the paint had begun to peel on the frame. When had that happened? Ronny was usually so anal about maintenance. Maybe I'd been gone years instead of hours, trapped in some sort of time warp that had taken me far into the future.

Beyond the shit that was about to go down.

"If only." I took a deep breath and reached inside my purse for the key.

I had just got it in the lock when the door swung open, pulling me and a few dead leaves along with it. "Joy, where the hell have you been? I've been worried sick."

Mom's uncombed hair looked like she'd been pulling at clumps of it all night. Silvery salt trails scored her bone-white cheeks and her eyes were hollow sockets, with circles so dark they looked like Ronny had gone after her.

I wanted so much to reach out and hug her.

Instead, I started to lie. Speaking quickly, I said that Janice knew some people in Los Angeles that wanted to party after the concert. We'd gone by, hung out and started drinking but couldn't drive until we'd sobered up.

"Why didn't you call?"

"We were having fun. I wasn't thinking," I choked out, my tongue disappearing into the back of my throat. The look on her face was destroying my resolve and I needed to convince her that I had just been a stupid teen getting high.

"I'm sorry, Mom. So sorry.

Now a red-faced Ronny came up, angry eyes flashing. "Fucking whore!"

I had been holding it together until then. But now I stumbled, reaching for the wall to stay upright. "I fucked up. I'm sorry. I'm sorry," I repeated again and again. "I'm horrible. I know. A freak. A dog. I shouldn't have gone there. It was so wrong. Wrong. Wrong. I'm a horrible daughter."

"Don't you say that! You do stupid things but you're not horrible."

The sound of Mom's cracked voice slashed through any defenses I had left. Tears sprang to my eyes before I could stop them. "I didn't mean to worry you guys... I swear. I'm-so-sorry..."

Mom reached out for my shoulder and squeezed. I buried my face in my hands as long, agonizing sobs racked my body.

"Okay, kiddo. Enough of that," Ronny said, with a gentle punch in the shoulder.

I lifted my chin and tucked a strand of hair behind one ear, surprised that Ronny's anger had dissipated like Point Magu fog in summer.

"Go rest. We'll talk more later." Mom gave me a little shove toward the hallway.

Once in the bathroom, I stood for long moments, my arms hanging limply at my sides. Each gold fleck in the linoleum glittered like dying stars in a universe forever changed. They held my gaze until my bowed neck kinked and an overall buckle dug into my throat. I reached for the metal and then closed my eyes before undoing the clasp.

Yesterday, these had shone as yellow as the loquats on the tree next door, but today, soot dusted the jean fabric. If each cuff was ringed in dark grime, what stains might be smeared inside? I stopped, unable to the lower the bib. Instead, I gently removed Carl's necklace and laid it on the bathroom counter.

The ugly side of man. One of the reasons I'm here, he had said.

Carl had survived and so did I.

With that abalone sea to strengthen my resolve, I began to remove my clothes one article at a time. First, I undid each clasp and lowered the overalls. Next, I slowly stepped out so as not to turn them inside out. Now, with as much care as a grieving mother might give a stillborn's swaddling blanket, I folded them in half. Then in half again.

I smoothed the fabric with my hands and cradled it for a moment before placing it in the empty wastebasket. Repeating this with my peasant top, I hesitated before removing the rest. Behind me waited the mirror. Below, wicker, like a basinet of nestling cloth. To my right, the shower.

I slipped off the last two items and placed them atop the others before grasping the grey shower curtain. With the mirror continuing to loom behind, I averted my eyes as I turned to step into the shower. Prickling fingers from the blasting water hit me full in the face, to mix with the torrent of tears finally unleashed. I picked up the white bar of Dove.

Lather, scrub. Lather, scrub.

But even though the flying bird etched on the Dove bar melted away until the wings dissolved and glided down the drain, it wasn't enough. The bar turned to pulp, but I knew I'd never feel clean again. Squeezing the white mass between my fingers, I put my head under the shower.

Where I stayed until the water turned cold.

SIXTY-TWO

JOY

So, you're wondering why I didn't tell. I'm sure you're thinking, *You were home and safe. You should have reported it.* And you're right. I should have.

But I couldn't.

First, there were the lies I'd told. Ronny hadn't been rough in a whole month but if he found out... I couldn't do that to Mom. Counseling had made her so hopeful.

Then came the paranoia, this constant feeling of being watched. *They* had sentinels observing my every move and if I went public, they'd know and come after me and my family. Over the next few hours, flashes of looming figures appeared in my peripheral vision and twice, I saw a gun-wielding shadow in the hall. Heart pounding, I turned, sure that the nightmare was about to start all over again.

Huh? But they were there.

I might have been able to push past those fears if it weren't for the shame-encrusted shroud I now wore. And would never be able to remove. I was now sullied, tainted, a defiled stain. Forever debased, only a tightly shut mouth could hide what I was from the world.

Did I want to tell? Feel Mom's cradling arms rocking me? Brushing my hair with the palm of her hand?

Only every moment.

When I smelled the sweet waffles on the iron and heard the sizzling of bacon, I almost rushed from my room with arms outstretched. Then I saw my hand on the doorknob and remembered. Mold. Filth. Rot.

With a shake of my head, I changed my expression. Donning the mask I'd worn most of my life, I went to breakfast. And pretended.

———

Monday morning, I got up, smoothed every wrinkle in my sheets, making my bed so perfectly Mom raised her eyebrows, and then, although I'd taken two the night before, jumped in the shower. I stayed in so long that I was late and had to run a comb through my hair while trying to choke down some toast. Next, I full-on ran to the bus stop, getting there right before the last kid was boarding.

I know, a senior on the bus? Humiliating. But what choice did I have? Janice used to be my ride and that stopped after our blow-up. Lisa didn't have a car and I never quite made it to girlfriend status with any guy.

That thought made me want to shrink farther into my sweater.

I stood in the aisle trying to decide where to sit. In the front were a couple of freshmen, staring straight ahead as if looking my way might bring down the wrath of God. In the middle, a couple of band geeks with open instrument cases on their laps and heads together chittered away. I headed for the back, where stoners' splayed-out legs dominated the seats.

With a quick nod, I sat in front of a long-haired dude named Pete, who was under the false assumption that those long strings were hiding the zits on his cheeks. When he glanced my way, I wondered if he knew.

Do I look different?

The driver yanked the knobbed gearshift and the bus lurched forward. Then it stopped.

"Newbie. Get a clue!" Pete shouted from behind me as the poor driver ground the gears.

I fought the urge to exchange a glance with Pete, opting instead to shake my head without turning around. My nostrils twitched from the faint odor of bong water. Pete was notorious for spilling.

While the bus driver tried to figure out where second gear was, I pressed a cheek to the window. The glass was cool and beginning to fog from all the giggling mouths on the bus. I drew a squiggle in the haze, then more. Multiple curlicues appeared beneath my finger. A surreal roller coaster with no beginning and no end.

My stomach clenched and I twitched. In jerky movements, my finger continued etching a curved labyrinth over the glass. One I found myself lost in.

There was a nudge on my shoulder. "Joy, wake up. You high or what?"

"Huh?" I shook my head. We were parked in the bus lane. But hadn't we pulled out of my neighborhood only seconds before?

I stared, unbelieving.

With absolutely no memory of the drive.

I wish I could tell you that the rest of the day was better. That every friend and teacher was a comforting blanket. That I stayed after class with Mrs. Plante and sought solace in her wisdom. Or at least cried on Lisa's shoulder during lunch.

I did none of those things. Instead, I did what I'd learned to do for so many years. I masked my face in placid smiles, turning the corners of my mouth upward while my vacant eyes gazed at nothing.

And made it through the day.

The next few weeks went by in a fog. Every day was the same. I got up, showered, choked down a few bites, and rushed out the door. There was some comfort in the routine of it all. I even washed in the same order, starting with my feet and working upward. When I got *there*, I scrubbed roughly, wishing all femaleness would slough off and close, turning me into an asexual doll.

And that's kind of how I coped. By trying not to. Now, I can almost hear the wind whooshing past your fingers as you waggle them and scold me. You're saying that a kid who went through what I did needs to process, should seek counseling, ought to confide in friends. Blah. Blah. Blah.

Should. Could. Ought. Yeah, there are lots of 'shoulds' and 'oughts' in the world. My dad could have come around to visit more. Ronny ought never to have curled his hands into flying fists. Kyle shouldn't have had to wear a cast for six weeks. And I should have told someone.

But none of those supposed 'shoulds' happened, so why lecture me? The last thing I wanted to do was think about it. I just wanted to go back to being Joy Chapel, dork, stoner and sub-normal teen.

Still, in the coming days I started observing myself, you know, like from a distance? And I noticed one thing. No, this is not some *Go Ask Alice* or *Reefer Madness* preachy lesson on the dangers of drug use, but for some reason I didn't want to get high so much. The week after, Frankie asked me to cut third period to go smoke a bowl and I said *"Nahh"*. Then at lunch, I went with Lisa to the field, but barely toked half a hit.

You'd think it would be the opposite, that I'd want to be absolutely blotto. But when I reached for Lisa's bong, my hands started to quiver. The idea of hours without control freaked me out.

How was it at home, you wonder? Better, I guess. Ronny went to more appointments, so that was good. We didn't really talk about it, but I could tell when it was counseling day because he came home all drained, like. Also, I peeked at the calendar hanging on the back of the pantry door and saw the abbreviation R. C., which I gleaned meant counseling for him.

Then Kyle got his cast off and bitched and moaned about *muscle atrophy* and other jock shit. When he came in from the garage after working the weights, he flexed his freshman arm and said, "Look at this bicep. Thirty percent of what it used to be!"

"Wasn't exactly Superman to begin with."

"Hey!"

"Is for horses." I raised my eyebrows as if I'd just come back with the best quip ever.

"Very original. Some writer you are."

I flipped him off. Kyle could be so annoying.

Then I realized how wonderfully ordinary Kyle being a pain in the ass was. Little brothers were supposed to bug you. That's normal, a part of life.

Life. For everyone, that's all there was. And for better or worse, this was mine.

I headed straight for my room and closed the door. I pulled my journal from under a stack of books and began slow, the writing dribbling like a leaky faucet. It dripped down a driveway before trickling into a steady stream, until soon it poured winter storm gutter pages.

I wrote it all. How the bong years began. The memories, both good and bad. The horrors and the joys. Friends and tormentors. Carl and Angie. Ronny and Mom. Kyle and Cheryl.

Lisa and Janice. Catch basins teemed with urban run-off and inky tributaries swelled, as I became the San Gabriel River spilling into the Pacific toward my Catalina sanctuary.

I set down my pen, fisted and extended cramped fingers, and pulled out the drawer on my nightstand. I dug under lipstick tubes, old tissues and Juicy Fruit gum wrappers to find the buried abalone necklace that I'd shoved in there after I'd taken it off that first morning. I placed it in the center of my palm, gazed at the colors, and returned to the island.

Thankful for that memory.

Thankful to be alive.

THE END

Dear reader,

We hope you enjoyed reading *Finding Joy*. Please take a moment to leave a review, even if it's a short one. Your opinion is important to us.

Discover more books by Laurie Woodward at https://www.nextchapter.pub/authors/laurie-woodward-childrens-fiction-author

Want to know when one of our books is free or discounted? Join the newsletter at http://eepurl.com/bqqB3H

Best regards,

Laurie Woodward and the Next Chapter Team

ACKNOWLEDGMENTS

This book would not have been possible without the support of several friends and family. First, I would like to thank Next Chapter, and its CEO, Miika Hannila, for taking a chance on me. It is an honor and privilege to be part of a publishing company that respects and supports its authors. A huge debt of gratitude goes out to Debbie Stiles and Tony Bartholow. When my computer crashed with the final copy of this novel trapped inside, you invited me into your home so Tony's technical wizardry could retrieve it. I owe you!

I'd also like to thank the Coastal Dunes Branch of the California Writers Club. This book took me to dark places, and I would have given up on several occasions, had it not been for your support and encouragement. Very special thanks go out to my go-to reader, the talented screenwriter, Leland Zaitz. Your patience, sharp eye, and honed craft have long helped to mold my work into the best it can be.

Once again, I would like to acknowledge my students both present and past. Your beautiful hearts continue to give my life meaning while inspiring me daily to find the joy in all of us. Also, to my fellow educators and school personnel: your hard work and dedication makes me proud to call myself an educator. Your extraordinary gifts often go unsung but know that children are finding the magic inside themselves because of what you do.

Most of all to my son and daughter: Nicholas and Jessica. All your lives, you have patiently waited while I scribbled away at my notepad or bent over the computer keys. Sometimes I was so lost in the dream that you might have had to call me twice to bring me back to reality. But neither of you ever complained. I think you always understood that when I got a distant look in my eye, I was not forgetting you. I was just dreaming of other worlds. But these worlds could never have taken shape without the love we share. And finally, to my mother, Claudia Stuart. So young when I was born, you hardly had a childhood. Yet you still endeavored to do the best you could. You have always modeled strength for me. For this, I am eternally grateful.

Finding Joy
ISBN: 978-4-86745-919-5

Published by
Next Chapter
1-60-20 Minami-Otsuka
170-0005 Toshima-Ku, Tokyo
+818035793528

18th April 2021

CPSIA information can be obtained
at www.ICGtesting.com
Printed in the USA
BVHW071341100521
606942BV00006B/991

9 784867 459195